Copenhagen Tales

Copenhagen Tales

Stories selected
and translated by

Lotte Shankland

Edited by

Helen Constantine

OXFORD
UNIVERSITY PRESS

OXFORD
UNIVERSITY PRESS

Great Clarendon Street, Oxford, OX2 6DP,
United Kingdom

Oxford University Press is a department of the University of Oxford.
It furthers the University's objective of excellence in research, scholarship,
and education by publishing worldwide. Oxford is a registered trade mark of
Oxford University Press in the UK and in certain other countries

Published in the United States of America by Oxford University Press
198 Madison Avenue, New York, NY 10016, United States of America

British Library Cataloguing in Publication Data
Data available

Library of Congress Control Number: 2014936758

ISBN 978-0-19-968911-8

Contents

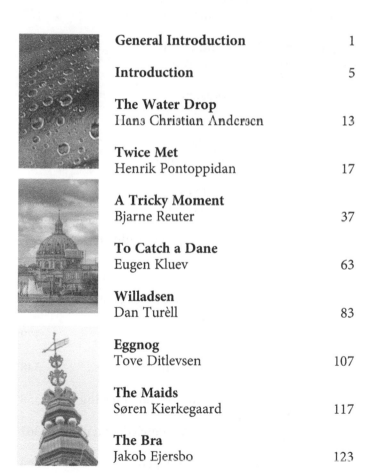

Picture Credits

General Introduction

The Danes have been telling stories for a very long time. In the magnificent National Museum in Copenhagen you find yourself surrounded by the stuff of myth and magic and history. Take one story, poetic as well as eerily logical, which comes down to us from around 1500 BC. Archaeologists have pieced it together with evidence from abundant carvings and images of the Sun Ship.

It is the story of the journey of the Sun around the Earth. At sunrise, fish pull the Sun up over the horizon out of the night ship into the morning ship; they swim along with it for a while before being consumed by birds of prey; then the Sun horse takes over the task of pulling the Sun on to the afternoon ship; later the snake takes his turn and hides the Sun in his coils before submerging him once again in the night of the ocean.

Another story you will encounter in the National Museum is not myth but history. One summer day in around 1370 BC the corpse of a slender girl of about seventeen, now known as the Egtved Girl, with short blond hair and wearing a short blouse and a cord skirt, was buried in a coffin. She wore a belt with bronze decorations, and had a thin ring at her ear; in a bark bucket was a mixture of beer and wine made from wheat and cranberries. Also found with her were the half-cremated bones of a five-year-old child. Before the lid was closed, someone placed on the edge of her coffin a small yarrow flower.

Who was she? Why and how did she die? What is the significance of the yarrow? Who was the child and why was it buried with her in the same grave? This is Danish *noir*, Bronze Age-style.

Besides the National Museum, visitors to Copenhagen will probably make for the most recognizable emblem of the city—the Little Mermaid, whose story, which will not be found in this collection, is recounted in the tale by Hans Christian Andersen. The mermaid fell in love, so the story goes, with a seafaring prince and, by means of sorcery, exchanged her tail for a pair of legs. This much-photographed statue sits in the harbour on rocks close to the shore by the fortress of Kastellet, where, if she were to turn her head, she would see factories and warehouses across the water, rather than the marvellous fronds and forests of the deep as in Andersen's story. Hans Andersen is represented in this volume by two short fairy-tales, 'The Water Drop' and 'The Naughty Boy', which will probably be much less familiar to English readers.

That the Danes are still great storytellers is evident to all from the phenomenal international success of some recent Danish TV thriller series. *The Killing* and the Danish-Swedish co-production *The Bridge*, or the hard-hitting political drama *Borgen*, all set in Copenhagen, have kept millions enthralled, taking us deep into a city and a milieu with which few were familiar. Now, with this generous selection of Copenhagen tales dating from the early nineteenth century to the present day, readers can discover for themselves from what a rich literary tradition this native storytelling genius springs. For sheer mesmerising willing read Karen Blixen's 'Conversation One Night in Copenhagen' or Benny Andersen's 'The Trousers'; for perfect control of their touching material try Tove Ditlevsen's 'Eggnog' or Dan Turèll's 'Willadsen'; for the evocation of a memorable character read Meïr Goldschmidt's 'Nightingale' or Bjarne Reuter's 'A Tricky Moment' or Jakob Ejersbo's 'The Bra'. Those who thirst for the excitement of Scandi *noir* will not be disappointed either: Naja Marie Aidt's 'As the Angels Fly' does not spare the reader the city's seamy side. Modern life in the capital, whether tragic or exhilarating, funny or passionate, is amply represented.

Despite Denmark being one of our closest neighbours, and despite its markedly Anglophile population, most of whom speak excellent English, 'wonderful' Copenhagen remains relatively unexplored by British visitors. Fortunately, and most especially for an outsider, there is no better route to understanding the deepest nature of a city than through the literature and art it has generated. This selection of short fiction, put together and translated by a Copenhagener born and bred, goes a long way toward that.

Readers will find, as always in this series, evocative photographs accompanying each story, notes on the authors and their texts, and a map at the back marking many of the locations brought to life in the tales.

God læsning! Happy reading!

Helen Constantine

Introduction

'Copenhagen contains within it everything which in other countries is distributed amongst several other cities. It is the capital and the seat of the sovereign and his government, the country's most important commercial centre and the main fortress of the land; here is the one university serving two kingdoms; here is the fleet and naval arsenal; all significant manufacturers and factories are concentrated here; here is the Academy of Fine Art and the theatre; in other words, everything that is curious and interesting in Denmark can be found in Copenhagen.'*

These are the opening words of the first comprehensive guide to Copenhagen, written just over 200 years ago by Rasmus Nyerup, a great bibliophile and irrepressible enthusiast of the city. Of course all Danes who are not Copenhageners will rightly dispute his concluding claim, yet it remains the case that Copenhagen is still the only big city in Denmark (and surely the liveliest and most beautiful in

---

* *Kjøbenhavns Beskrivelser,* Copenhagen 1800.

all Scandinavia) and still very much the heart and soul of the country's commercial, political, and cultural life. To reflect this continuity, these tales by some of our finest writers of the past two hundred years are loosely grouped according to Nyerup's broad categories, opening with stories of political and social import (1–4), followed by three exploring questions of work and class, while those touching on the city's cultural life and its role as 'seat of the sovereign' and 'main fortress of the land' compose the last four. 'Curious and interesting' might apply to all these stories, but I attach it in particular to the longer sequence of six tales (9–14) presided over by Cupid, or Eros, Hans Christian Andersen's 'Naughty Boy'.

Nyerup's encomium to the city was written at the very start of what has come to be called Denmark's 'Golden Age' (see 'Amelie's Eyes'), an era of exceptional brilliance in the arts and sciences roughly coinciding with the first half of the nineteenth century, the same century that under the pressure of intensive urbanization would see the city grow from small capital of a small state into a modern metropolis.

Until 1851 the rapidly expanding population was still confined within the ancient ramparts (*volden*), and this is the 'big city' packed with cannibalistic 'creepy crawlies' which the disgusted trolls examine through their magnifying glass in 'The Water Drop', a typically ironic tale by

Hans Christian Andersen which opens the collection. Through their own lenses most authors in this anthology find plenty to corroborate the two old trolls' impression in later generations. Copenhagen, like almost any other modern city, turns out to have a population and culture divided by inequalities of income and expectation, trivialized by the conformities of consumerism and the media, menaced by the desolations of drug and alcohol abuse and pornography—and on top of that cursed with a political class remote from its electorate. The sole tale by an outsider, Eugen Kluev's 'To Catch a Dane', makes bitter fun of the prejudice which immigrants often meet with in today's Denmark.

But, redirected at other corners of the city, and into other hearts, the various authorial magnifying glasses discover enough decent individuals or innocents struggling to live their lives against the worst trends of their times, or within themselves. In short, not all in the creepy-crawly city are creeps like Kierkegaard's seducer closing in on his next victim on a sunny Sunday afternoon in Frederiksberg Gardens, let alone the horrific 'Creepy' in Naja Marie Aidt's tale. Besides, as the reader will discover from the very first, a rich vein of humour runs through nearly all these stories. Perhaps, for the inhabitants of a small country surrounded by mighty neighbours who with depressing regularity have defeated it in wars and football and much else, a sense of humour is a matter of necessity. As well as great writers, Denmark has produced some very great caricaturists.

A further positive is that Copenhageners live in a very beautiful city, at least in its old centre. Even in his very dark tale of political betrayal in the aftermath of an attempt on the life of the deeply unpopular conservative Prime Minister Estrup in 1885, Henrik Pontoppidan is unable to resist giving an awed description of the sea approach to the city of memorable spires. With less lyricism but comparable accuracy, other stories take us deep into the working class districts of Vesterbro, formerly the main slum area ('Eggnog'), and Nørrebro with its lively new immigrant quarter so different to opulent but dull suburbia ('To Catch a Dane'), leafy middle-class Frederiksberg ('The Bra'), the vast dock area ('The Trousers'), the trendy bars and cafés of the centre ('Is There Life after Love?') and chic Bredgade, the city's most elegant eighteenth-century street, with its art galleries and auction houses ('Amelie's Eyes').*

Besides a wide variety of subject matter, epoch, and voice, there is variety in the short story form itself, ranging from Katrine Marie Guldager's subtle minimalism to the

* Danish *vej, gade, stræde* = road, street, alley; *plads* = square; *torv* = marketplace; *borg* = castle, palace (cf.'Borgen' for the parliament building Christiansborg, in Tale 3); *have* = gardens, park; *bro* = bridge.

more expansive art of great practitioners like Benny Andersen, Anders Bodelsen, and Bjarne Reuter, and the striking experiments of their younger contemporaries Jan Sonnergaard, Naja Marie Aidt, and the late, very talented Jakob Ejersbo. As opportunities for total immersion, I have included two longer tales by two of the city's very greatest storytellers: Meïr Goldschmidt, the Danish-Jewish novelist who in his student days notoriously crossed pens with the formidable Kierkegaard, and Karen Blixen (pen-name Isak Dinesen) of *Out of Africa* and *Babette's Feast* fame.

Goldschmidt's 'Nightingale' is set in and around the city's greatest cultural institution, det Kongelig Teater, the Royal Theatre, and in the still extant little streets and alleys nearby. This perfectly told tale, in which Copenhagen is still a compact middle-size city where seemingly everyone knows just about everyone, also gives an insider's glimpse of the rise of the city's small Jewish community from its humble Ashkenazi immigrant origins (still traceable in its speech) to comfortably off bourgeoisie. From this same background was to emerge the great radical literary critic Georg Brandes, one of the most influential thinkers of late-nineteenth-century Europe.

Karen Blixen's wonderfully atmospheric evocation of mid-eighteenth-century Copenhagen is set in the second year of the reign of the unstable Christian VII (the 'mad king' of the recent very successful film *A Royal Affair*). Lost in the city one wet and eventful night the novice monarch stumbles upon the slightly older but far more worldly wise poet Johannes Ewald in the company of his favourite whore. In the pair's schnapps-heightened 'conversation' about sex and myth-making, might and mortality, Blixen revels in the triumphs and absurdities of their macho world as if it were her own. Indeed 'Isak' Dinesen identified very strongly with Ewald, Denmark's first great lyric poet, who wrote his finest work while resident in the old inn at Rungsted, the Dinesen family home in which she was born.

The last 'tale' is not fiction at all, but a fine journalist's retelling of a fairy-tale moment in the history of her city. 'The Night of Great Shared Happiness' captures the joy and spontaneous need for togetherness—rare in the life of any great city—suddenly unleashed by BBC London's surprise announcement, on the evening of 4 May 1945, that the five years of Nazi occupation were at an end. Events unfold against the backdrop of some of the most familiar streets and squares and public buildings of the inner city: the historic power centres of Christiansborg and the royal palace of Amalienborg, the great public spaces of Kongens Nytorv and Rådhuspladsen (the Town Hall Square), and two important cultural icons at opposite ends of the city centre: the Royal Theatre on Kongens

Nytorv, and the head office of the daily paper *Politiken* on Rådhuspladsen.

In translating these stories, most of them for the first time, I have hoped to demonstrate the versatility, range, and also beauty (four writers here are first and foremost poets) of a great national literature very little known beyond Scandinavia, and here encapsulated in seventeen tales set in my ordinary and extraordinary city.

Many people have been instrumental in bringing this collection of stories together: my sister Trine, the indefatigable reader; great friends and Denmark lovers, Fleur Griffiths and John Lowe; the special little enclave of friends in Skamlebæk. Particular thanks go to my brother Jesper for his scholarly and excellent help and advice, also to my nephew Kristian whose beautiful flat in the centre of the old city he generously lent us, and to Rune Backs, who took many of the wonderful photos for the book. Thanks also to the helpful librarians in Odsherred Library, Asnæs. And finally, above all, thanks to Hugh, my husband and fellow traveller through life as well as the canon of Danish short stories, without whose help this book would not have seen the light of day.

Lotte Shankland

The Water Drop

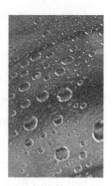

Hans Christian Andersen

I dare say you are familiar with a magnifying glass, that kind of round spectacle lens which makes everything a hundred times bigger than it really is? If you hold it up to your eye and look at a drop of water from the pond you will see over a thousand queer creatures you never normally see in the water, although they are there and they are real. It almost looks like a whole plateful of shrimps jumping around, and they are so ravenous they tear the arms and legs and tops and tails off each other, and yet they are happy enough in their own way.

Now, once upon a time there was an old man whom everyone called Creepy-Crawly, for that was his name. He always wanted to make the best of everything, and when that didn't work he used magic.

One day he was sitting there, holding a magnifying glass to his eye and looking at a drop of water taken from a puddle of ditch water. Goodness, how everything was creeping and crawling in there! All the thousands of little beasties were jumping and skipping about, pulling at each other and eating each other up.

'Oh dear me, that is quite disgusting', said old Creepy-Crawly. 'Can't they be made to live in peace and harmony and all mind their own business?'—and he thought and he thought but nothing seemed to work, so then he had to use magic. 'I must colour them so they'll be easier to see', he said, and so he added something that looked like a little drop of wine to the water drop, but it was magic blood, the very best for two shillings; and this turned all the queer creatures pink all over, and now it looked just like a whole city full of naked savages.

'What have you got there?' asked another old troll who didn't have a name, and that was what was special about him.

'Well, if you can guess what it is', said Creepy-Crawly, 'I will make you a present of it; but it isn't easy to discover if you don't already know.'

And the troll without a name looked through the magnifying glass. It really did look like a whole city full of people running about with no clothes on! It was horrible, but even more horrible was seeing how they pushed and shoved, all picking and pecking, biting and tearing at each other. Whichever was underneath had to be on top, and whichever was top had to be bottom! 'Look, look! His leg is longer than mine! Slash!—off with it! There's someone with a little pimple behind his ear, a harmless little pimple but it's tormenting him, so let it torment him even more!' And they pecked at it, and they pushed him over, and they ate him for the sake of that one little pimple. There was another one sitting as still as a little girl, only wanting peace and quiet, but the little girl had to go, and they pulled at her and they tore at her and they ate her up!

'That's exceedingly droll', said the troll.

'Yes, but what do you think it is?' asked Creepy-Crawly. 'Can you work it out?'

'That's easy to see!' said the other. 'It must be Copenhagen, or another big city, they're all alike. A big city, for sure.'

'It's ditchwater!' said Creepy-Crawly.

Twice Met

Henrik Pontoppidan

He went far up into the mountains of Norway—an odd-looking lanky fellow in threadbare clothes with a permanent grin on his lean face. No one could make out where he belonged—not whence he came, not whither he was bound. But when the 'Long Dane', as they came to call him, every spring and autumn without fail came striding through their valley with his thin oilcloth knapsack on his back and that stumpy pipe smouldering under his nose-end, not a few on whose doors he knocked to ask for a match or a beaker of water could resist the temptation to invite him in—to be entertained by his many far-fetched stories and his altogether curious figure.

On the other hand, one wouldn't particularly have wanted to meet him on a lonely path in the hills or the

woods. It was generally agreed there was something unsettling about the way those tiny dark eyes of his flickered
behind his glasses. His grin wasn't altogether above suspicion either, and his hair hung like a tangled mane all over
his ears and neck. The girls up in the summer pastures
squealed in terror when he stuck his long, slightly inebri-
ated nose through a crack in the door.

No, truth to tell, it was not easy to figure out what the
devil he was doing roaming about this foreign land, all
down at heel, when somewhere or other he surely had
hearth and home waiting to welcome him inside so much
more warmly. Most people considered him a bit of a 'queer
fish'. Others were of the opinion he had likely forsaken his
place of origin on account of some misdeed or other—
possibly even murder. He looked capable of anything, that
fellow! But if you asked him straight out, he would just
grin and say in his quaint speech that it was so 'much,
much bonnier in Norway'.

Once at some festivity where he had been invited in off
the road they finally managed to worm out of him that he
really did come from Denmark, was even a Copenhagener!
When, however, they went on to enquire whether he felt
homesick or ever had thoughts of returning to his native
land, a peculiar dark flush suffused his jutting cheekbones;
and after gazing silently at the ceiling a long while he
answered, 'Yes, when I am needed.'

He was a riddle.

Come winter, when the snow and the cold drove him down from the mountains, he betook himself to Kristiania where he found work in his old profession: bookbinding. There, every night, he could be found sitting in a modest basement tavern, always in the same out-of-the-way corner, bent imperturbably over a newspaper which he studied from end to end, shrouded in ever thicker fumes from that half burned-out little pipe which so rarely left the corner of his mouth. But at the very first signs of spring the irresistible longing for adventure awoke in his breast once more. He strapped on his oilcloth knapsack and struck out for the mountains.

Well now, last summer he turned up again in the usual places, where little by little people had got so accustomed to his arrival that they almost felt he belonged to spring in the same way as the starling and the stork. Only this time he was the shadow of his old self. His tall spare frame was now almost skeletal, and the little dark eyes flitted hither and thither distractedly as though his thoughts were forever far away, in foreign parts. No less striking was how relentlessly he pressed people everywhere for tidings of Denmark and the frantic eagerness he showed whenever he caught sight of a newspaper and then begged permission to read it. On the other hand, if you broached the subject of politics, the parlous state of affairs back home in the land of his birth, the coup d'etat, the king and the possibility of a revolution, he would straightway fall silent and go all black around the eyes.

And then it came, that October day with the appalling news from Copenhagen: Assassination attempt! Prime minister shot at! The story shook up even the Norwegian peasants. Now all hell will break loose, they opined. It's surely the last straw! And each morning, caught between suspense and concern, they picked up the paper and thought with commiseration of the old sister country.

But where, all of a sudden, was the 'Long Dane'? He had vanished into thin air, right from under the noses of the good people of Hallingdalen.

In fact, at the very first wind of the pistol shots, he had set out to cross the mountains by the shortest route to the sea. Without pause night or day he had tramped through valleys and towns, forest and heath, in an unfamiliar landscape, until toward evening after three days' hard march he came to a little coastal town in the west country. In one of the many sailors' taverns along the darkened quayside he discovered a German captain whose old tub had just taken on a cargo for Riga, and who, after a good many objections, in the end agreed to take him as a passenger to the waters off Copenhagen.

They weighed anchor at break of day the very next morning.

It was a misty November afternoon when the ship finally entered the Sound under a mild north-westerly. Reinald—for that was the Dane's name—stood beside the mainmast on the wet and slippery deck, blue with cold, with his numbed hands thrust into the sleeves of his tightly buttoned coat and his hat pulled down over his lank hair above those tiny feverish eyes which seemed to flare up each time he glimpsed a section of the familiar autumn-brown coast through the mist.

Most of the interminable crossing he had spent in more or less the identical position, and on the selfsame spot. Once in a while he had allowed himself a little exercise, pacing to and fro in the tight space between mast and rail; but when his impatience and agitation became too much for him he had sat down on a coil of anchor cable with his face buried in his hands. At night he slept below in the fo'c'sle between a sailor and a cabin boy who had enjoyed a good laugh at the expense of this baffling passenger who thrashed about in his hammock like a fish on the line and screamed aloud in his dreams.

In any case, there had been little chance to become acquainted. They ran into the foulest weather, with rain and gales over the North Sea, and fog over the Kattegat. For two days they lay off Hesseloe, compelled to keep sounding the ship's bell; and when the fog finally lifted enough to dare set sail again, they were forced to heave to once more in the lee of Kullen to await a pilot. Not until late morning did they slip past Kronborg—and now the Sound lay all about them like a thick, lead-grey, rocking waste over which the ship slowly crept along.

It was almost evening before Copenhagen loomed out of the mist far up ahead.

Reinald's bony body gave a start when he saw the first spires rise like fine needles piercing the grey gauze of the horizon. Instinctively his hand went to the small of his back—to make sure the well-honed pointed knife still sat snug in its leather sheath under his coat tails. His entire body started trembling with impatience as little by little the city emerged from the mist: Vor Frelser's slender corkscrew spire, the brickwork cone of St. Paul's, the plump dome of the Marble Church. And later: the Stock Exchange, the Cross of Our Lady, the crane on the old battlement of the royal dockyard, and the snow-white roofs of the bacon factories.

For twelve long years he had not set eyes on the city of his birth—not since those momentous days at the beginning of the seventies when, as a very young man, he had thrown himself into the socialist class war, never doubting that the time for the great reckoning had finally come, the dearly bought vengeance of the suffering, the oppressed, and the wronged. Right in there, between St. Peter's and Our Lady, high up in a wretched little garret he had lived with his poor, deceived, and abandoned mother to whose one sole lapse from virtue he owed his existence. Up there, day after day her joyless grey eyes had dripped that bitter hatred into his soul which made his cheeks blaze and his brain glow. And it was from there that he had stormed out to the great rallies, where under the eyes of the leaders themselves he had delivered his own fiery speeches to the listening thousands.

And then he had left—broken, disillusioned, full of loathing, branded by all the newspapers' inky lies, pursued by the gloating grins of treacherous comrades and the vigilant eyes of the police. Not long after, his mother died, and with that his last tie with his hated hometown was broken.

And yet... and yet wherever in the world he happened to set foot, in Germany, in America, and latterly in the mountains of Norway, he had unfailingly kept one sleepless ear cocked in the direction of the old places, waiting for the day when the people's patience would finally snap. And now at last it had come! The summons had sounded!... Or could it even be that the wondrous and ineffable had already occurred? Had the sentence been passed, the punishment carried out? It seemed to him that an eerie and eloquent silence brooded over the city as it gradually opened up to his gaze, with the long rows of pale lights under the still factory chimneys stark against the sky.

Could it, *could* it have happened?

On the stroke of six they dropped anchor in the inner roads. Darkness had fallen. Hundreds of ships' lanterns bobbed to left and right of the Trekroner beacon's penetrating beam. A tramp steamer came splashing out from the harbour with its fiery red and cat-green eyes riding above an incessant hissing and creaking. From within the glowing city sounded a far-off restless hum.

Staggering like a drunk, Reinald got down into the dinghy, which swiftly carried him ashore.

The first person he came across was a uniformed messenger standing under a lamp by the custom house steps, deep in a newspaper. But the blue, bloated face betrayed nothing, and Reinald did not have the courage to approach him. The customs officer, a sulky little fellow who inspected his knapsack wordlessly, likewise left him none the wiser. But as he hastened out into the deserted foggy street where once in a while a solitary figure brushed past him under the wan street lighting with coat collar round his ears, he was struck anew by the uncanny silence that hung over the city.

Next moment, through the fog he caught sight of a row of large posters on a nearby hoarding. People's revolution!— flashed through his mind as he hurried over. But then by the dim light of a far-off street lamp he made out:

Madame Popper Menter! Last concert! Theatre! Burlesque!
Chung-Chang the equilibrist! Breathtaking aerobatical per-
formances! Musse is coming!!! Bedbugs eliminated!...

A dry cough sounded a little way off. He looked round and
glimpsed a policeman's helmet slowly approaching from
the direction of Grønningen. Quickly he turned a corner
and was almost immediately in Store Kongensgade. Here
there was no lack of light or people. Hansom cabs and
drays thronged the street. Shop bells jingled, boys whistled
'The Happy Coppersmith'. On one corner a fat policeman
stood and yawned.

Reinald was astounded. He gazed at all those fine
gentlemen sweeping past him in their new promenade
furs, the imposing perfumed ladies with flashing eyes
roaming behind cherry-red veils. He gazed at the placid
urchins gathered wistfully in front of the bright shop
windows, at the workers quietly making their way home,
at the womenfolk and apprentice lads standing about in
doorways and gateways chatting together and smoking.
And he peered down into cellar tap-rooms where people
sat crowded together, drinking and laughing.

He could make no sense of it. What was the meaning of
this gaiety? Was it a cover under which the bullets were
being forged?

Where should he seek information? Whom did he dare ask?

He turned down one of the side streets, and at once his eyes were drawn to light streaming onto the street from a big house some way ahead. Knots of people were gathered on both sides of the arched entrance, and carriage after carriage drove through it and drew up.

'What's happening?' Reinald asked a shoemaker's apprentice after watching a while in amazement the ladies in ball gowns and the men in white ties skipping from the carriages into the garlanded vestibule.

'It's the liberals.'

'The liberals? Who are they?'

'The liberals? Huh, get away with you!'

'They're dedicating the flag', piped up a little old dame in a bonnet and long cape, and she nodded portentously up at him.

Reinald gazed down at her wizened trembling mouth, as though unable to believe his own ears. Dedicating the flag! Then had some sort of victory been won?

He felt utterly at a loss. As if in a dream, he roamed a long while through a succession of dark streets, almost unaware of walking. At last he halted outside a deep basement tavern. And being thereby reminded he had eaten nothing all day, he pulled himself together and descended the steps.

It was a grubby little room with a spittle-dotted floor, at that moment void of customers. From the centre of the blackened ceiling dangled a drowsily fuming bare paraffin lamp, and seated in one corner in shirtsleeves was the stout tavern keeper, fast asleep. The sound of the doorbell woke him, though, and he eyed the stranger in befuddled surprise. Reinald sat down at a table close to the door, and ordered a plate of sandwiches and a bottle of beer. With much effort and audible grumbles, the fat man rose from his chair and shuffled across the floor to a hatch in the wall, where he remained standing until the order was thrust through the hole.

'Bad times, eh?' he gasped as he slumped into a chair opposite the newcomer, and, still half asleep, bit off a good three inches from a stick of chewing tobacco which he fished from a trouser pocket.

Reinald nodded assent, bent over his sandwiches.

'Nothing seems to be moving. Just strikes and bankruptcies and mischief and misery wherever you look. And all just because of politics! Can you beat it?'

At the word 'politics' Reinald pricked up his ears.

But the fat man was suddenly wide awake too, and darted a hard look at his visitor out of the corner of an eye.

'Well—so what's *your* opinion about all this here politicking?' he asked.

Reinald replied that he had only that very evening arrived in the city from abroad and was therefore in complete ignorance. But he would appreciate some information; he had heard so many rumours.

'Did you also hear about the new emergency laws?'

'No!'

'About the gendarmes? And the police?'

'No! Has...has something happened? I mean— something really serious?' Reinald stammered out.

'Eeh, God preserve us!' cried the fat man in horror. 'What more could possibly happen? Isn't it dangerous enough already? Thank the Lord I don't bother myself with politics and that. To my way of thinking the Right or the Left would be equally good, if they could only agree. That's what they should be thinking about, that lot over there in Parliament, and start understanding it's us tradesmen who suffer. You tell me what's the use of all their fuss? Previously I could dispose of a half or even a whole barrel of beer in a single night, just to labourers and workmen. But now everyone's keeping well clear of public places so as not to run into trouble over what they say. It's easy to let slip a word or two when you've had a drop too much, and a spy can jump on it and use it to harm a man. So that's why they're all stopping at home, unless as like as not they're setting up secret societies and hush-hush clubs.... And as though that's any better! Watch out, or before you know it we'll be the same here as over there in Russia, what with them nillylists and dynamiters.'

'You really think so?' asked Reinald eagerly.

The publican again gave his customer a searching look. Then he winked a couple of times and said in conspiratorial tones:

'Who knows what might be going on in these strange times. Could be something new pops up sooner than anyone thinks.'

'What do you mean?'

'Hm! I'm not saying nothing', he said, and stared hard out into the room.

But a moment later he turned back to Reinald and laid a hand confidentially on his arm.

'Know how to keep a secret?'

'Me? ... Yes, of course.'

'Then listen to this. Up here on the second floor lives one of the leaders ... of the opposition, naturally—'

'Here, in this house?'

'On the second floor, aye. Take it from me, something's afoot up there. There's been no end of running up and down them stairs in recent days! And they go whishing and whispering and putting their heads together soon as they come out on the street. The other day—but don't quote me!—the other day there was a proper meeting on, with a good two dozen—and ladies and all, naturally! You

can be sure things were up for debate there! 'Cos *there* the
police can't go poking their noses in, am I right?...Bah!
Go ahead, is all I say! I don't go meddling in what's none of
my business. I'm neither nilly-this nor nilly-that, me, and
according to my way of thinking both lots are as good as
the other in those opinions they happen to hold, right?
Fair enough, eh?...So will it be another beer?'

'No thanks', said Reinald, getting to his feet.

'A bit of baccy?'

'No thank you...How much do I owe you?'

'Forty-two øre.'

He counted out the money—his bony fingers were
shaking—bade farewell, and left the cellar.

Once he was out in the street he first looked warily
about him, then went through the entrance and quickly
climbed the stairs. On the second floor he found a large
brass name plate on the door. He recognized the name,
which he had often seen in the papers, and softly rang the
bell. A maid opened the door and looked him up and
down suspiciously.

Was the master at home?

No—yes—but he wasn't receiving today. He had to go
out, and was dressing right now. But tomorrow morning
he would be available for consultation in his office.

Yes, yes—but all the same he would very much like to
speak to him this evening.

Was it not something she could pass on to him—for he was busy right now.

No, he absolutely had to speak to him in person.

She pulled a grumpy face and went away after casting an eye over the coats and cloaks hanging on the hall rack.

When she came back she instructed him imperiously to wipe his feet on the mat, after which she showed him into a large, beautiful, elegantly furnished room with rugs on the floor, armchairs upholstered in velvet, engravings and costly paintings—all softly lit by a red-globed lamp suspended from the ceiling. In one wall was a curtained doorway, and through this stepped a fair-haired middle-aged portly gentleman with a big moustache, dressed in tails, white satin tie, cream-yellow gloves, and with a large rose in his buttonhole.

'You wish to speak with me?'

'Yes'.

'Aha! Now I see, it's about the dance. So have you managed to get the bouquets and posies for the cotillons arranged to your satisfaction?'

'No—I am a traveller.'

'Is that so?' The fair-haired gentleman took out his pince-nez. 'May I ask you to be so kind as to be brief. My carriage awaits in the entrance, and I must away.'

Reinald, white with excitement, proceeded to explain his presence in naive detail. He started with his youth, the rallies, and his departure, and told how this very evening he had arrived from Norway where he had spent the last years, and how up there he had followed the course of the struggle and now had come back to offer his services to 'The Cause'.

At this a broad smile of understanding spread out from under the big blond moustache to the pale eyes which at first had lingered impatiently on the peculiar-looking stranger, inspecting him with suspicion all the way from the mass of unruly locks to the down-at-heel bespattered shoes. Reinald's story had touched him, and he stepped up to him, deeply moved, and gave him his hand.

'All you tell me delights me more than I can say—delights me more than you perhaps may understand. I bid you most heartily welcome! Believe me, it does all of us good, and fortifies us in our efforts, to meet with such fine proof of a true and devoted love of liberty.... Oddly enough, at the very moment you called I was endeavouring to find a suitable opening for the speech I have the honour of being asked to deliver tonight. And truly, if you will permit me to mention your heroic arrival on these shores I am convinced it will arouse universal sympathy. For—yes indeed!—it's as you say, there is a war on in this country—we are at daggers drawn! And that is precisely why it is so fine, yes, magnificent, when a man so unhesitatingly rallies to the banner at the hour of danger ... Once more, a hearty welcome! Be assured, we do not underestimate your contribution.'

And he wrung his hand again with genuine warmth.

But Reinald, heartened by this, now looked around the room and asked in a whisper:

'No one can hear us here?'

'Hear us? No, I don't believe so. But why?'

'Because... well, I wanted... I want to know right this very night how you wish to use me.'

'Use you?... What exactly do you mean, my good fellow? I could hardly have been more precise...'

'I am totally at your command. I am ready for anything!'

'Ready? How so? I don't quite understand you.'

'You can safely rely on me, Sir. My lips are sealed. I know... I know you had a meeting up here... the other day...'

'Yes, quite correct—the social committee gathered here in view of tonight's banquet... But how—in what connection did you imagine that you—?'

'There is no need to be afraid of me. Like I said, Sir, I've known how to keep my mouth shut all this time. Give me any task you will. I'll take on anyone, even if it be—the man himself! I have an old score to settle there, I can tell you.'

'But what does the fellow mean to *suggest*?' cried the fair-haired gentleman of a sudden, instinctively taking a step back towards his desk. Horror-struck he stared at that pale, quivering apparition, those two tiny coal-black eyes glowing at him above the dark stubble. 'What are you saying? What is it you want?...Are you out of your wits, man? Do you mean to...Have you come here to...? No, no, no, I apologize!' he promptly checked himself with a breathless little laugh, extending a reassuring hand when he saw the startling effect his outburst had had on the stranger. 'I got quite...I thought by God for a moment you...Well, do forgive me. The thing is...in these times, when excitable thoughts are bound to surface...'

And now that he had regained his composure he started to pace back and forth over the carpet, speaking with broad gestures as though rehearsing a public address.

'As I say—we deeply appreciate the fact we can count you amongst our ranks. In such times as these the country needs every one of its sons who are true to the constitution. For now has come the moment for all truth-loving men to join together, all those who by precious ties—ties of patriotism and the goal of liberty—inextricably belong together. We know the current situation. We are starting from scratch. There has been an infringement of the constitution—a clear and incontrovertible infringement of the constitution! But we will fight the battle with lawful weapons, which will, which must, which *have* to prevail. We stand firm upon our sacred rights and the truth. And in this battle each one of us is called to do his duty to the full. You too—my dear friend!—will honourably play your part in our ranks. Support us to the best of your ability in our struggle on the ground. Become a member of our constituency organization, support our papers, attend meetings regularly, give your mite—be it never so modest—to our funds...And you shall see, victory will be ours one day!'

Shortly afterwards, Reinald slunk down the stairs. As he stood in the street a carriage rolled out of the gate.

He looked after it for a long time, with a rueful smile.

A Tricky Moment

Bjarne Reuter

Aksel stared at the back of his driver's neck. Of all necks his driver's was the one he knew best. His knowledge was based on seven years' study, which included the man's eyes in the rear-view mirror. His eyes, and the back of his neck. Constants to rest the mind: watery blue eyes, powerful neck. Thus proving there was nothing new under the sun, but for the fact that Aksel could not remember the man's name. His name would obviously turn up again, it had to be lurking somewhere. Like a shoe absentmindedly kicked under the bed. Nothing to fret about, least of all now Aksel had so much else to occupy his head. The text, for instance. Not that he needed to learn it by heart, still he would like to get a feel for the right tone of voice. As he'd said to his secretary: 'You don't want to screw up when reading Hans Christian Andersen. Balance of trade figures and inflation projections maybe, but not Andersen.'

The driver mentioned something about the weather, and Aksel answered in the affirmative. This by and large was the sum total of their exchanges: the weather and the Super League. On a good day both might even be combined. They had always called each other by their surnames. How this came about was lost in the mists of time, but it felt natural.

But what was the man's name? ...

The ministerial car drew up in front of TV City where the Christmas glitter was beginning to wear off. Aksel said as much to the driver, who asked what time he should be back. Though he could equally well stay around and wait.

'Don't wait, I don't know how long they'll want to keep me, but you're on no account to wait for me.'

The driver said his evening was ruined anyway.

Aksel looked at his watch, uncertain whether to take the remark as a reproach or a sample of dry humour.

He opened the car door.

'Well, see you soon then, in any case next year.'

The driver nodded: 'Happy New Year, Frederiksen, and regards to the family.'

Aksel gave the driver his genial smile to make up for the name which for some reason still escaped him.

She was standing by the desk, waiting for him as agreed. Aksel hadn't seen her before. She looked dependable. Even sported a little three-cornered hat on her head, and a bunch of streamers in her breast pocket.

'My name's Suzy, welcome and thanks for taking the trouble to be with us.'

He put his arm round her.

'You do realize, Suzy, before an election we'd all sell our souls for the sake of sixty seconds.'

Her smile became a trifle forced. He realized he shouldn't have put his arm round her. It was a relic from a bygone era. Something he needed to remember. To quit doing. They were so touchy these days. Nice enough, but on their guard. The more belly they bared, the more buttons they unbuttoned, the more on their guard. There was a certain logic to it.

He suppressed a yawn, and was rewarded with a shiver. He said to himself: you are just as clapped out as this building. Looks like something from Walter Ulbrecht's time. Not so surprising if a name slips the mind now and again. The fatigue in his head had spread to the rest of his body. He thought of his couch back in the office, and also of the people sitting at home. The people he should be with. Except they weren't sitting at home. They were in Trørød. He had jotted down the address, to be on the safe side. Why hadn't he written down his driver's name?

On the way down to the studio he greeted two people he recognized as they hurried by in the other direction. He needed to sit down and put his feet up, preferably with a pick-me-up, but that of course was out of the question. Suzy said something about a New Year's Eve mood, but Aksel couldn't make out whether or not she meant it positively. He had seen her before. On children's TV. Maybe she was older than he'd first assumed. She looked the sort who goes in for aerobics. Big muscles, strong legs. Well upholstered. A strapping lass with a tired smile.

'I believe', he said, 'I believe I know the text pretty well, but then that'll turn out not to be the case. When we get started I'll no doubt have forgotten it all. I said something to my driver about that. We should form the Amnesia Party.'

'The Amnesia Party?'

'It was just an idea, a silly notion, they come and go these notions. So it's okay if I read out the story?'

'Of course.'

Suzy walked fast. Aksel had to shift gear to keep up with her.

Dentist's receptionists, he thought. The place is crawling with them. You never get to see the dentist.

'I'd prefer people to see that I'm reading. To be more myself, you know—Suzy—warts and all.'

She smiled and opened the door into the studio.

'Now we'll see what the bigwigs have to say.'

He took a seat in the chair she indicated, while the lights came on. At least he had remembered the book. His secretary had underlined a few things which should help him through the text. A beer wouldn't come amiss, especially now the rest of the population were sitting in party hats getting blotto. Eleven minutes, he thought, eleven piddling minutes. Would it do any good? Change anything? Deep down he very probably fancied it could. The bright young things in the office had said it was an offer he couldn't refuse. Was he called Frandsen, the driver?

Aksel sat back, shut his eyes, and thought of all the phone numbers he knew off by heart.

'Something to drink, Aksel?' Suzy was standing there with a bottle of mineral water.

'That would be great. Or a cup of coffee, though I suppose the canteen's closed?'

She sat down beside him. Aksel was quite certain he'd seen her before. On children's TV. Something about brushing teeth.

'Were you on B&U, Suzy?'

'Have I been on B&U? No, never.'

'It was something about remembering to brush your teeth. Along with Jimmy.'

'Jimmy?'

'Jimmy Stahr'.

She smiled and said they'd had a little think about his clothes.

'My clothes?'

'They say it might be an idea to consider something other than a lounge suit.'

His driver wasn't called Frandsen, though something very like Frandsen.

'I think I look rather becoming in my Christiansborg uniform.'

He had wanted to say something different, but was too tired to think clearly. Precision had gone out the window.

Absentmindedness, he thought, is a persistent problem, a condition in its own right, impossible to shake off. The entire time we're somewhere else. He told himself that was worth remembering, might be useful in some other circumstance: modern man could be defined as an individual who for reasons unknown exists in different places. You stand with your feet far apart. Your left leg is here. Your right's somewhere else. The splits! Excellent expression, the splits. That isn't the main problem, though, seeing that in actual fact you're nowhere. Interesting thought. Make a note about not being anywhere. Physically of course he was present. He was demonstrably sitting in TV City, but his thoughts were in Trørød. Yet if the truth be told he was also still in his office. Or with the man whose name he'd forgotten?

He pulled a face. The splits can make us disloyal. He would make a note about disloyalty. Disloyalty towards one of his staff whose name he couldn't remember...

'Yes, that's what you'll do'.

'What I do?' Aksel looked up. 'So sorry Suzy, you were saying something about I should...I didn't catch the last bit.'

'I know what!'—Suzy clapped her hands—'I've got a suggestion, we go down to the girls in make-up. Josey, she's from Minnesota, she's a total miracle worker. What do you say?'

'Why of course. Is there a particular hurry?'

'No, no rush. This way.'

He hastened after her, stumbled over some cables and tumbled into the neon-lit room.

'Two secs, and she'll be here.'

Aksel gazed at himself in the mirror, turned round in his chair and started rummaging in his pockets for the slip of paper with the Trørød address. He'd been there before, dammit. That was when Lene's grandchildren were small.

'My wife has three grandchildren,' he mumbled.

Was the driver called Mouritsen? No, he was called something else. Aksel steadied his nerves by proving that at least he could remember the grandchildren's names. Children were given the most peculiar names these days.

Was the driver called Meinertsen? No, nobody could be called Meinertsen. In that case Mikkelsen?

'Bloody hell, my wrist hurts!'

He had said it out loud. 'Two hundred New Year cards. It affects the wrist.'

Was memory located in the wrist?

Another girl had turned up in the mirror. Somewhat older than Suzy. Dark and pretty. She introduced herself as Josey and apologized for her accent.

Aksel gave her his genial smile. He had practised that smile. He had been advised to do something about his teeth. Especially the lower ones. The know-alls reckoned his lower teeth were too aggressive. In our day people were fitted with a brace to straighten their choppers and make them like everybody else's, but it was far too late now. He had seen his own smiles on video. All five of them. Per from the secretariat had come straight out with it: You look like you've got a belly-ache, you screw up your eyes too much, try lowering your head a touch, try to look more appealing, don't turn up the left corner of your mouth, it looks like a nervous tic. Can't you push out your lower lip a bit? Think of your childhood, think of that old dear who sends you sweets at Christmas. Think of your summer house, your dog, your lunch pack, and all the happy memories from the Nordic Council.

Aksel had managed a smiling compromise between the doorstep salesman, the child molester, and the bluff docker.

'I have an accent myself'—Aksel pushed out his lower lip a bit—'although it's a dialect. But it goes, did you know that, Josey? And it's your fault. Well, not yours, but the fault of television. My wife says there's still a little trace of Kolding left when I get excited. One's own speech risks the splits.'

Josey smiled. Pityingly. Aksel thought he ought to learn to keep his mouth shut.

'Can I ask you something, Aksel?'

He set his briefcase on the floor.

'Ask away. That's why I'm here.'

'Your sideburns, may I take a bit off them?'

She placed her hands on his cheeks. Her touch reminded him how tired he was. But he was a workhorse, wasn't he? Was he called Finsen, the driver?

'They make you look—I won't say older but...'

'My wife likes them.'

'That's the odd thing', said Josey, 'it's the wives who are more conservative. People think the opposite. I suggest we put it to the test.'

The battery-operated machine was already at work.

First the left side, then the right. It went so quick.

She blew away the hairs and studied him in the mirror.

'Now if we trim you just a little bit above the ears it will be spot on. And it will save you a haircut.'

'One is a creature of habit.'

She took a spray and moistened his hair. Told a joke about an actor who had begged her to make him ten years younger.

'Half an hour later, well, he was ten years younger.'

Aksel laughed. He had nothing against being ten years younger.

'And it's New Year's Eve after all.'

Josey flashed him an enviable smile. So confidence-inspiring, so professional and warm. Aksel tried to guess how many percentage points a smile like that was worth.

'You have good hair, Aksel.'

'I have dead hair, Josey. It was Josey, wasn't it?'

'I'm really called Josefine, and you certainly don't have dead hair. I'm just taking the ends off, and a bit each side, to give you a more sparky look. I won't touch the rest.'

Aksel took the book out of his briefcase. He had seen Josey before too. Was it at Bakkens Hvile music hall? That couldn't be ruled out. He definitely wanted a sparky look, whatever that meant.

'Might one be allowed to read a bit while you trim?'

'All you want. That little thingummy you have under your lip—shall we hold on to it or what?'

'I did have a full beard for many years. That's the last stubborn bit left over. In the ministry they call it my ... '

He stopped short, stared into the mirror and went over all the phone numbers he knew off by heart.

'Your what?'

'My wisp.'

They didn't call it his wisp, but something much more amusing.

'So what'll you be reading?'

'*The Little Matchgirl*. I know it's a bit sentimental but I actually think it's suitable for tonight. Am I wrong?'

She rolled her eyes.

'I don't know it. How too embarrassing.'

Aksel smiled and said that all the same the story was part of our common heritage. He thought about the word 'actually'. Why had he said 'actually'? It was unnecessary. But he had acquired the tendency, this bad habit, of moderating his language all the time. His wife had said it came from perpetually pandering to the electors. Aksel had defended himself, though he was old enough to remember a time when politicians had dared to stand up to people. That was the time before television dictated the terms. TV had laid an egg, out of the egg came the fickle population, the wandering tribes of the opinion polls, the beast in the dark, King Kong atop the Town Hall tower. In the sixties you betrayed them by talking over their heads, today the betrayal consisted in agreeing with everything they said. But that was easy to say if you happened to be sitting in Trørød, home and dry.

Aksel watched the little tuft land in his lap. All it took was a onceover with the machine. The change was astounding.

'What's it about, Aksel? The story?'

'Oh, it's just a, what can I say, a melancholy mood-picture. Reminds us to, well, think of those who have less than most of the rest of us. Probably rather ill-timed. As a boy I lived in...'

He stopped short, for Suzy had returned. She gave Josey a knowing look.

'I'll be quick, Suz.'

Suzy pulled up a chair so that she was sitting sideways to Aksel.

'Up in the control room they're saying it might be a good idea to try a different story. What do you say, Aksel? It's entirely up to you.'

'I was just saying to this nice lady that I...Look, I've done my homework on it now.'

He laughed at his own reflection, thinking that the change truly was astounding. Hadn't they said his intelligence resided in that little tuft? They were so high-spirited in the office, especially Per, who had a past in advertising. Aksel had nothing against an easy-going manner. It came with the young, who got younger and younger. Age, he thought, is the great handicap. You mistime things, or rather, what timing you have no longer fits the bill, you get there too late, too early, or not at all. You resort to copying, but timing can't be copied, you lag so far behind they say you're past it.

He closed his eyes and thought about an old advert for beer. He felt as thirsty as the man in the poster. Could he really manage to read the whole text in eleven minutes? He repeated that he'd done all his homework, actually.

'Yes, I'm aware of that', Suzy gave him the kind of look you bestow on a child desperate for praise. Her voice confirmed it.

'But up in control . . . up in the control room they think it's a bit, you know, rather bleak for New Year's Eve. We're on at 9.30. It's a tricky moment.'

For the last phrase she had switched to English.

'Is it a tricky moment?'

'Yes, it truly is. It's really rather, well, tricky.'

Aksel wondered how to interpret this. What was the sense of 'tricky' in Suzy's mouth? Awkward, perhaps? Tense? Dangerous, challenging? Maybe something quite different. Something generally agreed. He had considered saying no to the offer. But you don't turn down TV. That was inscribed on page one of the handbook. Even if it was ten seconds after midnight. You turned up, danced to their tune, adjusted your calendar, your rhythm and your language, all for ten seconds on the News. In *Borgen* the joke was you got your daily exercise by running after a cub reporter from the local paper. In that regard he was in good trim. He had driven from Copenhagen to Hirtshals to explain an EU directive with the North Sea breakers as a backdrop. The item had been scrapped in favour of an extended weather forecast.

He thought about the phrase wear and tear. Excellent phrase. Television had that effect, the medium wore you out. You had to watch your step. Suddenly word goes out: *We don't bother with him any more.* Metal fatigue set in at his age. But metal fatigue was only the next worst thing. The worst was: *Seems things have gone a bit quiet around Aksel Frederiksen...*

'Okay, I'm amenable, there's plenty of other stories to choose from. It's just that this seemed fine, the right length. It was eleven minutes, wasn't it?'

He found the note in his pocket. It was sitting right next to his mobile. *Trørød, Sverigesvej 18.* The house was red with a thatched roof. But what the devil was his driver's name? In any case not Meinertsen. He smiled and shook his head. He had gone to school with someone called Meinert. Which must be why it kept popping up.

'They suggest dropping Hans Christian Andersen.'

Suzy leaned into the mirror and straightened her three-cornered hat.

Josey rolled her eyes. 'Isn't everyone sick of him?'

'Aksel is a really good singer.' Suzy winked at Aksel.

'Oh, please!'

'No, you have a good voice, Aksel, you truly have.'

'Listen, I'm bloody well not doing any singing. I mean to say, if you want to get me to sing Lene will skin me alive.'

'Lene?'

'My wife. She's staying up late with the children in Trørød.'

'Okay.' Suzy leaned into the mirror and studied her lips. 'We have eleven minutes, max twelve. Actually rather a prime time, we've two million viewers watching.'

'No more?' Josey applied rouge to Aksel's cheeks.

'People are a bit on and off. We're between a movie and a comedy show.'

Aksel pushed the note back in his pocket, aware he was thinking of the wrong house. To start with it didn't have a thatched roof.

'What do you say, Aksel?'

'To what? Fair enough, I'm with you about dropping *The Little Matchgirl*, if that's what you reckon.'

Suzy lowered her voice. 'They say it's for your own sake, Aksel.'

'Who?'

'The people up there in control.'

Aksel laughed. 'But I can't just get up and sing like that, at random.'

'You're not going to. Finish here with Josey, and then I'll see you out in the lobby. Raul will come for you. And he is a genius.'

Aksel stared at his reflection. He thought he had too much rouge on his cheeks and the mascara was too thick.

Josey said to bear in mind the powerful lighting.

'I look like an old tart.'

Josey tossed her head back and laughed. She had a great set of teeth. Very large, almost too large for the rest of her face. Still it suited her. Gave her a fresh and confident look. Yes, like something out of Bakkens Hvile.

'"Grandma", cried out the little girl, "oh take me with you, I know you will be gone when the match has burned down!"'

He gazed at Josey in the mirror.

'But that's been dropped. I do understand. Most likely would have been terrible. Everything considered.'

Josey pressed her cheek against his.

'Saved by the bell.'

She too had switched to English.

He went into the lobby and sat on a yellow sofa and dreamed of a cup of coffee. Despite having sworn to forego coffee. With coffee came the need for nicotine.

A young man arrived, hauling along a clothes rack. Aksel guessed it was the person called Raul, and that Raul was in his late twenties. Wasn't there a footballer called Raul?

'You a size 56, Aksel?'

'Yes, that's about right.'

Raul eyed the rack.

'This was all I could find. Most of it's with the drama department, they're working on *Summer in Tyrol*.'

Aksel leaned back. His fatigue had gone to his forehead now. Probably that was what had blanked out the driver's name. The trouble was that when he finally managed to get to bed now he couldn't sleep. In the old days he'd slept like a log, but that time was long past. Now everything went spinning round. Everything that had broken loose.

'Can't I get away with just taking off my tie?'

'That would definitely help.'

'Do you mean that, Raul? I think in that case I might keep it on.'

'I'll just call Suzy...'

Raul disappeared into the studio. He was wearing very large trousers. The arse trailed along the floor.

Everything had gone very quiet. At the end of the corridor a so-called person of different ethnic origins was struggling with a trolley stacked with furniture. Apart from that it was remarkably empty. And quiet. Aksel noted the place seemed a bit shabby. Excellent word, shabby. And the lad had all of Russia in his trousers.

'Here time is running out, and you can see it', he muttered.

The words dissolved into letters which disappeared in the gloom of the corridor. Meinert had shared the same desk with him at school. Lived in Algade 42, second floor on the left...

'And you never got your espresso', Suzy sat down in the yellow sofa.

'No, but I quite see why the canteen is closed. And just as well. Your coffee has never been any good.'

He laughed loudly and considered bumming a fag off her, only of course she didn't smoke. Or else used to smoke like a chimney and had taken a cure, but still had a hash problem, three children and an illegal immigrant husband on social security.

'Aksel, honestly and truly, it's just so cool you're giving us a song, and we've got hold of the pianist, Tim Lauberman. Up in control they say it would be terrific if you tried out this one.'

Suzy passed him a piece of paper.

Aksel sank back into the sofa.

'No, you've got to stop it now. You can't mean it. Suzy, you can't be serious.'

'They say you can do it, it'll be just the ticket.'

'I bloody well can't...'

'You know the tune, I bet.'

'Yes, but by God I hadn't imagined...'

'Aksel, it's so sweet. So truly sweet. It's a goosepimply kind of song.'

Aksel shook his head and looked around imploringly.

Suzy had pulled out her mobile, saying she had twenty messages on standby. She turned her back, keyed in a number and got connected to someone.

'Ditte, it's me', Suzy sighed. 'Sure, I went to Field's but I didn't get them. Someone beat me to it. I hate the place. Was it chocker? I tell you, it was *chocker*. Have to run, say hi to the others. Tell Freddy it's his treat next time. Bye.'

Aksel rubbed his forehead. Felt something or other oozing out. Presumably his powers of resistance.

'Sorry Aksel, did you say something?' Suzy put the mobile in her pocket.

'I don't believe I said anything, but don't you think there's a, what can I say, a certain discrepancy? To put it mildly.

'A discrepancy, Aksel?'

'Yes, a discrepancy between me and the words.'

'Sure. And the, well, discrepancy's what makes it so totally fab.'

She laid her hand over his, but removed it again quickly. He was thinking he couldn't remember when he had last taken such a whipping.

'A man bloody well can't sing that song,' he muttered, 'you're too young to remember Grethe Thordal.'

He wished he'd said something more. Something more convincing, but his voice withered in the empty foyer. He thought of the teenage Grethe Thordal singing about how she looked forward to her first ball. His hand crept into his pocket to check the bit of paper with the address was still there. He saw his plastic grandchildren sitting at the decorated table. Masters of aloofness. He had mentioned this to Lene: 'It doesn't matter what I do, I could even stand on my head. It's this aloofness. As though I am a stranger. Even though I've only damn well known them since they were born.'

Suzy patted her hair, and appeared to be thinking of something else. Aksel pinched his eyes. But why argue with the receptionist? At bottom she couldn't care less. Would rather get home to the kids and the benefits handouts.

He felt a latent resistance. Said to himself, I truly can't stand Suzy's type. Possibly it's unfair, but I find her attitude repulsive. You only have to look at her. Thinks she's streets ahead of me just because she's twenty years younger. Could twenty years accomplish that? All right, thirty. But she was the type you always got stuck with. Because Suzy was manufactured in the great media factory which that punk girl from the Red-Green Alliance called the Planet of the Apes. Cheeky bitch, that girl from the Red-Green Alliance. Green hair, ring in her nose, unbelievably sharp at the repartee, turned everything back to front and hit the target every time. Never ran after the local paper. Maybe there was still time to get Josey to dye his hair and move his wedding ring up to his nose.

'Suzy, might I say something? I think you ought to drop the idea of ... '

'Aksel'—she sat down next to him—'listen up. It's no big deal. They suggest you sing only the first and last verses. There's no need to learn it off pat, on the contrary, it'll be ten times better if you're just standing there with the words in your hand. Wasn't that what you said yourself?'

'Yes, but it has to be a girl who sings it. It's a girl's song.'

Suzy looked up at the man they called Raul. He said it had taken one hell of a time digging out the clothes, but it was always extra hassle when they were doing karaoke TV.

Aksel looked at the man's trousers and remembered a tent for two he'd once had.

'Drama has taken most of it', sighed Raul, sinking onto his other hip, 'and they're not parting with anything at any price. I'm so fed up with them.'

Suzy bent forward.

'Trust me, Aksel, you're in good hands, Raul knows what he's doing. It's going to be great.'

'What's going to be great?'

'Your costume.'

'I'm not putting on women's clothes, Suzy, I'm not putting on a dress.'

Suzy looked at her nails.

'Shit! Broken again. My little fingernail keeps breaking. What's your suggestion, Raul?'

'I found a blue number which I think looks rather fetching.'

'Not blue, the decor's blue. Got a nail file, Raul?'

'How about white?'

'White would be perfect.'

Aksel gave a loud laugh. 'Am I allowed to say anything?'

Suzy looked at her stopwatch. 'Of course.'

'You've a bloody cheek.'

He fumbled in his pocket for the note with the Trørød address. Was so tired that his words didn't match up. The word dementia came into his head.

Suzy was filing away at her little fingernail. Raul said he was familiar with the problem.

'Blame vitamin B. You're not getting enough vitamin B.'

Aksel leaned forward.

'Sweet Suzy,' he began.

'In control'—Suzy put the file down—'in control they're wild about the idea. You come on last, we've scrapped the other acts.'

'Suzy, you need to think again, girl.'

Aksel shook his head and had a glimpse of himself from the outside. He was sitting on a yellow sofa and shaking his head as he heard Hans Schreiber's popular number coming from the studio.

Suzy was presented with a bottle of lotion by Raul who said he rubbed it on his hands four times a day.

'If I forget they dry out completely. If there is anything I hate it's dry hands.'

Aksel stared at Suzy who was rubbing her hands together. She said the tune was very beautiful.

'It's genuinely beautiful, Aksel.'

'Yes, it is beautiful. But it shouldn't be sung by a middle aged man. My dear children, now let us...'

He stopped short and thought of the word dementia.

What had he been about to say? He had been about to say, Now let us pat the horse.

The dress fitted perfectly. It was possibly a shade too big, but Raul sorted that out with a strip of gaffer tape.

Were they wearing paper hats in Trørød? Were they celebrating? Perhaps they were watching TV. Waiting for him to appear. Lene and her grandchildren. Aksel's plastic grandchildren. The ones with the ambitious names: Frederik-August, AnnCeline, and Chelsea-Margrete. The trio that invented aloofness.

But what was his driver's name? . . .

'Gaffer!' He said it out loud.

They were always using gaffer out here.

Aksel sighed and looked round at the gaffer institution. Piss and paper and adhesive tape.

'Are you called after that football player?'

Raul was studying his hands.

'Me? Ah. Who? Oh, him. No, I'm not. To be quite honest I don't know who I'm called after. Perhaps my uncle. I'm from Macedonia. Take this little cap for your head, if we set it at a slant we avoid a wig. I'm not one for wigs. I draw the line there.'

Aksel wondered where he drew his own line, and swore that this was the last time. The last time he discussed his performance with a world-weary chain smoker from the Planet of the Apes and a homosexual lotion expert from Macedonia.

Suzy appeared at the entrance to the studio.

'Three minutes, Raul.'

On the stage stood two plaster figures and a grand piano. The backdrop represented a flowering meadow.

Aksel went over to stand on the little cross on the floor he had been shown. The lights were extinguished, leaving only the one spotlight shining where he was standing.

He screwed up his eyes.

'Hello, what about my shoes?'

'They can't see your shoes.'

Said who? A voice he hadn't heard before.

'Shouldn't we have rehearsed it first?'

'Control is happy. Twenty seconds.'

Aksel got a nod from his accompanist whom he had met on a previous occasion, to be exact at Nyborg Strand, in 1998. The delegates had sung the *Midsummer Ballad* to the Shu-Bi-Dua tune. No one could remember the original version. The pianist looked dry and unconcerned, as though he couldn't wait to get home. He suggested a key.

Aksel rubbed his eyes and felt something snap, presumably the gaffer.

A voice asked for silence in the studio.

Aksel cleared his throat, took a sip from his glass of water, and stared out into the darkness.

To Catch a Dane

Eugen Kluev

They decided to go out at dawn to catch a Dane.

'It's best to catch them early, while they're still fresh', said Donut.

'What do you want a Dane for?' asked Giselle, who was in the process of applying war paint to her face with poisonous Indian ink. Giselle was just what she was called, no-one had a clue why.

'For the sake of the thing!' said Donut sternly. 'To see what they're like. Everyone talks about them: the Danes, the Danes ... but no one's ever seen an actual Dane.'

'The grown-ups have seen them', said Giselle, quickly adding, flustered that she might have lied: 'Some grown-ups.'

'How could they have seen them when no Danes ever come here?' said Donut incredulously. 'You can find them out in Hellerup. And in Gentofte. And along the coast. But this is Nørrebro, and there are no Danes here.'

'So it's not here we catch him? Then I expect it might be best along the coast...'

'I'm not allowed to go that far', warned Small. 'I'm only allowed here. Or they'll string me up from the chandelier, my dad says.'

Small was seven, and that limitation you had to accept. Eight-year-old Giselle and particularly the ten-year-old Donut looked down on him, but put up with him. Small was Giselle's brother.

'Rubbish, they won't string you up,' promised Donut on behalf of the absent father.

'And anyhow', said Small, 'I'm not bothered about catching anybody, I want to roller skate!'

'Typical!' said Donut. 'Third generation refugees-and-immigrants! They do nothing but roller skate... So just skate through life till you're old. And when you are old, you and your roller skates will be a burden on everyone.'

'How do you know?' asked Small, scared.

'It's what people say'.

'About me?'

'About everyone!' pronounced Donut.

Well, if that's what people said about everyone obviously Small could hardly object. And in any case, if that's what people said then it must be true.

The idea of catching a Dane had originated with Donut's oldest friend who went by the name of Shitface, but not so long ago Shitface had gone off to 'the third world', and before leaving he had, so to speak, bequeathed the idea to Donut. What 'the third world' was Donut did not know, but just to be on the safe side he told Giselle and Small that Shitface had died. Giselle had been about to burst into tears, but when Small also looked glum she stopped.

Personally Giselle wasn't that keen on the idea of catching a Dane, because it made her feel sorry for the Dane. Only from everything Donut said they were duly bound to catch a Dane.

'Is it on account of Shitface?' she asked warily.

So then Donut said it totally wasn't on account of Shitface, and Shitface had nothing to do with it. They needed to catch a Dane because they *had* to, and they had to because all three of them, Donut, Giselle, and even Small, were refugees-and-immigrants. In other words, people bound to 'create problems'. It was all over the newspapers and talked about on TV. And that meant that was how it was, for the papers and the telly don't lie.

'But what if I don't feel like creating problems?' Giselle wanted to know, as she stopped in front of the bicycle shop window and gazed in horror at her painted face in the glass.

'Do you think they intend to ask if you feel like it or not? I told you we just *have* to because refugees-and-immigrants always create problems. If not, you're not a real refugee-and-immigrant.'

'I am, too!' said Giselle, offended.

'Okay, so if you're a refugee-and-immigrant, start creating problems.' Donut was merciless. 'No one else will create them for you, it's up to you. And not just you, every single one of us—all refugees-and-immigrants.'

'But I'm still a child!'

'The young create even more problems', Donut snapped back.

It was pointless trying to argue with Donut, for Donut was the most important person in the yard. And not just the yard, possibly the entire block—the whole street even. Sometimes it felt like Donut was the most important person in the whole of Nørrebro. Donut had arrived in the country when he was a babe in arms—perhaps he was a year—and he always said he'd had time to experience loads of things before that. Giselle and Small would listen to him with bated breath: being born in Nørrebro they had nothing to remember. On top of that, Donut came from a totally foreign country which no one had ever heard of. According to him the people in that country consisted entirely of his family, and in fact the country had been set up for them alone. And when they went away the country was immediately abolished, since there was no one left to live in it. Sometimes he would start speaking to his parents in his mother tongue—and then everyone went all quiet, they just could not see how anyone could speak that way. And after that not one of them dared say anything in any language at all.

All in all it was a great honour to have Donut for a friend. And for that matter, so long as her parents gave permission, Giselle could easily have married Donut on the spot—not actually because she cared for him that much, more to stop someone else getting him. But it was still too early to marry Donut, and there was nothing else they could do together—at least in the near future—other than catch a Dane.

At the filling station kiosk Donut bought sweets for the money they had, mixing all the most lurid-looking ones together in a great big bag. They straight off sat down by one of the pumps to eat the sweets.

'We're not allowed to sit here', said Small. 'This is where they put the petrol in cars.'

'Maybe some people aren't allowed', agreed Donut, 'but we can and we must. Because the law wasn't written for people like us.'

'Why wasn't it?' asked Giselle, fishing some toffees out of the bag.

'Are you still wanting reasons?' said Donut crossly. 'Because we are refugees-and-immigrants, can't you understand that? I mean don't you ever read the papers, don't you ever watch telly? We're the ones responsible for breaking all the laws of the land!'

They were silent a long while, busy with the sweets.

'I feel sick', said Small. 'And my mouth's all sticky. We should've bought apples!'

'Don't be so bloody weird!' sighed Donut. 'You're supposed to live an unhealthy life and have harmful habits. Eat up and stop moaning, just look how thin you are! The children of refugees-and-immigrants should be overweight, like me—that's because we eat too much. And the wrong kind of food. They all say that!'

Small was almost choking to death on a wine gum.

Hiccupping after finishing all the sweets they left the petrol station and went over to the shopping centre where, according to Donut, it was time to *hang out*. 'Hanging out' just meant wandering back and forth in the shopping centre, spending the time sitting on benches for a bit or messing about with all the stuff on display.

'So what sort of problems do we create if we catch a Dane?' Giselle was absorbed in trying on a lady's boot size 45, reduced.

'Just you wait and see', sighed Donut importantly, hauling Small out from under a pile of cardboard boxes he had collided with on his roller skates. 'We find out once we're there. To start with we'll have a really good look at this Dane—see what he's made of. We'll investigate everything about him—tickle him—see if he laughs or not. But we've got to be in national costume.'

'What's that, "national"—?'

'Surely you have some national costumes at home.'

'I've got a tiger suit', said Small cheerily as he started unscrewing one of the legs of the bench they were sitting on. 'I wore it for carnival.'

'A tiger's not right, it's not national. You need feathers and stuff, necklaces out of tusks, fur... like for instance the Red Indians. And faces have to be painted—like yours', said Donut pointing at Giselle. 'We can dye our hair as well, that looks national. It's all so the police will know straight off we're refugees-and-immigrants ready to create trouble any moment.'

'Will there be police, too?' queried Giselle, sounding scared.

'Of course!' Donut's voice boomed proudly. 'There's always got to be police wherever there's refugees-and-immigrants.'

'But what if the Dane we're going to catch is scary?' asked Small suddenly, and shivered.

'He's most definitely scary,' Giselle piped up promptly. 'The Danes are altogether scary. My best friend saw a

Dane once and nearly fainted! She, I mean the Dane, didn't even have legs, just a tail with scales on, like a dragon.'

Small, who had managed to unscrew the leg from the bench, suddenly let out a loud wail:

'I'm scared of—of catching one like that, she'll kill us with her tail!'

'Quit hollering', scolded Donut. 'Just get on with screwing the next leg off. Like I said, we'll catch him—or her—at dawn, while he's still asleep! And we'll be in national costume.'

'With tusks and claws—and feathers? We don't have stuff like that at home…So maybe we shouldn't really even try to catch one?' Giselle did her best to avoid Donut's eye.

'Typical!' he said. 'You don't want integration.'

'Yes, I do want integration,' said Giselle. 'But integration, that's when you have to go to work, not when you…catch a Dane.'

'You're so dumb!' Donut said, exasperated. 'Refugees-and-immigrants never ever work in their entire lives, they aren't capable—everyone says so! They're not on this earth to work—they're just on this earth to hang out for days on end. But integration, that's another thing altogether, that's when…when refugees-and-immigrants study the people of the country. That's what we'll do, see…catch a real live

Dane and study him. We find out how he's put together. And then we tell everyone else.'

'And what if he grabs us and puts us to work!'—Giselle set the boot back where she had found it and followed Small's progress with interest, for he had already managed to half unscrew the second leg of the bench.

'He won't do that!' Donut assured Giselle. 'For starters, everybody says it's totally impossible to get refugees-and-immigrants to work, get it? They said that again on the telly just last night. And then they showed a refugee-and-immigrant who all of his own accord chose to go to work. Wow, did he look sick! And for another thing, there isn't anything at all to do actually, not for anyone. There's only very little work left, everything's been worked to death already.'

The bench collapsed, and they landed on the floor, right in the middle of the shopping centre. Small let out another ear-splitting wail. As though he hadn't known how it would end!

On the whole Donut understood for himself the need to cause a bit of trouble. When Shitface suggested some-how catching a Dane and studying him, Donut had pre-tended to understand perfectly well what it entailed. But he hadn't understood too well. To be honest, he hadn't understood a thing: not what sort of people these Danes were, neither how to go about catching them. The grown-ups all round him never stopped saying the most terrible things about the Danes. Donut had looked all around him as carefully as he could, but failed to see anyone especially terrible—at least nobody with a tail...and absolutely no one with scales. Danes never came to this neck of the woods, he had told himself, they'd all settled somewhere by the sea. Donut, of course, had never been to the sea. In the emptiness of life without Shitface he had decided that if the Danes really lived by the sea it would be best to catch them with a net. Donut had read how people used to catch all sorts of sea monsters with a net: you threw out the net, the monster got caught in the net...job done!

But what were you supposed to do with it once you had it? Studying was another thing everyone was supposed to be able to do, and Shitface had said he knew how to. But Donut didn't. Just one time, he remembered, he'd made a study of a cockroach—by tearing off one leg after another. But the experiment hadn't been very successful: the cockroach died. What if the Dane died too?

'We're not going to hurt him, are we?' asked Giselle, as though she could read Donut's mind.

'Why should we do that? We—we're going to measure him.'

Phew! Suddenly everything fell into place. Donut straight off thanked his foreign god, and likewise—just in case—the local one too, for whispering in his ear: of course, studying means measuring! You just had to take measuring instruments along—a ruler, a tape measure, and whatever. And then—well then you used them to measure the sleeping Dane—length, width, height, and what was it called ... diameter? And if he had a tail then the tail would have to be measured on its own, or similarly wings, and so forth. Measure, and then write it down—and that way you'd clear up the mystery.

'We need to clear things up', said Donut.

'So where did they actually come from, these Danes? Or have they always been around?' asked Small without much interest, while fiddling with his sister's mobile phone.

'From Denmark, is that so hard to understand?' Giselle took the phone off him. 'There's a country called that.'

'There was', clarified Donut. 'That was in the olden days. It was where the Vikings lived—they're the ones with horns. I have a book at home with "Denmark—Land of the Vikings" written outside and there's pictures of these Vikings in it. They look like beetles. But later their horns dropped off and they became extinct - same as the country, so I read. But the Danes—they're entirely different— they pop up all by themselves in any old country.'

'With horns?' asked Small. Just to be on the safe side.

'Most likely without.' Giselle, who having waited in vain for Donut's answer now supplied it for him. 'Definitely with tails, but I'm not so sure about with horns...'

The horns will have to be measured as well, if they have them—Donut silently noted to himself.

'Perhaps we ought to check up first, Donut? After all it's better to know in advance, if they have horns or not...' Giselle gave Small a clip across the ear, he'd pinched her mobile again.

'The ones with horns, they butt you', Small warned them, and showed how.

'Have you both gone crazy?' said Donut, and shook his head. 'Do you want everyone to know? That will be the finish!'

Darn it, what a bummer it was that Shitface had gone off to the third world—these little kids didn't have a clue. How daft to suggest it. Go out to the coast where it's teeming with Danes and gawp at them all... they'll catch us in a second and gobble us up—it's no accident they say they live on raw meat. Shitface told a story about how he'd once seen a Dane in the cinema: he was standing up by the screen in a black suit holding out some sort of raw meat... ugh! And the kids didn't have national costumes; he'd have to get hold of some himself, or even worse make them! Also he'd somehow have to get hold of a net.

*

Ingerlise Annemarie Vildmark Jensen—all skin and bone, eighty-seven years of age, unmarried—naturally had nothing personal against integrated refugees-and-immigrants. To be sure, in all her long life she had never met a single integrated person, and not a single refugee-and-immigrant for that matter, thank the Lord. Here, on Zealand's north-east coast, where she lived in her villa 'Valhalla', which she had inherited from her parents, no refugees-and-immigrants were ever to be observed, not even in good weather. But on the television Ingerlise Annemarie Vildmark Jensen could look at them as much as she wanted, and she had noted that there was a startling variety in the looks of refugees-and-immigrants. They consisted of both men and women; old, middle-aged, young, and even very small children; slit-eyed and some with normal-shaped eyes; thick-lipped and some with hardly any lips at all; hairy, moderately hairy, and some completely bald; tall, short, and extremely short... some simply pitiful; black-skinned, red-skinned, yellow-skinned, white-skinned... This last group in particular struck her as more dangerous than the rest: integration had clearly succeeded so well for them that they could easily be mistaken for members of the indigenous population, including Ingerlise Annemarie Vildmark Jensen herself.

Even so, naturally she had nothing personal against the integrated white-skinned ones; they were welcome, she opined, to settle somewhere or other along with the rest—only just not here. After all, there were special places—like Nørrebro, or Ishøj—where it was suitable for that sort to live. But Kokkedal, for example, was in her view wholly inappropriate. Why should they live so close to her?

All the same, for a while now the media had been talking of nothing but how things were not going so well right here in Kokkedal. You only needed to turn on the television, and in no time up popped one refugee-and-immigrant after another on the screen smiling a crafty smile... aimed what's more directly at Ingerlise Annemarie Vildmark Jensen. It was as though they were all of them saying, Hello old Ingerlise Annemarie Vildmark Jensen, how are you, are you *still* doing okay?

It was the 'still' which alarmed her so greatly...

And one time Ingerlise Annemarie Vildmark Jensen's secret but entirely platonic admirer, the tanned golfer Ejvind Julienne, had told her that driving along the Rungsted coast road in his Porsche he had sighted two refugees-and-immigrants: there they were in broad daylight standing right in the middle of the road indulging in a long multi-ethnic kiss.

After this disagreeable story Ingerlise Annemarie Vildmark Jensen had immediately contacted the very definitely not publicly listed company 'Andersen & Sons', which specialised in the delivery and installation of alarm systems. Rather rashly taking advantage of their winter discount, she ordered their package deal, complete with all appliances, and a service contract which went under the trade description of 'combined coastal surveillance'. The combined coastal surveillance turned out to cost nearly one quarter of all the savings Ingerlise Annemarie Vildmark Jensen had set aside for her still distant old age.

Just a week later Villa Valhalla had become unrecognizable. Ingerlise Annemarie Vildmark Jensen was particularly pleased with the four long-distance cameras of impressive dimensions now mounted on each side of the building. They captured and relayed to the audio-video database all movements carried out by whatsoever randomly selected multi-ethnic object within a radius of thirty miles. 'Naturally I have nothing personal against integrated refugees-and-immigrants', she confided to Andersen Junior, 'but you do understand, young man...'

The young man understood only too well. From now on whatsoever randomly selected multi-ethnic object merely had to set foot anywhere within a radius of thirty miles to set coloured lights flashing on and off all round Ingerlise Annemarie Vildmark Jensen like a disco at midnight, so that she was constantly called to the screens; and there virtually all the tedious goings-on of the north-east coast lay revealed to her gaze. And as for any movement by whatsoever randomly selected multi-ethnic object proceeding in the direction of Villa Valhalla itself, it instantly set off sirens which started to hoot, groan, sob, and wail in a whole variety of registers.

To live in Villa Valhalla had become impossible, but safe. Ingerlise Annemarie Vildmark Jensen wept for joy. But after a while—chiefly due to exhaustion caused by the neighbourhood dogs who accompanied the sirens' chorus with appalling howls—she started knocking the sound system off the alarm at night. There was no danger in that, as her body had learned to react to movement by whatsoever randomly selected multi-ethnic object within a radius of thirty miles without any help at all from the ultra-modern equipment. Nor did Ingerlise Annemarie Vildmark Jensen need to start to hoot, groan, sob, and wail in various registers, though if necessary she could manage that too, for now she was all but indistinguishable from the digital apparatus she was surrounded by.

It did, however, become necessary to alter her daily routine; from now on Ingerlise Annemarie Vildmark Jensen slept during the day, whereas the entire night— between the hours of 11 p.m. and 7 a.m., when the alarm was disconnected—she spent on the roof of Villa Valhalla. On cold nights, with her legs swathed in a woolly blue and green tartan plaid and her head encased in a warm hat à la Viking with vigorous horns projecting on either side, In-gerlise Annemarie Vildmark Jensen hauled herself right up on to the roof ridge, from which vantage point she was able to react with her—now almost digital—body to any movement made by whatsoever randomly selected multi-ethnic object within a radius of thirty miles.

Seen from below she looked like a little flying mermaid with horns.

Around six o'clock that May morning Ingerlise Anne-marie Vildmark Jensen's digital body all of a sudden started to register certain external disturbances—it started trembling in tiny convulsions, threatening to cause the human shape on the roof ridge to lose balance. 'Here we go', said Ingerlise Annemarie Vildmark Jensen calmly to herself, pullling out a pair of heavy binoculars...

This was precisely as she had imagined them, the unintegrated refugees and immigrants. With painted faces, undersize, dark-skinned, covered in animal hides, with feathers and necklaces made of tusks and claws, they advanced slowly with a net in their hands—quite evidently meant for her, Ingerlise Annemarie Vildmark Jensen, a person of eighty-seven years of age, unmarried. At a short-legged, jerky pace the unintegrated refugees-and immigrants covered the distance between the station and Villa Valhalla, and then—suddenly catching sight of the little flying mermaid with horns up on the roof ridge—they screamed like crazy.

But all in vain: Ingerlise Annemarie Vildmark Jensen's digital body answered with a chorus of sirens, hoots, groans, sobs, and wails, which was immediately accompanied by the howling of every dog in the neighbourhood.

And within no more than a few seconds the combined coastal surveillance team in the shape of a dozen police officers, arriving on the scene in four cars, had surrounded Donut, Giselle, and Small.

'Don't be scared', whispered Donut to Giselle and Small. 'It *has* to be like this. Clashes between refugees-and-immigrants and the police are entirely normal. But the police are powerless, says the telly... Charge!'

'Ch-arge!' yelled Small excitedly. At that very moment he had finally fully woken up, and with great menace swung a future crucial exhibit above his head.

A school ruler.

'*A flat plastic weapon ten centimetres in length.*'

Willadsen

Dan Turèll

'If I wrote novels I would write Willadsen, the novel'

– Peter Laugesen, January 1966

1

His name was Willadsen, Svend Willadsen Nielsen. The first time we saw him he was draped over the shoulders of a removal man who knocked on our door and asked if it was here Mr. Willadsen was moving in.

It was. We had been tipped off by the owner, and obviously had known for a long time that there was a room empty where we lived on the second floor of an enormous villa in Lyngby, a decadent ancient overgrown enormous villa with towers and terraces, now let out room by room—with two families on the ground floor, two on the first floor, a couple in an annex, and four rooms on the second floor. Four rooms, of which we lived in one, Peter and Jeanette in another, and a fellow called Ole and a girl called Annie, joiner and hairdresser, in the third—both very rosy-cheeked and very optimistic archetypal 'young Danes', as though for some reason deliberately misplaced there amongst us wolves and outsiders (second floor was *the* outsider floor in the house)... They were in the third, and the fourth had been standing empty for some time.

So when the removal man arrived fairly late in the evening with the more or less unconscious Willadsen over his shoulder we were on the case. We laid Willadsen on our bed, and went downstairs to give the removal man a hand lugging Willadsen's shit up to the second floor.

While we were struggling up and down the stairs, he, the removal man, told us how he had spent the entire day driving around with Willadsen. How he had picked him up at a house somewhere on Ordrup Jagtvej where all the other tenants (it was a house much like ours, and with the same owner) were apparently pig sick of him and had put all his belongings out on the pavement to be ready for the removal man's arrival around midday. They loaded up and climbed aboard, and at that point Willadsen couldn't remember where exactly he was supposed to be headed, but gave the removal man the key to his new room, his destination, saying they only needed to drive around

Lyngby a little while and he'd be sure to find it, he'd seen the house before and would recognize it...But he had been drinking heavily all day, and having finally achieved his goal he had evidently passed out with undisguised, no doubt mightily relieved, indifference.

So there they were, late in the evening, and after their Buster Keaton entrance we humped all Willadsen's chattels up the stairs. It wasn't as though his belongings amounted to much—at any rate no more than the rest of us possessed, but he was that much older: somewhere between forty and fifty, very thin and grey and wrinkled and worn as he lay there on the bed. We got the door unlocked to a very small room, the smallest in the house: his, where his table, bed, chair, and chest of drawers (all dilapidated stuff, as worn as the man himself), together with some piles of books, an old typewriter, a radio, and a few boxes of clothes, china, and a medley of other stuff, all managed to fit in.

There were some odd things amongst them. Odd things which showed up bit by bit as we carried them upstairs in the balmy darkness of a summer's night. The chest of drawers was full of small lined boxes which in turn were full of small speckled and mottled *eggs*—and most of them, nearly all of them, cracked. There were a lot of notebooks, thick and scarred and stained, with wobbly utterly illegible handwriting outside and in. And curiously, amongst his otherwise shabby standard baggage there were several binoculars and a set of photographic equipment with expensive looking lenses. And the very few books were odd too, special, scientific—and written in several languages, definitely French, English, German, and Spanish.

We dumped the lot in there—Peter and Jeanette, the removal man, Kirsten and me—then went to our own room and had a beer and chatted a bit about it all. Later, after the removal man had gone, we put Willadsen to bed, in his own bed, with his possessions stacked up around him—there wasn't much else to do—and went to bed ourselves.

And all night I dreamt about the thin, grey, worn, almost invisible man with the bony face and the many boxes of eggs.

2

Over the next days we got a little closer to him. He came in person to apologize—in a terribly mild and polite fashion—for being so 'indisposed' at the time of moving in. He thanked us for the help . . . He had lunch with us. His hands shook so much he dropped most of his food while trying to eat.

He began to sort out his stuff and threw out the cracked eggs. We talked with him quite a lot (I don't think any of us were working at the time), and bit by bit more or less managed to piece together his story, at least assemble the bare bones of it from the snippets he unintentionally let drop from time to time. It transpired he was divorced from his wife, wife number two, but was still hopelessly in love with her—no children, she was ten years younger, and he was paying for some sort of training for her. It transpired he was a chronic alcoholic—that was why his hands kept shaking, and why at times he would lose it and just keel over in a coma like the evening he moved in—or true to form *was* moved in, like part of his own worldly goods. It transpired he seemingly didn't really have 'anything to live for', and was just a very lonely man somewhere between forty and fifty, with no wife, no 'family' in any sense of the word, far removed in time and space from the friends and society he must once have frequented—and at present unemployed and thrown out of the house he'd been living in because the people there were fed up with his drinking and his comas, and thrown into our house since that was the place where the owner (the future very notorious property shark Jacques Bassan) gathered most of the dregs, or to put it as he so inimitably did in his cynical-cum-charming way: the place where the most tolerant of his lodgers lived.

It transpired that Willadsen had been or was an orni-thologist (the birds' eggs, the binoculars, the photographic equipment), and that a good many of his boxes contained yellowing periodicals like *The Ornithologist* or *The Field Ornithologist* of which he kept stacks lying about, years' worth of copies. Also that he had taken countless measurements and studied the migration and flight paths of birds in every possible way, and that for many years he had been working on an enormous opus about his favourite bird, *Rex regulus*, King of the Birds—working at it on and off between his worst alcoholic bouts (the notebooks). And that in addition he was writing a 'treatise' about something as weird and abstruse as Gundsømagle Lake and its 'limno-ecological changes' over the past twenty years— which he therefore must have measured or observed or what the fuck else you do when investigating 'limno-ecological changes'. (The words are still etched in my mind, they were the precise words he used—and he sat very quietly in his little room surrounded by his battered furniture and dented suitcases talking about these things slowly in a drawling monotonous voice while sucking on an ancient eternally juicy pipe, drinking beer all hours of the day and listening to his radio softly playing assorted dance music till the end of time...)

Day by day that summer disappeared, the summer of 1965, I think it was. The sun shone like crazy, a drowsy heat hugged the houses and hedges of Lyngby. Everything was waiting just around the corner, Peter and I wrote poems no one wanted to print, and the world was very beautiful.

And Willadsen drank beer for as long as he had money, very often dropped whatever he was holding, got a little greyer and more haggard inside his dry skin, spoke less, and less coherently, and his eyes stared out from ever deeper sockets.

When he ran out of money—wherever the devil he got it from—he'd start to sell off or pawn his binoculars and photographic gear to the tobacconist and the grocer, or at the very least deposit them as security for his purchases—chiefly Danish fruit wine. He did this very calmly and politely, like when he apologized the day after moving in—as if deeply regretting having to inconvenience the shopkeepers in this fashion, but seeing unfortunately there was no other way... They nearly all agreed to what he asked, and stored his things at the back of the shop.

I spoke with the tobacconist about it—how you could see, no, *smell* rather, how tormented Willadsen was, how even the way he moved his hands showed how thoroughly sick he must be. And we spoke about how at the same time you could always see by his face that he knew what he was doing, and that there was no other way open to him. We both realized he was in another world, way out there: he would never have hurt anyone, no one but himself—for the world around him didn't actually *exist* for him that much.

All of us had the feeling that all we could do was wait and see what happened. And we learned a few things from it. Through Willadsen we learned that a good many alcoholics convert to fruit wine if they are skint but still too grand or too choosy to touch meths or wood alcohol. Danish fruit wine was then selling at 9 kroner a bottle, cheaper than anything else (this was before the era of cheap plonk from supermarkets like Irma)—and still with a hellishly high alcohol content. Sticky stuff... Through him we learned how the alcoholic suddenly goes under, how he can sit for hours and clearly not be anywhere, just be away, far away from everything. From him we learned all over again, in a new variation, how Fate—what we would later call Karma—can mould people after its own image. We saw the disciplined way he sold off his binoculars and books, and knew and could tell (as he himself later confirmed, needlessly) that he had done this many times before—that he knew the routine and it was a regular routine. Right down to the bottom until every penny and every pawnable valuable is gone, then up again and start over, recoup the gear and get a job and drink nothing but tea and coffee—until after a while it's back first to the beer and finally the fruit wine, long pendulum swings to and fro lasting a year or six months, with ever fewer and shorter intervals between the spells.

3

The days passed in their divinely obscene way as they have done since forever right until now, ten years on, and we were all doing our 'own thing' or at least whatever chance seemed to hold out for the moment. At the time Peter was a proofreader at *Berlingske Tidende*, the daily paper, Kirsten was working at Bleggaarden dry cleaner's, and that summer I was a window cleaner. The days passed, one thing and another happened, the summer drew towards its inevitable close, and one day Peter and Jeanette left for Odder and moved into a house there. They went from Bagsvaerdvej 65 in Lyngby to 'Solbakken, Ballevej, Odder', and were lost from sight.

And just as Peter and Jeanette were moving out Willadsen finally cracked up and asked us to help get him admitted to hospital, so that all at once it felt like the whole of that summer's second floor was falling apart in the early autumn—falling apart and, like flecks of dust, forming a different pattern elsewhere. Departure was in the air, wild and unsettling, 'The Times They Are A-Changin'' as Dylan was singing in New York more or less at that very moment...

And so Willadsen asked to be admitted. He had come full circle now, he said—there was no other way. He needed to be admitted to Rigshospitalet, the state hospital, and he knew he couldn't manage it on his own and there was no one else to ask, simply no one else to ask, so he had to beg us to go along with him and get him admitted. He'd reached the end of the line, social services had finally given up on him, and there was no point in dragging it out. Tomorrow we must get him admitted, he said over the last bottle of fruit wine. Tomorrow we must get him admitted to Rigshospitalet and have the Salvation Army collect his things, so he could 'start afresh' when he came out. When he came out and had kicked the habit and had work again he would get it all sorted. We *must* promise to get him admitted the very next day, even if he happened to change his mind in the night...

The very next day we got him admitted, and it did in fact take a day. From the early morning, when he was shaking and just needed a little drink, and then a little more, and then just needed to wait a little and sort out a few little things, and then change his shirt (three times...), and then have a little bit more to drink—and so on... When we were out in the street and on our way (he still with a bottle in his hand), we just had to make a little detour to look up his friend Skov, his one and only friend, to say goodbye to him. And Skov lived in the same house Willadsen lived in before coming to our place, the one out on Ordrup Jagtvej on the edge of the wood, near the racecourse—and anyhow it was on the way to Willadsen's doctor who we had to call on for the referral chitty.

So we set out on our way, moving along like a weird caravan right from Lyngby to Ordrup with Kirsten and me on either side of Willadsen. And the birds sang like crazy that day, sang like crazy all along the long stony suburban streets with their long fancy driveways. And at last we came to Skov's place, and Skov and Willadsen said good-bye, and Skov thought it was very smart of Willadsen to quit his boozing.

And Skov suffered from a persecution complex. He told me how a conspiracy had been got up against him. He had been a jockey at the race course, but had fallen off a horse and hit his head, and from that moment on he had been persecuted, partly by the doctors and the psychiatrists at the county hospital (though in effect by doctors and psychiatrists everywhere), and partly by a whole series of top people from Prime Minister Krag to ombudsman Hurwitz, and even high court supremo Carl Madsen. They had all refused to help him, and were consequently in cahoots with the doctors—and with the newspapers which had never wanted—or dared—to relate the true story about the conspiracy against him, Skov. And it wasn't as though he hadn't tried to work up interest in his case! He'd done *everything*! He produced letters from Krag, Hurwitz, Bomholt, *Ekstrabladet*, Aksel Larsen, Villars Lunn, the chief of Gentofte police, the Lord Chamberlain's office—all very similar sounding letters which all regretted they were unable to do anything for him. He was of the opinion I ought to write an article about him—if I were really interested in some good stuff which—so he said—'could make my name'. (He carried on sending me letters and documents about the case for a long, long time after...)

We managed to tear Skov and Willadsen apart and continued on our way to the doctor—an extremely brusque elderly man, straight-backed, tough and grizzled, 'a southern gentleman' they would have called him in an American movie. 'All a waste of time', the doctor said to Willadsen. 'Waste of time, man... You know the drill... You've tried it four or five times before... Useless', said the doctor. And to me, 'Young man, you're wasting your time too over all this... But if he *insists* on being admitted... I am not entitled to deny him, but I tell you again: it's a waste of time, *it is a waste of time...*'

So we got the referral chitty and took a tram down to Rigshospitalet—a tram I hadn't ridden since we went to the international against Sweden when I was in second grade at school, and had to queue for six hours with a packed lunch in high spirits and with placards saying things like 'Come on Jens Peter, make them sore / you have beaten Swedes before', and I lost myself in a fog of memories on the tram... We smoked cigarettes that day, and Hasse, he went and broke a tram window with his

elbow, oh man...My childhood...Tickets punched, off
we get and it's straight into Rigshospitalet, through the
entrance and down the long corridors where Willadsen,
totally at home, finds the right ward in a jiffy and is met by
a doctor he knew from 'last time'...And it was the same
old story: 'Waste of time...You know as well as I do...'
and so forth, until finally they resigned themselves to
admitting him, and Willadsen—very small, grey, and
thin—waved goodbye to us from the doorway with a
nurse at his side shaking her head. The last glimpse
of him there, waving with a Chaplinesque melancholy
(if Chaplin had happened to be Slav), waving and waving,
so little and worn and disappearing into the big white
hospital corridor...

4

Kirsten and I moved to Vangede only a couple of weeks
later, when Bassan—not unexpectedly—threw us out of his
house because of an article I had written about his specula-
tions. Every so often we sent a letter and some tobacco to
Willadsen, and every so often got a letter telling us things
were on the mend—he would soon be out and find some
work and 'get everything back in shape a bit'. Autumn
set in, and it was late, dark autumn when Willadsen came
out and moved back into Bagsvaerdvej 65, into the same

room on the same second floor where now not one person was left of the original occupants he had known.

He found a job, and a pretty fortunate job. It was in a lab which worked for Brüel & Kjaer, qualified technician's work which he turned out to be good at—being half- or three-quarters trained as a laboratory worker, as it transpired. They were pleased with him. He drank less, managed to pay some bills, got stuff back out of pawn. He worked in the daytime, wrote his treatises in the evening, and got up early every Sunday morning to see the birds migrating.

Once in a while he rode out to Vangede on an old moped, a recent acquisition, and would spend the evening sitting and chatting, and seemed calm enough, although his hands still shook. On such evenings he showed—in brief, nervous flashes—what we had previously guessed at through the alcoholic haze: that he knew an awful lot, that he was well up on the most diverse subjects. You'd be sitting listening to the radio, a jazz record which chanced to be playing, and all of a sudden Willadsen would start talking about what an incredible pianist Art Tatum was— all of a sudden he'd be sitting there talking about Art Tatum's piano technique as though all he had ever done was hang around digging Tatum. Almost no matter what the topic of conversation, he would modestly put in 'as you probably know' and then go on in his mild and unassuming fashion (yet tough and stubborn somehow, enough at any rate for you to sense that once he must have been strong and tough and stubborn)—and then go on to say something scientific in a matter-of-fact way which no one, obviously, had a clue about, but which for each of us clearly breathed *knowledge*.

He would all of a sudden produce a treatise he'd had printed ten years back—a treatise about why the cuckoo was called what it was called in all the languages of the world, and what the name meant in the folklore of the various languages. He spoke or read many languages, or snatches of them. He could talk anatomy for hours on end, and had his own particular anatomical theories whose points I didn't understand, but which he planned to work out in more detail once everything was back in shape again and he had time to acquaint himself with some of the literature in the field which he hadn't yet read or been in a position to buy.

He began to buy his books back from the second hand book shops. He acquired more and more French and German books about the King of Birds, fat volumes about 'limno-ecological changes' (not many used the expression 'ecology' in everyday conversation then, and I heard it first on his lips), books on anatomy—weighty tomes with graphs and plates and diagrams. He worked on his book about *Rex regulus*, and he could show you several hundred closely written pages, typewritten and in pencil, with drawings, photos, and countless notes in the margin... Many years' work, absolutely fascinating even to those still unable to distinguish between a *Rex regulus* and a sparrow... He was paying off his debts and 'sorting things out', or starting to anyway.

Then something or other happened, and I don't know what and was never told. Perhaps there was nothing that 'happened', as such... Perhaps nothing happened, and the doctors and hospital staff were right: perhaps that's just how it *was*. Perhaps that's just how it *was* for Svend Willadsen Nielsen, there in his little dark room, between forty and fifty years old, still so helplessly in love with his divorced wife whom he never saw... Perhaps that *was* just how it was, that he *had to*, he was doomed to start drinking again. All of a sudden the weird alcoholic glow was back again, like a blue mist before his eyes and all round his body, a tent he lived in, a remoteness separating him from all others... and all of a sudden he would again shakily get up from his chair and say: 'Excuse me... do you mind if I pass out?' in a pathetic, almost self-effacingly polite voice (as though he was sorry to interrupt some fantastic per-formance...) before next moment collapsing on the floor in a coma. And you would wonder how come, seeing he had been there several hours and not drinking—until you found an empty bottle or two behind the toilet, between the toilet and the wall, hidden behind the pipe. So he must have grabbed the booze out of his coat in the hallway and taken it out to the john, discreetly, perhaps feeling vaguely guilty...

5

Things got worse again. It was the same routine we had seen once before, and we did what we could, and we couldn't do much. At any rate it wasn't enough, and maybe nothing would have been. Kirsten was pregnant, we weren't getting on very well at the time, and in reality didn't want the child. Kirsten stopped at home, pregnant and on edge, at times crazy as hell, and I was working in a bloody laundry—a ten-hour shift in piss-awful heat, steaming hot premises that melted the brains out of you and boiled up your thoughts, and I was so fucking frustrated with that job and all the hours boiling away... Oh, *I* was a child. And Peter and Jeanette were stuck out in Odder, in more or less the same situation, and in one of his letters from Odder (Peter was constantly writing letters then, endless letters ten or twelve pages long which always made you very happy, for they were enormously liberating and said so much about what you weren't able to say yourself, but could always see so well as soon as it was said...) Peter and Jeanette were stuck in Odder and all the same never so very far away, and it was in one of those letters that Peter wrote: 'If I wrote novels I would write Willadsen, the novel... Willadsen is you and me, abandoned and alone... It sounds precisely as sentimental as it is...'

And I thought about 'Willadsen, the novel', an old story—the Outsider's story, or the Loser's story, or the Saint's, the reluctant Saint's story. The story of a person who has totally given up on himself, and therefore has such sad, such distant eyes—a person who is as infinitely and hopelessly, as unostentatiously *lost* as anyone can ever be.

Things followed their course. Willadsen's visits became fewer and fewer, once more his work dropped out of the equation, his books and binoculars and equipment vanished from his room, his correspondence became irregular, his handwriting more illegible, and he resorted to fruit wine again. There came more and more blank stretches, black hours, and you began more and more clearly to sense how his consciousness was screwed together, and why there were those kinds of big lacunae which were nothing but empty—quite simply those periods when he drank all day, or had drunk all day, and had no idea what else had happened. Black zones—like when in the middle of a political discussion it turned out that Willadsen knew nothing of the Soviet occupation of Hungary in 1956, which I myself vaguely remembered as something the grown-ups talked about over the papers at the breakfast table while you eyed front page pictures of tanks rolling by. Willadsen knew nothing about Hungary 1956 and what came after, because that was one of the empty stretches—just one of them, and just one way of discovering them. Black zones, and more were on the way.

He slowly faded away, vanished from sight. The last time I saw him I drove him home late at night on a motorbike in a snowstorm—the winter of 1966. The road was devilish slippery, and Willadsen was enormously drunk and had become almost disjointed, the way he (and other alcoholics I've known) sometimes became when a bout had reached its climax—as though his legs couldn't really carry him anymore, as though they folded under his negligible weight, as though his arms couldn't even manage the simple movement of reaching out, as though his hand would inevitably break if you put anything in it. He was already in that state, numbly rubberized, when he crawled onto the bike, and he flopped on and off it and overturned it twice on the way down Nybrovej, in the snowstorm, until I parked up the bike and practically carried him home, shoved him onwards through the snow, yard by yard. For he was desperate to get home—there were too many people in our house, too many he didn't know, and the radio stood ready and waiting to play the eternal dance music he always listened to, the old radio stood ready for yet another night with the bottle in the little dark room with the bed, the desk, the chair and the chest of drawers with the last and latest birds' egg collection, still intact...

He moved to the provinces and infrequent letters followed from first one and then another town. For a while there was something in Nykøbing Falster (I think), something vague about a girl there, a new note in the letters (Peter wrote: 'Willadsen is you and me...any one of us without the others')—but nothing came of it. Something got in the way, or maybe something happened quite different to what we imagined, or maybe it was just Willadsen, who for a while thought something was happening, or tried to convince himself it was.

In any case, shortly after this the letters petered out entirely. And a while later, a couple of years after that and in a roundabout way, we got to hear that Willadsen had died.

6

Willadsen left nothing. Nothing, neither children nor family, not even a will, and no one knows where his things are gone. Not so much the bed or the chest of drawers with the cracked birds' eggs, not so much the German doctoral thesis on anatomy or the old radio or his greasy coat, those are not the things I'm thinking of—they've no doubt wandered their sensible way to a second-hand shop of an appropriate kind. But the 300-400 sheets with the carefully handwritten and typed notes about *Rex regulus* or the almost equally thick manuscript with the countless maps and measurements of Gundsømagle Lake over twenty years—no one knows what's become of them.

Someone must have them, or have been given them, just as Peter was given his collected Shakespeare when they left, or as I was given his Bible the first time we got him admitted—a large, beautiful, compact old bible which I don't have any more either . . . I was forced to tear it up one winter's night five or six years later, when a paranoid dopehead we had taken under our roof turned out to suffer from some sort of persecution complex regarding bibles, and I had to tear all the pages out, one by one, to calm him down (and I saw how this simple tangible action really did liberate him . . . as though it really *helped* him to see how something which had plagued and tormented him, something which had so evidently oppressed and dominated him, could in that way, simply and symbolically, be ripped to shreds, bit by bit . . .) The handsome empty brown leather binding was all that was left, and I later sent it to the artist Henrik Have as a postcard, as a 'Bible of Zen Buddhism', a friendly joke, and Henrik has very probably still got it, for Henrik likes his possessions . . . But that was how Willadsen's Bible disappeared, and that is most likely what has happened to most of his stuff, or something much the same.

The last solid reminder of Willadsen was his old type-writer, a big heavy indestructible one which I bought off him back in 1965 for 30 kroner and a bagful of beers, and used for at least five years and wrote my first books on, and only last year gave away to my girlfriend's sister (and now she's no longer 'my girlfriend' either ...)

And I believe the way these things ended is how the whole of Willadsen's life had been. The way these things ended their perambulations is I think possibly how 'Willadsen, the novel' might have looked. The way his things kept wandering back and forth, and he himself followed his own routines or his one routine, perfectly resigned to whether they were with him or not pro tem—and all the time was able to see his own situation, see his own movements very clearly and concretely, see his own movements mirrored in these things wandering off to the pawn shop or getting sold, out for ever or back again into the room, his little dark room on the second floor, or perhaps the unknown room where he ended his journey, perhaps still with fragments of his life's permanently mov-able possessions around him ... The unknown room in some provincial town or other, the room in some hospital or other or in an institution, where Svend Willadsen Nielsen left for ever Gundsømagle Lake and that King of

Birds he must have loved with such a great and beautiful and strange love...That room with that bed with the white sheets where Svend Willadsen Nielsen, the thin grey man with the sunken eyes finally *died* quite unobtrusively, at last ended his cycle and became invisible...

Eggnog

Tove Ditlevsen

The child was standing on the back stairs with both hands on the banister, leaning over, stock-still, listening to the yard door opening down below and the far-off footsteps she convinced herself were her mother's right up until the moment they halted a couple of floors beneath and the slamming of a door crushed her hopes once more.

Now Hansen from the third floor was back home, and Ketty from the soda works, and Fireman Henriksen's wife who worked at the Carlsberg factory together with Mum and who surely would come up to tell her if anything had happened. But perhaps she didn't have the heart to, or simply didn't know. Nearly every day the ambulance drove off tooting with someone or other—and it was, after all, such an enormous factory.

In her agitation she trod down on her toes, hard, and held the position a long time to explain away her tears which tumbled down in great drops all the way to the basement. The same thing happened every day for shorter or longer periods of time, depending on how much the mother was delayed. The child was always there at her listening post a little while before the mother could reasonably be expected back.

Her still, white face shone dully like a dimmed lamp in the darkness. From behind the open kitchen door came the soft bubbling of potatoes on the boil. In the small living room the table was laid for two. The flowering begonia had been moved to the centre of the oilcloth, which always made her mother smile her habitual wan smile, for potted plants belong in the window not on the dinner table.

Just as the child released her fierce grip on the banister and sat down on the topmost step despairing of everything and crying out loud now as if to persuade fate she had been tried hard enough and deserved a little bit of good luck, she heard the street gate opening, and the faintest indefinable little sound, perhaps only the scraping of a shoe on the yard cobbles, which made her jump up and run into the kitchen and switch on the light and turn off the potatoes, in a fever of indescribable exultation: Mum's coming! Now she would be putting her bike in the shed, now running up the stairs, nearer and nearer. The world filled with light, her heart with peace.

She was standing with her back to the door, her hair down her cheeks like two black wings, engaged in tipping the steaming potatoes into a soup plate when the mother came in and banged the door shut behind her.

'Brr—its freezing out there.'

'I've fried the meatballs, Mum, they just need warming up.'

Her voice was as husky as a boy's in early puberty. She was almost as tall as her mother, but lean as a sick dog from having to look after herself all day long. Her face was small and perpetually worried, with a pointed chin and grey unhealthy skin. Only the eyes shone, large and deep blue and serious in the small ugly face.

The mother made no comment on the mention of meatballs. In fact not another word passed between them before they sat down at the table, at which point the mother with a little wan smile on her painted face set the all-important begonia back in the window. As she sat back down she chanced to bump against the naked bulb which swung to and fro a while, sending shadows up and down the faded wallpaper.

She ate quickly, with two deep furrows between her thin plucked eyebrows. Her peroxide hair had roots of some dark indeterminate colour without sparkle, like her tired near-sighted eyes. The days had been so much alike in the past dozen years that she had hardly noticed the changes wrought in her face. Red for cheeks and lips, a dirty powder puff passed across it, and a little black brush to rub over the sparse eyelashes: in front of a chipped mirror in the grey morning light time seemed to have stood still, each day identical to the one before. If the rouge ran out she could buy another box, and there was powder enough in the world to dust that ravaged face white for all eternity, and there were enough thirsty men in the world to ensure that the stream of empty bottles in need of rinsing kept flowing down the remorseless conveyor belt for far longer than her nimble hands would be able to grab them and rinse them clean. It could be called a sad life, but when she complained it was less because she acknowledged its bleakness than simply out of habit, and because after all it was good form to complain about everything. In its own way it was a secure life, because of all the powder, and all those thirsty men, and sometimes it was good because of the child to whom she had so little to say.

All the time she was eating the child's gaze never left her face. The mother would be gone in the morning before she was awake, and it was only in these precious hours before bed they could be together.

The child didn't remember the father. A sailor is always a visitor in his own home, and in any case she had been barely three when she last saw him. Inevitably she harboured the same hatred for him as the mother. Perhaps that too was a matter of convention and habit: 'The lousy swine', said the women at Carlsberg and on the staircase, and 'He'd never dare show his face here again', said the mother, to go one better. But the child's hatred was vaguer and arose from the protective tenderness she felt for the mother.

When they had finished the meal she cleared the table and rinsed the plates. She always left the full washing up until the following day when she got back from school.

Her mother's purse lay open on the kitchen table, a few coins spilling from it. The child's relationship to money was a mixture of awe and resentment. For the sake of this money the mother was gone all day long; it was to blame for the endless hours of work, fear, and loneliness. Each coin taxed the mother's strength a little more, and her eyesight too, ruined as it was by constantly having to hold bottles up to the light to check they were clean.

She hadn't been so very old when she asked the mother why she went to work when it was after all so much nicer to be at home. So then she was told it was to be able to buy food and clothes for them both, and on the Sunday the child had asked anxiously if they would be getting any food that day, seeing the mother was home.

She wondered a moment why the purse had been thrown down so carelessly on the kitchen table, and quickly went to pick it up. She was putting the coins back inside when suddenly she became aware that the mother was standing behind her. It made her start, because she hadn't heard her coming. In her confusion she let go of the purse and brushed her hair away from her face with her forearm before meeting the mother's hostile and suspicious gaze. She flushed a deep burning red and stared back wide-eyed and horrified, a look the mother returned with anger, then defiance and uncertainty, until a glimmer of shame passed across her face, and no longer able to bear that look of terror she turned away with a shrug of mingled embarrassment and irritation and went back into the living room.

The child remained standing mute and motionless next to the purse and the dirty plates. Her breath came fast as her thoughts tumbled over each other behind the pale hot forehead: She thought I wanted to steal, she thought I was taking money from her—maybe she thinks I've done it before—as though I don't cost her enough already—if only her purse hadn't been there—if only everything would go back to normal—dear God, let everything be like it was before—let it never have happened.

'What are you standing gawping at out there?' shouted the mother from inside the living room. Her voice was irritable and hostile like her eyes had been, with a brittle note of injury to guard against the self-reproach and tenderness she had never learned to express. She got out a work bag from the sideboard behind the table and after a while arranged a cloth over the bright bulb before sitting down in front of the stained tablecloth and pulling a stocking full of holes from the bag, after which she fell to gazing at it as though baffled as to how a single stocking can have so many holes. She listened out anxiously for any sounds from the kitchen, with her coarse painted mouth set in a pained expression. She could not acknowledge that anything special had happened, but an unease grew in her heart, as when an animal lifts its head on scenting danger and cocks an ear in that direction.

Then she called the child by name in a queer soft voice which sounded strange even to her own ears. The child came in and sat down opposite her with a vague glimmer of hope on her thin little face, not unlike when she stood on the back stairs in the dark trying to convince herself that the steps she heard were the mother's, right up until a door banged shut somewhere else in the building.

'Now she has to say something', she thought to herself.

The silence in the room was unbearable. She glanced nervously at the clock ticking heavily as though the noise it made could hold back the unknown redeeming words hovering on her mother's lips. Obscurely, the child felt these strange words never uttered before had to come from the mother; not because it was she, the mother, who was in the wrong, but because she couldn't manage it herself. She couldn't say: I wasn't stealing, partly because that would make the thing so tangible and never afterwards could you pretend that nothing had happened, and partly because those were the very words a thief would use—no one could prevent her using the same words if she really had stolen, or had wondered about it. It was this utterly new as yet unspoken truth which stopped her short and opened up terrifying visions of future injustices which could ever after be done to her.

Open-mouthed, she hung on the mother's lips. Those lips far too red and coarse which had seldom quivered with tears, and whose lines had never been softened by tender and loving words. A factory girl's hastily kissed and forgotten mouth.

Still gazing at the stocking as though she has forgotten what she is supposed to be doing with it, she feels the child's silence as a painful shattering of the established order of things. She doesn't quite know what has happened, but the child's distress reaches her by unfamiliar, secret paths. Helplessly, thoughts cross each other in her brain. She doesn't know we can always help the one we love. She lifts her eyes and meets those of the child. And her own eyes are beseeching and scared in the way of a child whose clumsiness has toppled a precious vase to the floor. Then she clears her throat and says softly:

'You could fix yourself an eggnog.'

And she sees the pale pointed face relax and break into a smile as the child leaps up and runs into the kitchen with a bounce in her long straight legs:

'I'll make one for you as well, Mum, I'll make one for each of us.'

Then she calmly goes to work on the stocking.

The Maids

Søren Kierkegaard

When summer comes and the maidservants set out for the
Deer Park, it is generally very little pleasure to behold. They
go there only once a year, and therefore want to derive
maximum enjoyment from it. They don hat and shawl
and comport themselves dreadfully in every possible way.
The merrymaking is wild, ugly, lascivious. No, then I far
prefer Frederiksberg Gardens. They go there on a Sunday
afternoon, and so do I. Here all is decorous and decent, the
merrymaking itself more calm and dignified. Indeed, any
member of the masculine gender who has no feeling for
maids loses more hereby than they do. The mighty army
of maidservants is really the handsomest militia we have
in Denmark. Were I king, I know what I would do—I
wouldn't trouble to inspect the troops. Were I one of the

32 members of the municipal council I would at once insist on forming a welfare committee, which, with insight, advice, admonition, suitable rewards, in every way endeavoured to encourage maidservants to attend to their appearance with good taste and care. Why squander beauty, why should it go unnoticed through life, let it at least show itself once a week in the best possible light! But above all, taste and restraint. A servant should not look like a lady, in this I agree with the esteemed paper *Politivennen*, though the reasons they give are quite fallacious. If one dared to promote a desirable improvement within the class of maidservants, would this not in turn have a beneficial effect on the daughters in our homes? Or is it too bold of me to imagine a future for Denmark which in truth might be called wondrous? Would that I were granted the joy of being alive in that golden year, then in good conscience I could pass all day walking about the streets and lanes and delight in all that meets the eye. How broad and bold my thoughts do swarm, how patriotic! But that must be because I am out here in Frederiksberg, where the maidservants come every Sunday, and so do I.

First come the peasant girls, hand in hand with their sweethearts, or in a different pattern, the girls all hand in hand in front, all the lads behind, or in another pattern, two girls and one lad. This company provides the picture frame, they like to stand or sit by the trees in the large square in front of the pavilion. They are all hale and hearty, their colours clashing only a little too strongly, in their skin as well as their clothes. Next pass the girls from Jutland and Funen. Tall, straight-backed, rather too sturdily built, their attire somewhat mismatched. The committee would have much work to do here. Never lacking is the odd representative of the Bornholm division: capable cooks, but it is not advisable to get close to them, whether in the kitchen or in Frederiksberg, their manner being rather haughtily forbidding. Their presence is therefore by contrast not without effect, I would not be without them out here, but rarely associate with them.—Ah, but now here come the troops to quicken the heart: our very own girls from Nyboder. Not as tall—buxom, fine skinned, gay, happy, vivacious, talkative, a little flirtatious, and above all bare-headed. Their attire aspires to that of a fine lady, with just two notable distinctions, they do not wear a shawl but a scarf, and no hat, at most a cocky little cap, but by preference they go bare-headed . . . Well, hello there Marie; fancy seeing you out here! It's been a long time since we last met. Are you still at the privy councillor's?—'Oh yes'—That must be an excellent position?— 'Yes'—But you are here all on your own, no one to walk with . . . no sweetheart, did he not have time today, or are you expecting him? What, not engaged? That's impossible. The most beautiful girl in all Copenhagen, a girl in service with a privy councillor, a girl who is an ornament and a model for all maidservants, a girl who knows how to make herself so pretty and so... elegant. What a delightful kerchief you have in your hand, made of the finest cambric... and what's this I see, with embroidered edges too, I know it must have cost 10 marks... Many a highborn lady does not possess the like... French gloves... a silk umbrella... and a girl of that sort not engaged... It's truly an absurdity. If I am not much mistaken Jens was rather taken with you, you know Jens, the broker's Jens, the one from the second floor... See, I hit the mark... Why did you two not become engaged, Jens was a good-looking fellow, he had a good position, perhaps with the broker's influence he might have made it to policeman or fireman in the course of time, it wouldn't have been such a poor match... It must surely be your own fault, you must have been too hard on him... 'No! But I got to hear Jens had been engaged once before to another girl, and they say he didn't treat her very nicely...' What's this I hear, who would have thought Jens such a bad chap... Yes, those hussars... those hussar lads, they can't be trusted... You did absolutely right, a girl like you is really too good to be thrown away on just anyone... You are bound to make a better match, I vouch for that... Now how is Miss Juliane doing? I haven't seen her for a long while. My pretty Marie can surely oblige me with some information... Just because

one has been unlucky in love oneself, one needn't
be unsympathetic to others ... But there are so many people
here ... I don't dare speak to you about this, I fear someone
could be spying upon me ... Listen a moment, my pretty
Marie ... See, here is the place, on this shady path where the
trees entwine to hide us from the others, here, where we see
no one, hear no human voice, only a faint echo from the
music ... here I dare speak my secret ... Isn't it true, if Jens
hadn't been a bad person you would have walked with him
here, arm in arm, listened to the pleasant music, maybe
enjoyed an even higher ... Why so upset—forget Jens! ...
Do you really mean to be unfair to me? ... It was only in
order to meet you that I came out here ... Only to see you
have I been coming to the privy councillor's ... You must
have noticed ... every time it was possible I always went to
the kitchen door ... You must be mine! ... The banns will be
read from the pulpit ... Tomorrow evening I shall explain
all ... Up the kitchen stairs, the door on the left right opposite the kitchen door ... Goodbye my pretty Marie. No one
must know you have seen me out here, or spoken with me,
you know my secret now — She really is lovely, something
could be made of her. When once I gain a foothold in her
room I shall read the banns myself from the pulpit. I have
always endeavoured to cultivate the noble Greek concept of
autarchia, self-sufficiency, and in particular to dispense
with a priest.

The Bra

Jakob Ejersbo

I answered an advert in the free paper, and I had to go for an *interview*. I mean, hello?!—I've been cleaning for people since I was fourteen. I went along—a big two-room first floor flat in Frederiksberg: KIRSTINE BRODERSEN.

She opened the door: so dead CLEAN, so tastefully dressed—slacks, T-shirt, blazer, high-heeled sandals with narrow leather straps over the toes—no strap at the back. Short blonde hair—beautifully kept—discreet make-up, barest hint of scent. I stood there feeling like a bag lady.

She was so *slim* and *firm*; maybe just two years older than me, but with the kind of body I can only dream of now. I mean, once you've had a kid, and have to study as well as work, you might as well kiss your body goodbye for a year or two. There's just no time to firm it back up.

Then I remembered something. If she was ever on TV she's the very type my man would call a 'frigid career whore'. That was some comfort—she didn't represent any competition in the battle for my guy, even if my clothes are worn and baggy.

Mine and Henrik's whole flat is the size of Kirstine's living room, and her living room is clinically clean—not one speck of dust. On top of that she has a big bedroom, a big kitchen and a big bathroom. *Everything* brand new, no sign of wear. She showed me round the first time I went there, all was perfect.

Piet Hein's ellipsis table and six Arne Jacobsen ant chairs. Over the table: some kind of map behind glass in a gold frame. Actually there are just four pictures in the entire flat, all big and behind glass in the identical gold frame. No knick-knacks, no family photos or holiday souvenirs, no personal stuff *at all*—like she doesn't have a past. For me it was a bit of a culture shock. I mean, our flat is *overflowing* with stuff—gadgets, knick-knacks, souvenirs. Sofie's toys everywhere, chunks of coral reef from Bali, Portuguese olive bowls, a big Firestone neon sign Henrik got from his uncle Torben who deals in car tyres. How can she *live* like that?

A Montana bookcase, elegant vases, hand blown fruit bowls in coloured glass, three gigantic plants—like in a head office, I imagine. But no flowers in the vases and no fruit in the bowls.

'This is how I like it', said Kirstine as she opened the door to the bedroom. The double bed was made up in a very special way. The pillows were at the head of the bed—fair enough—but the two single duvets: they were folded in half and then turned through 90 degrees, so they sat there like two rectangular parcels with one edge facing the foot of the bed and the other finishing halfway up the mattress, and the covers had different patterns on their two sides, so with the duvets folded that way the patterns matched up when you saw the parcels from the side. It looked dead posh. Above the bed: a reproduction of Claude Monet's *Water Lilies* framed behind glass. I wouldn't mind trying to live like that someday—that's what I was thinking: all cool clean lines.

After that we sat down on the futon in the living room, not next to each other and not even at opposite ends, but with a kind of gap between us. It felt so weird sitting and talking like that, having to turn your head to see the other person. I would have preferred a chair so we could have sat facing each other, only there *was* no chair; there was just the futon, a square chrome coffee table with a dark blue glass top, and that was it. On the table: a neat stack of glossy magazines lined up with one corner of the table, a big candle in a shiny stainless steel holder plus a couple of coffee-table type books. Over the futon: an Asger Jorn reproduction.

She sure put me through my paces: Did I have much experience of cleaning—was I reliable? I delivered on both scores. You use a dry duster—fine weave so it leaves no fluff behind—for dusting round. For certain things you need a well-wrung damp cloth: first dip it in hot water with just a drop of detergent, then take it in your two hands—palms up and pressed together, like a beggar. Next, grasping the cloth firmly between both hands twist it out of that position with the sides of your hands rubbing against each other right up until your wrists are crossed and the backs of your hands are facing upwards—point being that's the only way you can wring out a cloth without doing violence to your wrists. You dust first, then you hoover.

After we'd been sitting there a while I was so gagging for a cigarette, but I couldn't see an ashtray anywhere and didn't want to ask. Luckily she's a smoker too—Marlboro Lights. She went and fetched a little black ashtray, beautifully polished—later I found it's the only one she possesses. I'm sitting there thinking: I wonder what kind of lighter she has? Instead she used *matches*. I told Henrik when I got home. Tordenskjold matches, the most common make in the land.

'Blow me if she doesn't show signs of having a personality after all, or at least some form of...*style!*' he said. Well, I'm sure it shows something, I thought.

'There's just one thing you should check out', said Henrik. I should check whether after striking a match she brought the flame straight up to the cigarette, or if she let the sulphur burn off first so as not to inhale the poisonous fumes.

'I reckon she won't know about that', said Henrik—apparently it's one of those things men notice. But he was wrong. She lets the sulphur burn off—calm as anything—until all the smoke is gone, and then she brings the flame up to the cigarette.

She only ever wears new clothes. After her clothes have been washed a few times they get thrown out—the moment they show the first hint of ever having been worn. She puts them in a bag she keeps behind a curtain in the corridor. Behind the curtain is a kind of cubby hole—a messy corner—where the vacuum cleaner stands; though of course it's not the least bit messy. She washes her cast-offs before putting them behind the curtain, and when I arrive the following week the bag has gone.

'Do you think she just chucks them out?' I ask Henrik when we're sprawled on the sofa watching Okay Tone on DR2 after finally getting Sofie off to sleep.

'Let's hope she gives them to the Salvation Army', he says, and then reading my thoughts he says: 'Go on and ask her!'

'I can't do that', I say.

'No, you're right', he says, 'and besides it'd seem just too bloody impoverished. If instead you'd been an illegal Mexican immigrant in Los Angeles you could have.'

'How's that?' I ask.

'Because then she would know she'd never bump into you wearing her old clothes—you'd either sell them or save them to wear to mass on Sunday.'

'I just wish we had a bit more money—I could really do with some new clothes', I say.

'Fuck her clothes, and fuck her matches!' says Henrik, and pulls me close. 'We've got a life—she's got nice clothes,' he says, and gives me a smacking great kiss on the cheek. And it's true—she does come across as leading a pretty superficial life. But I could still do with some decent gear.

Whenever I bike over to her flat I'm always a bit keyed up—all agog to see if anything's happened. Take for instance the big candle on the coffee table in that hugely stylish steel candle holder—I dust it every Friday, the candle too—it has never once been lit, and I'm *certain* of that, for I made a little nick in it with my nail. And it's been fully six months since I started cleaning for her.

One day I told Henrik I'd become pretty potty about cleaning for Kirstine.

'When I'm up at her place I move around with a kind of—total concentration.'

'A bit like you're paranoid?' asked Henrik.

'No', I said, and then: 'Yes—in a way. I just so want everything to be perfect for her', I said.

'That sounds a bit sick to my way of thinking', said Henrik. So I gave up describing the feeling for him. It isn't sick. It's more because... well, if I give her place a good clean everything ends up perfect, but when we have a good clean-up at home the paint's still peeling off the coffee table legs, Sofie's squiggles are still on the walls at child height, there are still food stains on the wood floor, holes in our clothes, loose wallpaper in the entrance.

'Try and guess what kind of music she has', I ask Henrik. And he guesses right, Elton John, Whitney Houston, Celine Dion, and masses of Complete Dance CDs—in fact the only one he misses out is Toni Braxton, who he doesn't know.

'Has she got any nostalgia CDs?' he asks.

'Yes', I say, and again he guesses right: Tøsedrengene, News, and Dodo and the Dodos. The radio is always tuned to Voice.

'So what does she read?' I ask.

'Trick question,' he answers. 'She doesn't read—*at all*!' And that too is about right. In the bedroom she has two Danielle Steel books and Peter Hoegh's *Miss Smilla*. In the living room there are only coffee-table type books: *Key Moments in Fashion: The Evolution of Style—Lighting: Creative Planning for Successful Lighting Solutions—Making Faces*—Kevyn Aacoin reveals how the famous look their best with the help of make-up. Winona Ryder, Janet Jackson, all sorts of models—all somehow looking like hookers in different price ranges—mostly expensive.

Finally, once in a while I find certain manuals to do with her work, which presumably she has to study in her spare time—for instance: *Marketing for Kids*. God, that's just so sick! But the worst of it is when women like her have their own kids. A baby fucks up their entire control trip. That's a quote from one of our nursing lecturers at Bispebjerg Hospital, where I've just started; she says local councils have started taking on extra health care workers to help out the rich and oh-so-cool first-time mums, because they can't get their heads round caring for kids. They simply don't *get it* that a baby can cry *after* its feed. Or that a child won't fall asleep at exactly the same time every day.

Maybe someday it'll be me who gets her as a client, and then I'll have to sit her down and explain that you can't run a baby according to a time manager—they scream and they yell and you get shit all over your fingers—which doesn't smell too nice. It'll totally freak her out, I'm afraid. All the same I can't quite stop myself embroidering the picture: cleaning lady goes back to former employer, only now with the authority of chief consultant on all things pertaining to babies.

Kirstine's perfumes: Calvin Klein's *Eternity, Gio* by Armani, and Yves Saint Laurent's *Paris*. I had a similar arsenal before Sofie came along. All Kirstine's creams are exclusively Clinique, and the same goes for her make-up. Clothes by Sand, Bruno & Joel, Carli Gry, Bruuns Bazar. Shoes by Calvin Klein and ONO—around 40 pairs. Bags by Louis Vuitton. Bras by Marie Jo.

The bra situation is actually a whole separate chapter. I get to do a wash for her once in a while. Her whites are white. Her underwear has to be washed separately in a special net so it won't spoil. So much for her big environmental worries: two bras and two pairs of knickers in a single wash!

Personally I have my one and only bra, well worn. I only take it off to wash it, and then I go about with dancing boobs like some hippie on the make. A top quality bra with matching knickers costs 600 kroner; I used to always go round in that kind of stuff when I was really young and worked in a cafe and got loads of tips and had no overheads. Now I'd have to clean for her for a month to afford a set like that—I go there once a week and make 150 kroner a session; that's for three hours' work, though I get through it in an hour and a half, but that's also because I'm now expert at it, seeing I know exactly how she wants everything.

There's so many things about her—she's a source of endless fascination. I go straight over there from Bispe-bjerg Hospital where I'm doing my training. I don't even need to hurry, as Henrik fetches Sofie from the day nursery when he finishes at the State Hospital—he's a porter there. Kirstine is never around when I'm cleaning—I think she finds it a bit embarrassing that I need to clean other people's houses to make ends meet. She doesn't have the time, either; I mean, after secondary school she went on to commercial school and then to the famous Niels Brock, and so walked straight into a job with this big market analysis firm where she works now. Naked careerism: eight to five every day, lunch at the Café Europa or some-where equally swanky, then on to tennis or aerobics, or a body therapist. On the other hand—what total bliss: good job, loadsa money, super stylish home, time to keep in trim, get into town—no *obligations*.

When I get to her place I always find the 'mess' from her breakfast sitting there. Mess in this context means a toaster with no crumbs at the bottom, a plate with just a crumb or two, a dirty knife and a perfect teacup with just a hint of tannin on the inside. She drinks Medova.

Henrik doesn't believe she ever menstruates.

'You can't begin to menstruate if you have just one piece of toast for breakfast', he says. But she *does* menstruate; there's both Tampax and Always Night in the bathroom—she's as clinical as the girls who do the sanitary towel ads on TV2.

'She's one of their target group', says Henrik, and goes on about how he's waiting for the day when he gets to see an ad for sanitary towels where there's a dirty great punk wringing out a towel with cascades of blood welling up all over the place.

'And the punch line will be: *Always – sucks you dry!*' And he explains how the ad would then go on to show a model—dehydrated, borderline anorexic, botoxed lips— draped picturesquely in a corner, smiling beatifically.

'What the hell do they need all that blue liquid for?' he demands, adding: 'This is about *blood*! Blood-sucking sanitary towels!'

'Stop it', I giggle—I reckon Kirstine would disinfect the entire flat and sack me on the spot, if she knew I was living with a man with such a filthy mind. Still, she does hide it well—her period. Of course she keeps a chromium-plated bin in the toilet, and that gets me thinking how it is for me, the way I have to wrap the towel in loo paper, and when we have people round I have to very discreetly carry it out to the kitchen and cram it deep down in the rubbish bin. And each time I think what do my girlfriends do if they're on their period when they drop by—do they carry the used towel around with them in their handbags? How embarrassing—I mean for me. And still I haven't got round to buying a bin. The thing is there never *are* used towels in her waste bin, only cotton wool pads with a smidgeon of make-up on. Not even a cotton wool bud with earwax.

Then we write notes to each other, Kirstine and me. The first time I wanted to ask her something I needed a pad of course, so I was forced to look in the drawers in the Montana bookcase. There was nothing in the top and bottom drawers, and in the middle one an empty pad. Luckily I had a biro in my jacket pocket. So then I write:

Was it okay the way I ironed your sweatshirts and tracksuit bottoms?

Yes, she writes back, *they are only for wearing round the house.* Now fancy that! She wears freshly ironed clothes round the house. And she leaves notes for me too: Would I be able to stay on an extra hour next time, as she is going to the wedding of Count So-and-So and Miss Pipsqueak in some castle or another. *There is so much ironing to get through, we are staying the whole weekend,* she explains in the note. You'd think she was kidding. Or: *I like the way*

you fold the towels so they fit the shelf exactly. You'd think
she was kidding even more; I'm so glad I'm not like that.

Her kitchen ware is also hyper cool—loads of steel. She
has the weirdest stuff. Just one example: a Georg Jensen
gadget for trimming the foil off the necks of wine bottles. By
and large all the bottles in the wine rack have proper corks.
The drinks cabinet would make Henrik hyperventilate.

The food in her fridge: Gaio, Parma ham, Wonder-
white sliced bread, Kærgården butter mix, Harild mineral
water, plus little sachets of espresso coffee for the big
Presto machine from Tefal: in matte black with loads of
gold. And then of course I have to go and drop the big
glass shelf from the fridge when I'm cleaning it one day,
and a corner as big as half a sandwich breaks off at an
angle. Naturally I was sorry about it, though it didn't really
show if you turned the damage inwards. I left her a note.

Not to worry, she writes back. A couple of weeks go by,
and then Henrik asks:

'Well, has she got that fridge shelf changed?'

'No', I answer. He nods meaningfully, and says:

'It has set in.'

'What?' I ask.

'The rot', he says. 'The shelf's the first sign. From now
on it's downhill all the way with her.'

So I carry on cleaning like my life depends on it. The hoover is a miracle: a mint green Panasonic MC-E751 with a perfumed filter—the scent of flowers.

The Montana bookcase has to be sprayed at a distance of 20 centimetres with Sterling Furniture Spray—some kind of wax made of silicone and perfume which 'enhances the glow of the wood', as the can says. Afterwards you polish the wood—that gets done once a week. The plants get sprayed with Substral Leafshine. All in all there's heaps of spraying. I also iron her clothes with a steam iron that's like something out of *Star Trek*. Certain clothes first have to be sprayed with Bio-tex, Pre-Ironing Treatment. She also has a spray called Swimsuit Cleaner to protect her super expensive swimsuit.

'No bloodstains on the walls, by any chance?' asks Henrik, when I tell him about the spray-and-ironing routine.

'No, why?' I ask.

'She sounds almost like a Danish version of American Psycho,' he says, 'I bet there's something kinky about her.'

He could be right.

I don't know if she wonders about what makes me tick just like I wonder about her. Maybe she feels sorry for me because I have a kid already—I can imagine that, and it was actually a bit early—Sofie wasn't planned but I do love her, even when she mucks up the whole flat. I don't know what to say...but in some ways it's just as unnatural to live the way she does.

Some things I'm not allowed to touch, for instance the Piet Hein table.

'I polish that myself every Friday when I get back in from work', she explained to me the first time I was there. So far as I can tell it's only a simple melamine table top. I've had a look in the cupboard—she treats it with Trend Massive Oil which has to be rubbed in with a dry cloth and polished over afterwards—once weekly.

I've told Henrik about it—over time he has become fascinated with her too.

'I *promise* not to do anything obscene', he says when he begs me to take him along to see her flat. But I can see in his eyes he has dastardly plans, and even though it might be fun it wouldn't be right.

'Do you think she fucks in the dark?' is the kind of thing he can come out with. Don't get me wrong, he says it to get me in the mood; I'm one of those gals who likes the lights full on—I want to *see* what I'm up to...and what's being done to me.

It's hard to tell with her. In some ways she comes across as probably finding sex far too dirty a business to get mixed up in. On the other hand...I mean, you'd think she must...*do* it. I know she pops Mercilon contraceptive pills—they're kept in the bathroom, and you can see they get used. And she *does* have some form of boyfriend, because once in a while there's some of his gear among the laundry: T-shirts with film posters printed on and daft boxer shorts with Mickey Mouse characters and such. The weird thing is I've found long black hairs in her bed. I just can't imagine her having a boyfriend with a long black ponytail, so that gets me toying with the idea she has a *Latin lover*. I almost hope so; I'd be turned right off if I went and bumped into Mickey Mouse just before the crown jewels.

I can't help peeking inside whenever I find a clothes bag sitting behind the curtain. One day I find two bras in the 4–500 kroner bracket which are only just starting to look a weenie bit tatty—like my own clothes once I've washed them a couple of times, because we always wash everything together, all jumbled up. And there's worse to come: there's a pair of dead smart high winter boots sitting there; I could so do with a pair like that. I try them on— and they almost fit. They're a tad too big, but I've only got thin stockings on—with an inner sole or thick socks they'd do me perfect. Imagine being able to afford that sort of stuff...

I start on with the cleaning. Her computer has vanished—no doubt she's got herself a laptop. I hoover the kitchen. On the fridge door is stuck one of those magnet things with a plastic pig on. It holds a couple of menus for pizzerias and Thai food. It's got batteries inside, so if I happen to knock into it and it falls on the floor it says 'oink, oink' in an electronic voice—it's hugely irritating. She's also got this pair of completely worn-out slippers, shaped like a lion with a mane. So now I think I've pretty well identified the three items which express her personality. Henrik and I are agreed the oinking pig signifies: *I can be good fun too*; the worn slippers *Now let's have us a real cosy time*; and the matches *I have my very own style*. And that's it.

Next the phone rings and the answer phone comes on. I go over and turn up the sound to hear the message after the beep:

Hi there Kirstine, it's Gitte. Okay, you're not at home. Anyhow . . . things are crazy busy here too. Maybe meet up Saturday at NASA—if only I can make it. Talk soon . . . Byeee!

While I carry on working these pictures keep popping into my mind starring myself floating down the street in the boots behind the curtain. In sheer distraction I accidentally spray the TV screen with Sterling Furniture Spray. It takes a long while to rub off.

Anyhow, at long last I'm done. So I go behind the curtain to put Panasonic MC-E751 away. Oh heck, how those boots call out to me! I've got a short leather skirt on, because later I'm meeting one of my girlfriends at a coffee

bar. The boots would look great with the skirt and...
Okay, to hell with it! I pull on the boots, and then I pull
off my top and my old bra. The air feels cool against my
breasts, which still show traces of breastfeeding, but no
stretch marks and they're beginning to get back their
firmness, though of course they are a touch heavier, but
actually I like that—it's like I really have something to
offer. Henrik likes them too.

So I'm standing there in her boots and next thing I'm
trying on her bra. It really does something for my tits—
brings the best out of them. It's the kind of bra you'd like
to see a man's hands undoing. I stand there in front of the
mirror and sing:

'These boots are made for walking, and that's just what
they'll do—one of these days these boots are gonna walk all
over you!'—Nancy Sinatra—only I look loads better, with
my pout and my sultry turned-on look.

Then the intercom buzzer goes! It's her! Kirstine! I press
the button to let her in. PANIC, PANIC! I plonk myself
down on the floor to yank the boots off, but they are well
and truly stuck. Why the *hell* hasn't she got anything as
simple as a bootjack? I'm tugging and tearing and feel I'm
going to bust out in a fever. Finally they come off, but I can
already hear her on the stairs. There's nothing for it, I'll
have to pull my top on over her bra which now feels

welded to my boobs. I just have time to stuff my own worn bra behind my beaten up Fjällräv rucksack, which is also behind the curtain, before there's a knock on the door and I have to let her in. She's been shopping.

'Hi, I have people coming tonight,' and she explains she's a bit behind. I stand there wondering if I can really be certain—absolutely bank on her bra being intended for the Sally Army. Because of course it could easily be she has an uncool sister who gets her cast-offs.

'I'm nearly done,' I say, frantically searching for some excuse to stop a bit longer, so I can put the bra back. 'But I don't mind staying on a little, if you need help with anything?'

'Only if you have the time', she says.

'It's no problem', I say.

'Can you really be bothered?' She's delighted. Next thing I'm out in the kitchen slicing up a sea of vegetables with a perfect razor-sharp Raadvad knife with a wood handle, on a perfect chopping board, in preparation for what gives every appearance of promising to be a perfect Thai dinner. She has two recipe books, both coffee-table size: Meyer's *Køkken*, and *Thai Cooking* by Jackum Brown with a 'consultant' called Rachanee Boonthon! All authentic: packed with names of exotic spices such as 'galangal' and 'krachai' and obscure ingredients like 'tamarind water' and 'wonton wrappers'. Kirstine puts the shopping away and cleans the vegetables. There's no chance of somehow sneaking the bra off from under my top.

I slice the vegetables like a pukka chef, for I also worked in a café kitchen for a time. Kirstine is dead impressed. The funny thing is that when I look down at my hands at work my breasts take up more of the view than normal, because the bra gives them really good support, without squeezing or feeling tight.

Kirstine rushes round—in and out of the kitchen— preparing all and sundry; seemingly her guests are supposed to feel like they're in a restaurant. When we have people round they get a potato peeler shoved in their hand as they come through the door—we're friends aren't we, so chill out.

And then Kirstine comes dashing back into the kitchen to dice a piece of lean beef. She reaches out to grab a knife from the long knife-magnet that's screwed to the wall above the kitchen table. She's in such a rush that she doesn't get a proper hold on the knife, so then it drops and leaves a very visible nick in the table top which is wood. She freezes.

Oh my God, now we're in for a major crisis, I'm thinking, as she lets out a little despairing sigh. I hold my breath and watch her out of the corner of my eye. Then all at once she gives a shrug like she's shaking it off, and starts cutting up the meat. So now I can breathe again. Phew, I thought she . . .

'So, are you expecting some hunky guys tonight?' I ask to lighten the mood, but a bit also because I'm curious.

'Ooh . . . no', she answers, hesitating a bit before saying: 'My parents are on a visit.'

'So where do they live?' I ask, sensing straight off this isn't her favourite subject. Again she hesitates.

'Randers', she finally answers, 'they're coming over from Randers.' I'm just about to say something like in that case she can't get to see them so often, when she adds: 'But they are staying in a hotel.'

I'm not too sure how to react to this—whether it's good or bad. Instead I say something about cooking, and so we start talking about that. After a bit of time she even asks what Sofie eats, and then I chatter away nineteen to the dozen.

I'm still a bit nervous, for I just don't *know* what she's got in mind for her clothes. I decide to visit the toilet just before I go. So then I can take off the bra there and sneak it back into the bag when I fetch my Fjällräv from behind the curtain—and all should be okay. I don't reckon she'll spot I'm not wearing a bra when I come out of the toilet.

After chopping and preparing for half an hour, and smoking one of her Marlboro Lights and drinking a Corona she gives me, I go out to put on my worn-out health sandals—left lying on top of a box behind the curtain. She hovers in the kitchen door, saying:

'Thanks for the help, it was so brilliant you took the trouble.'

'No trouble at all', I answer, thinking this is the moment to say I'd like to use the toilet. I turn away to sneak my own bra out from behind the Fjällräv and stuff it down one of the side pockets without her catching sight of it, but I'm standing a bit awkwardly. And just as I'm about to haul my Fjällräv out of the cubby hole it suddenly strikes me that I have to visit the toilet without my rucksack, otherwise I'll have no reason to go back to the cubby hole to put her bra back in the bag. This makes me so jumpy that I go and tip the whole bag of clothes out into the corridor, and I can feel my cheeks going red hot as I start shoving the clothes back in the bag.

'Oh my, those old clothes!' says Kirstine, like it's something she'd forgotten. 'Perhaps I could ask you to do one more thing for me . . . I mean, so long as you happen to be going that way', she says tentatively.

'Yes, what is it?' I ask, standing there fumbling with the rucksack so she doesn't see the colour in my cheeks.

'It's just that bag of clothes', she answers, pointing. 'I forgot to take it with me to the clothes bank on my way to work this morning.'

'I'll do it, no bother', I tell her, bending down to fasten my sandals with her bra hugging my breasts like it was made for them. I can feel the colour draining from my cheeks, as I take a deep breath.

'Should the boots go too?' I ask in an off-hand way, as I hoist my Fjällräv on to my back.

'Yes, if you can cope with it all,' she says apologetically. If I can cope? You bet I can.

'Yeah, there's a basket on my bike—no problem', I answer, and she thanks me again. On my way downstairs my heart is thumping like crazy. On my bike too, and after pedalling a short way I pass a laundrette. I can't wait, and anyhow I really do need a pee now, so I get off and lock the bike. Luckily there are no customers. I go out to the toilet and sit down for a pee. I'm so impatient I try to pull the boots on while I'm still sitting there, and that makes me slide so far across the toilet seat I nearly piss over the side, which makes me laugh. So I have to wait a bit and dry myself before pulling on the boots. In the bag I also find a pair of knickers which match the bra, and—wait for it— right at the bottom of the bag is a natty silk shirt. It's actually a tad worn, but I tie the ends together in a knot just above my belly button, so my little potbelly sticks out, and it looks so cool—like something from the '60s. I can't tear myself away from the mirror, so I light up a fag and dig out the sunglasses I borrowed off Henrik, and then just stand there looking dead sexy.

I bike off in the direction of Nørrebro with a smile on my face, and I don't know what to say ... I mean, I just feel *so* on top of the situation.

There's a really cool looking girl on the pavement who quite openly turns round to watch me go by—I really have to force myself not to look back. Sitting outside the Blue Dog are two guys whose eyes follow me all the way as I cycle past—they try to hide the fact but they're not cool enough. It feels fabulous.

I decide I absolutely must upgrade my wardrobe—Henrik will just have to get used to it. I'm not going round looking like a bag lady the whole time.

By now I'm nearly at Flora's coffee bar where I'm to meet my friend. She's sitting out front. I park my bike, and I'm practically on top of her before she sees who I am.

'Wow!' she bursts out, as she gets up to give me a hug. 'You look bloody amazing!' And I smile. Carry on—I can take it.

H. C. Andersen fecit Juni 1848.

The Naughty Boy

Hans Christian Andersen

Once upon a time there was an old poet, such a very kind old poet. One evening, when he was sitting at home, there was dreadfully bad weather outside; the rain came pouring down, but the old poet sat warm and snug by his stove, where the fire was burning, and the apples roasting.

'They're won't be a dry stitch on all those poor things who are out in this weather!' he said, for he was such a kind poet.

'Oh, let me in! I'm freezing and ever so wet!' cried a little child outside. It wept and rapped on the door, while the rain came pouring down, and the wind shook all the windows.

'You poor little thing', said the old poet, and went to open the door.

There stood a little boy; he was quite naked, and the water was streaming out of his long yellow hair. He was shaking with cold; had he not come in he would most surely have died in the dreadful weather.

'You poor little thing!' said the old poet and took him by the hand. 'Come inside, and I'll warm you up! I'll give you wine and an apple, for you are a sweet boy!'

He certainly was. His eyes looked like two bright stars, and even though water was running down his yellow hair, it still curled so prettily. He looked like a little cherub, only he was so pale with cold and shaking all over. In his hand he held a splendid bow, but it was quite ruined by the rain; all the colours on the beautiful arrows were running into each other because of the wet weather.

The old poet sat down by the stove, took the little boy in his lap, wrung the water from his hair, warmed his hands in his own, and heated up sweet wine for him; so then he recovered, he got rosy cheeks again, and he jumped down on the floor and started to dance round the old poet.

'You're a merry little boy!' said the old man, 'what is your name?'

'My name is Cupid', he replied, 'don't you recognize me? There is my bow, I shoot with it, you know! Look, now it's clearing up outside, the moon is shining!'

'But your bow is ruined', said the old poet.

'That's bad', said the little boy, and picked it up and looked at it. 'Oh, it's dry already, and not the least bit damaged! The string is quite taut! Now I'll try it!' Then he strung the bow, fitted an arrow, took aim and shot the good old poet right in the heart. 'Now you can see my bow wasn't ruined!' he said laughing at the top of his voice, and he ran away. What a naughty boy!—to shoot the old poet who had let him into his warm living room, and who had been so good to him, and gave him the tasty wine and the best apple.

The good poet lay on the floor and wept; he really had been shot right in the heart, and so he said: 'Ugh! How naughty that Cupid is! I am going to tell all good children to watch out and never play with him, for he will hurt them!'

All the good children, girls and boys, to whom he told the story, took care to be on their guard against the bad Cupid, but still he tricked them, for he is a cunning fellow! When students leave their lectures he runs alongside them, with a book under his arm and dressed in a black gown. They don't recognize him at all, and they take his arm and think he is a student too, but then he thrusts his arrow into their chests. When the girls are preparing for confirmation, and even when in church taking communion, even then he is after them. Yes, he is constantly after people! He sits blazing in the big chandelier in the theatre, so people think it is a lamp, but later they know different. He runs around Kongens Have and Volden! Yes, once he shot your father and your mother right in the heart! Just ask them and hear what they have to say. Oh yes, he is a bad boy that Cupid, don't ever have anything to do with him! He is after everyone. Imagine, he even shot an arrow into dear old Granny, but that is long ago, and it is over now; but it's something she will never forget. Shame on you, bad Cupid! But now you know him! Remember what a naughty boy he is!

Is There Life after Love?

Jan Sonnergaard

It was that time just before winter turns into something resembling spring, and Ulla and I were walking along Nørrebrogade after a not specially successful and pretty expensive dinner at a restaurant out in Frederiksberg. Arguments, silences, and snide remarks had become the order of the day, every day, and long before then I should have realized which way the wind was blowing. Even more when she started on about the cook she knew from the time when she ... and now this cook had just left her husband and kids in order to move in with ...

'I know the type', I cut in, Lord knows why, 'the type of woman who runs from one man to the next leaving only death and destruction in her wake.'

And then it was as though all movement stopped, and my banal remark was left dangling in the air like a toxic cloud, and she gave me a look that could only mean I had just plunged a dagger into her stomach.

'Are you trying to make me feel guilty or what?' she said, on the verge of tears, and I should have said, Sorry, that was a stupid thing to say, and I should have been shocked and flustered and should have broken off mid-sentence. Thunderstruck, I should have asked if she was considering doing the very same thing. To me. But I just looked at her stony-faced, without saying a word.

She was just a fucking tart. Just a tart. A fucking tart. That's what she was. And nothing else. She was nothing better than that. A fucking tart. And a traitor, not someone to grieve over. The opposite. She was the type of person you should be only too pleased not to number among your acquaintances. You don't go making friends with traitors. You string them up, and then you cut them down.

So that's what I just can't understand. Why our break-up so completely knocked me for six. I can't think what made me do it, but I kept constructing different scenarios. So I'd phone her up and plead,

'Can't we see each other—all the same?'

The first few times she agreed, plainly with no great enthusiasm, and we'd meet for half an hour, an hour, and just once for an hour and a half. In bars, always in bars, even though I'd have much preferred meeting just about any other place. More private. My own place. Or hers. Or her parents'. But it always ended up being bars. Or restaurants. Every single time, and in the end I couldn't stand it anymore, that it had to be so anonymous and public. Why did we always have to meet up in places neither of us knew? Why always so cold? Can't you see how impersonal it is? And cold.

Later on she wriggled out by suggesting parties she never turned up to. Even when the invitation expressly specified I was not to show up until 'after dinner'. Or she'd invite me round to her flat and when I arrived she'd not be there.

'Why weren't you there?'

So I'd demand over the phone after a couple of days with no word of explanation from her, and even though I never got a proper answer it invariably ended up with me asking, 'So when can we meet again?'—even though I had every reason in the world to be livid with her, even though I ought to have slammed the phone down and forgotten all about her, and even though I knew perfectly well I'd be better off with absolutely anybody else. But always it ended up with my forgiving her and pleading,

'Just once more.'

The thing is I kept seeing her before my eyes, with her dimples, and her long blonde hair, the way she used to look when things were good between us. Especially at weekends I felt I just had to phone her, and also I began sending her letters or postcards saying things like, 'It doesn't have to last this long', or 'Remember the time we had lunch with the Hara Krishnas at Govinda's on Nørre Farimagsgade?'—and once I also wrote saying we could easily meet up in some bar just round the corner from where she lived. That way she wouldn't need to walk so very far.

But she kept putting me off. It would have been simpler to arrange an audience with Queen Margrethe. If it was me wanting something her lips were sealed seven times over.

'Couldn't we meet—this Friday?' I asked after I'd at long last got hold of her direct number at her new job. And she said she didn't wish to. No more did she try to sidetrack me, or avoid the issue, or lie. Very quietly she announced she didn't wish to.

'Why not?' I asked, and there was a three-second silence at the other end. Then she said,

'I think I'd rather not tell you', and it was as if it went on resounding in the room whole minutes after she'd rung off.

So I clammed up. When I was out. In the morning. And when I was home. At night.

Where either I listened to the same three records over and over again. Or late night programmes on the radio. There were just those two alternatives. I never ever listened to any of my own records, just the ones which weren't mine. For I had to get away, far far away, since I couldn't stand being at home. Especially not to eat. I had to get out. Out into town. To places with lots of people.

To libraries, or museums, or parks, or streets, or alleys. Until dark. Or to Govinda's on Nørre Farimagsgade. Or the Italian restaurant just round the corner on Smallegade. Or the wine bar a little further on. As though there was something comforting in everything being so anonymous, and so few people who knew me. And like as not I'd want to be in some other place next day. But wherever I happened to finish up I'd always be sitting there hoping that next moment...next moment she'd come through the door, in precisely this library. This restaurant. This bar. This coach on this train on my way to my father's in Slagelse. Or Funen where my mother lives. And she would fling her arms wide and hug me tight when she saw it truly was *me* sitting in this very coach, over by the window.

But it was air. Nothing but air.

All I had left was the music. The same records and CDs as back then. All the time I kept listening to the same records and CDs as back then, and most of all the last three which I'd been going to give her on the first of June, her birthday.

Most of all I'd listen to just those three records which were so specially meant for *her*. And the letter... I'd tell myself I needed to read her letter all over again. 'There is nothing wrong with either of us, and there's no reason to doubt it. The chemistry just isn't right. At least not for me... But don't get me wrong, I for one really do not believe our affair was a completely negative experience...' And then the classic remark that she hoped we could still carry on being friends. That bit I definitely had to read again, no matter what, because she actually thought I was a great guy, on no account must I get that wrong.

Once she sent me three postcards. All that, and she was holidaying with her parents for no more than a week. And seven months after we first met I took fifteen pictures with a little disposable camera, just the two of us. Abroad, or else out in the country. By the Brandenburger Tor. And in front of the Arc de Triomphe. Or hand in hand in front of a summer house my cousin lent us. And even when I was almost dropping with fatigue I still always contrived to stay up another hour staring at those pictures, with my music centre playing all the records from back then. Until seven in the morning. Even later.

And yet strangely enough I always managed to make sure the place was *clean*. Every second day I washed down the floors and windows, hoovered and wiped away every speck of dirt. And shaved. And brushed my teeth. And called 118 to check she was still living where she'd always lived. And when I was told she did and I was asked if I wished to be put through at the cost of one-and-a-quarter krone I always keyed in 1 for 'yes', and always waited until once more I was told the call wasn't wanted.

One day I decided to check the calendar to see how long it was since she'd broken up with me. And when I counted back I don't know how many weeks and months I discovered that not even once in five-and-a-half months had I fixed to meet up with another human being. No family, no old friends, nothing.

A sensible person would have been shocked, and if I'd been fully compos mentis I would have grabbed the phone and called up just about anyone still prepared to see me. Or anyone in my family. Instead I did something else. I took the car and drove into town and parked right in front of her flat in Sølvgade. And then I settled down to wait until she came out the door and walked off in the direction of Østre Anlaeg.

And three days later that's precisely what she did.

Because I could see the whole thing. How they left her block of flats hand in hand having a laugh at something or other, and she flung her arms round him. I saw them right there, walking off down the street toward the gates into Kongens Have. And they entered like all other young people newly in love—for at that point they hadn't yet spotted me—and twice I dashed out of the car to grab hold of them.

And failed miserably. Because they were no longer there. They'd gone off some place else. And this just had to stop. Stop right now. Let it go! It was all more than five months back. Relax.

By the sixth time I sat waiting there I could tell I'd been detected. They knew I was there. Except they made out they couldn't see me. They came out from her entry as always and set off down the street. Only now there was space between them. They weren't touching. Not in public. They weren't going to do that to me, despite everything.

And if at long last something or other came up which distracted me a little bit for a couple of days and made me think of something else. If, just once in a while, I managed to repress the urge to spy on them. Or listen to the records. Then suddenly some disaster happened which sent me right back on their trail.

Because even if I didn't want it, it still happened just the same. I left off lurking there in my car. Even I realized it was embarrassing, and restrained myself and managed to stop. It couldn't go on. But then it would happen just the same. I was sitting on a bus going up Vesterbrogade and I saw them together, hand in hand, walking in the opposite direction. She was laughing at something he'd just said, and she kissed him on the cheek, and I couldn't help noticing that this friend, or fiancé, or whatever he was, was holding something in his hand. A string fastened to a little creature. A puppy. A boxer pup, I think. It was enough to make you throw up, and it hurt like hell, and I got off at the next stop and started running back the way they went.

But I didn't manage to catch up with them. They were gone, and never would I find them, and most likely they'd gone further into town to find some café where they could be together. Or to a concert. Or a restaurant. It was the middle of the afternoon in the middle of summer and it was right now I could have been with her, we could have been walking side by side, hand in hand, and instead I was running wild round Vesterbro like a drunk, or a junkie or a madman.

And next morning when I woke and turned towards her I saw...no one there. And every night I went over all the times we'd been together and something had gone wrong. First I'd replay the scenes the way I remembered them:

'Do you have to tread on me, you mean cow!'

'You asked for it, you idiot.'

'What did you just call me? Are you calling me an idiot?'

And afterwards I'd go back over the scenes and play them the way they might have panned out if we had both been less hot-tempered:

'Sorry.'

'All is forgiven.'

'I didn't mean to...'

'I know, of course you didn't. Come here...'

And finally I'd play them the way we both in reality dreamed they should have happened:

'Don't you think we really should do it?'

'Do what, my love?'

'Move in together...'

'Yes!'

And sometimes both voices were shouting so loud that the person in the flat above started stamping on the floor.

I'm not too sure how long this lasted. I only know it never stopped. Even though life went on. Though maybe that was precisely what it *didn't* do. And even if it did go on, it was the same old routine.

Right up until one day something happened which never in my wildest dreams I had ever imagined. The phone rang, and straight off I knew who it was.

'Ulla...', I said, just that. And she sounded so strange, almost light-hearted, and so very strange, for she said,

'I'm so sorry I haven't rung you for ever so long.'

But so much had happened, she said, it was almost overwhelming, as if her cup were overflowing, and next moment she sounded alarmingly grateful when I asked her the question I'd asked her every single day for over three months, back in the spring, because she replied,

'Of course we must meet up, Anders! That's why I'm calling...'

She was so animated and excited that I could still feel it long after putting the phone down. She was very, very happy. Only it wasn't *me* who had made her so happy. And it wasn't him either, that jerk with his ridiculous boxer pup. It was something else. She was in such high spirits, higher than ever before—even higher than when she and I were together.

What on earth can make a person *so* happy? It was as though her joy redoubled, and kept on redoubling until it hit me at the other end of the line. That's how powerful it was. And *so* happy... Never before had she been like that. And for the first ten minutes I was infected by it, and I started whistling as I wandered around the flat, truly over the moon to be seeing her again. And then something flashed through my mind, and for the rest of that weekend one sole question haunted me:

Who on earth is making her so happy?

Her happiness was unclean, it was besmirched, and as such it would be wrong and despicable to respect it. I had to back off, I thought, it was vital to back off—because actually I knew only too well what the reason was. Yet when the day came I still went and bought that stupid bunch of long-stemmed red roses, and kept on at the girl in the shop to make the bouquet bigger, and more impressive, and more expensive. More red roses, please. And then I realized this was worse than anything I'd ever been through before. For my hands were already shaking before I left the shop, even though it was still early morning and there was a long while to wait before our meeting.

She was sitting there already, down in the corner in front of a bottle of sparkling water, and she lit up in a big warm smile the moment she clapped eyes on me. But the smile gradually faded as I came reeling over to her table, and she quickly turned her face away when I wanted to kiss her on the mouth, as though she could already smell everything I had been drinking in order to work up enough courage to actually show up for that meeting. She pulled back when I wanted to hand her that very beautiful bouquet which I'd bought before popping into that bar a little further down the street.

'I'm just so happy to see you again', I began, but she shook her head and said,

'That's not at all what I meant'.

I placed the bouquet before her. And tried hard to look as though I so totally shared her joy. As I headed for the bar. While desperately trying to exercise some control over this thing which long ago had turned into a nightmare, because of course I'd noticed she had put on a bit of weight. Not much, but just enough to show.

'Why are you doing this?' she asked when I came back to the table with a tray containing six beers and six small glasses of Old Danish. She looked straight into my eyes and was close to tears.

'What on earth are you trying to prove?'

'Would you like to hear a joke?' I replied, for something had to happen if this meeting wasn't going to go down the plughole. We had to start talking about something other than *us*.

'Have you read Jacob Rendtorff's article today? ... You haven't read it, have you?'

'In *Information*?'

'You really must. He defines what *life* is. You haven't read it, have you?'

She looked at me as though we'd never met before, and I looked away and swiftly knocked back another Old Danish. And I was already spluttering with laughter even before explaining that his definition of life was:

'A fatal illness which is sexually transmitted!'

But she was not amused. She whispered,

'Please don't humiliate yourself like this in front of me.'

And she was anything but happy now, that was obvious, and actually quite terrifying, but desirable too. In a way.

So I shouted for the waiter who of course did *not* react. Which was why it was such a good thing I hadn't paid for just *two* but *six* beers before returning to her table.

Very pointedly and very slowly I put one of the bottles from the tray up to my mouth and asked,

'Why freak out like that? Are you ashamed of something?'

And then I downed the bottle in one. It felt like a punch to the solar plexus, and I noticed there wasn't room for all of it, since something wet was dribbling out of the corner of my mouth. But better this than capitulating, I thought, so I wiped it away with the back of my hand, and when she didn't answer I said,

'You do know you've hurt me, don't you? You do know this is killing me?'

I stared at her, and then I also asked her,

'Have you any idea what you're doing?'

And when she didn't react at all, but just sat there weeping and muttering,

'You should be ashamed of yourself. You really should... It's too mean!'

—I simply took a beer in each hand, stretched up my arms, put my head back and poured beer all over myself... over my mouth, my neck, my hair, my chest, my shoulders—my entire body...

'Look—' I said, with all the anger and impotence I could muster, and then I picked up another beer from the table and poured it all over my face without making *any* effort at all to hit my mouth,

'Look what you make me do!'

'I thought you'd be glad to know', she said and looked at me in such a way it made me lower my eyes. For the second time that day.

So once more I caught sight of her little bump—and something must have shown on my stunned face, even though I did everything possible to mask it. For she reached across the table and tried to take my hand. I actually think she was trying to comfort me, for a brief second. But that was the moment it got really bad, for I caught her hand and squeezed it and held her tight and attempted to smile whilst begging her to forgive me, though I also wanted her to sit on my lap.

She tried to hit me to make me let go of that hand, and she started to shout for help while all the time I tightened my grip, for I couldn't let her go now. Most definitely not now. And in the end the waiter came running up and he dragged me out of my chair so I had to let go, and he shouted,

'Couldn't you have this argument in the bedroom instead?'

That's what he said. In all seriousness, and as though he was *blind*. It was pretty obvious that was the one thing we couldn't do, so did we really have to put up with that kind of comment?

I shoved him out of the way and reached out a hand for her again... And she walked off. Just like that: off she walked without saying goodbye. And when it dawned on me that was what she intended and she wasn't pulling my leg I prized myself free of the bar and ran after her, hell for leather. But she was already far away, and even though I stood right there outside the wine bar shouting after her she carried on down the street as though she was deaf.

There I stood, out there in the street, thinking what a crime it was. You can't do a thing like that. No way can you do what she'd just done. You just can't. Yet it was exactly what she did do. And I couldn't move.

And then for some reason, and I don't honestly understand why, I remembered a joke. Standing out there on the street as though turned to stone, I suddenly remembered the story about a little girl, no more than four, who is playing out in the back garden. At a certain moment her seven-year-old sister comes running up and shouts,

'Sister, little sister . . . There's a dildo on the veranda!'

And the four-year-old looks up at her sister in surprise and says,

'What does "veranda" mean?'

A Bench in Tivoli

Katrine Marie Guldager

As far as sex goes, Heinz normally solves the problem with a porno film or a magazine. From time to time he visits a porno shop in Istedgade. Today, for once, he doesn't look over his shoulder and walks straight in. The shop assistant is a young woman who looks up apathetically from her book. Instantly Heinz wonders what she can be reading. A novel? A manual? Heinz inspects the shop from one end to the other. Now he's here, he might as well make a thorough job of it. He picks up various gadgets, handcuffs, and whips, pondering and appraising them. Then he flips through the naughty underwear, but it makes him oddly depressed. It sickens him. The shop assistant clears her throat. Heinz assumes it means she wants him to pay up.

On his way home he passes a 7-Eleven and sees something is going on inside. He halts in front of the automatic doors which fail to open. Two people who look like drug addicts have been apprehended with their pockets full of all sorts, from packets of ham to sweets. The staff are trying to restrain them until the police arrive. The situation is at once desperate and utterly routine. People stand and stare, but not for much more than a couple of seconds. The customers are queuing up again already. The world doesn't come to a stop on account of a pair of junkies.

When Heinz gets home he chucks the magazines into his car and drives out to Vestskoven. He finds a place to park up and masturbates over a picture of a blonde in chains. He collects the semen in a handkerchief which he later throws away.

Heinz lives in a small flat near the Café Intime, not far from Frederiksberg town hall. He is a professional painter and decorator, but in recent years he has been cleaning in a bar on Frederiksberg Allé. When he comes off work he generally goes home and takes the dog for a walk, but lately he has taken to going to Tivoli. He has invested in a season ticket. A couple of days ago he chanced to meet a nice lady who happened to be sitting by the fountain opposite the concert hall drinking a mug of coffee from a flask she had brought along. Heinz sat down on the bench next to hers and asked,

'Do you have a season ticket?'

The lady smiled and gave an elaborate answer, and her answer opened so many doors that it was easy to carry on the conversation. Heinz told her he was a professional decorator, but for the past couple of years he had switched to cleaning. Funnily enough the lady had been married to a decorator and knew quite a number of the union people out at Lygten. In fact she had been there several times herself. The lady offered him a coffee and passed him a mug. In her lap lay a napkin with a check pattern, and she asked if he wanted a bit of powdered milk. Heinz smiled, convinced that the coffee would taste horrendous but he was pleasantly surprised. They were both surprised. In no time they realized they had been chatting for several hours, and Heinz offered to see the lady home. But the lady said she'd prefer to meet up with him the following day.

Next day, when Heinz enters Tivoli he fears he is too smartly turned out. He is freshly washed and shaved and has put his best clothes on, but then instead just as he is passing the Pantomime Theatre a picture from one of his magazines eats into his brain. A picture of a red-haired woman in leathers, down on all fours. Heinz halts right in front of the Pantomime Theatre and thinks:

Have I destroyed myself?

The lady is late. Heinz fidgets impatiently on the bench outside the Concert Hall. He falls into conversation with a young mother and her baby which keeps crawling off into the flower bed. The mother asks him to take a photo of the pair together. In the background is a balloon seller. After an hour the lady still hasn't shown up, and finally Heinz realizes he might as well leave. She isn't going to come.

When he gets home he collects the dog and takes a walk in Søndermarken. He can't get the lady from Tivoli out of his mind. Maybe he could find out where she lives. Maybe he could visit her privately in her home, just for a coffee together, some chat. But that might seem forward. That would seem much too desperate. He would look like the loneliest person on earth, and she his only salvation.

As the Angels Fly

Naja Marie Aidt

No one could deny that that winter was frost-clear and very cold, and we felt deliriously special as we sailed over the ice-bound streets in the late dawn light, thin and dressed all in black. Only the street lamps showed our piercing pupils, and in actual fact we were not sailing. We flew. But otherwise all was dark. Dark all the time. All we saw was each other's shadow, and every day our movements traced new patterns—gliding towards each other we hugged hard and tight, and pulled back to find new release in another encounter, a new body.

We did so want to fly. It lasted all winter, and that year the winter felt endlessly long. Long and white and cold.

The house was meant to be pulled down in the spring. Its rooms were big and dank, with paint peeling off the walls; lone words and phrases stood out from the masonry, sprayed on with black paint. An almost constant acoustic echo rang through the tall empty rooms.

The house was uninhabited. But people lived there. Creepy lived there, and several others. They lived on scattered mattresses, with their guitars and reptiles, their full and empty bottles rolling around the floor, their little white stashes of speed and cocaine and stuff in plastic bags and corked tubes, hidden in pockets and locked away in cash boxes. Mirrors and razor blades. Jewelry hung heavy from thin wrists and young tense necks.

We dyed our hair black or white or red, and dressed in tight rubber and leather. The girls' stockings were torn and finished half way up the thigh, because that was the look. That was how we wanted it; deeper and darker and more endless with each passing day. With each windy night. Letting our brains explode and seeing the light that always comes after. When visions and demons take over and the body follows those secret paths which are so full of painful desire.

Creepy was the only fixture in the house; the rest of us came and went. His room was at the very top of the building, you had to crawl up a narrow stepladder, and the only light he had was an ultraviolet neon tube suspended over a big cage. A kind of heat lamp. In the cage lived Plexus, a four-metre-long anaconda boa constrictor, fully grown and yellow with intricate black markings. Creepy fed it on rats and young guinea pigs. He never forgot its mealtimes, and didn't disturb it when it was digesting.

In the centre of the room lay a long black coffin lined with white satin, stained from years of use. For Creepy slept in the coffin, and he fucked in the coffin. He had drilled five or six holes in the lid, so you could breathe when you lowered it over you. The holes looked like small stars in a dark sky, because light came through when you saw them from below: a freaky purple light from the neon tube. A length of black material covered the small attic window in Creepy's room. It smelled in a special way of Creepy, his clothes and his semen and his skin, and of Plexus, the sand at the bottom of the cage, the remnants of its meals. Of dust and meat. From a nail in the ceiling dangled a white mask with a big red mouth, swaying. Clothes and shoes were heaped all over the floor. Apart from the coffin there was only one other piece of furniture: a low bookcase along one wall. It held a dead bird in formaldehyde and a little shrine made of dark wood.

That was where Creepy hid his gear. The click of the lock when he opened it and picked out a little bag. The sweet shivers you felt at the back of your neck.

All the girls were wild about Creepy, he was so ugly and so sweet and so brutal with us in the coffin, and we loved that too, for it was as though the madness lifted us all the way up to God when we lay there under the stars, naked on cool satin, and let ourselves be split apart. By Creepy's violent and desperate thrusts and the ferocity of his sharp nails raking red tracks across our skin. Creepy loved only Plexus, but he needed us. That's what he said. He said we were his dolls, and couldn't tell our names apart. But we were after all nameless that winter, so it wasn't an issue.

Creepy on the other hand had his name, and his own room, and he had Plexus. And he even had, alone of all of us, a job. He made rubber masks for horror films, and was so in demand he produced them for abroad too. The money he made was for the most part sugar white, and he earned a lot. He could snort as many lines as he liked, and that too was quite a bit. Even so he wasn't mean when it came to sharing the goodies; you could always count on a great fix if you went in the coffin with Creepy. We were really pretty crazy about him.

In the evening and all through the night loud, loud music boomed from the speakers and made the walls shake. We shook too, we danced and danced and banged our heads against each others' ringing skulls.

Our noses were dry and irritable from snorting up heaven. Our genitals were full of small scratches and sores, for we put the cocaine straight on them, and I have to admit it works. As a supplement to the real ecstasy. The restive rattling of handcuffs and chains grew out of the dark; when the music was over short shuddering shrieks broke the morning stillness. Crosses were torn off their chains and left marks on throbbing necks. We bit each other till we drew blood.

That was when spring was on the way with its harsh light. In the end only the sight and smell of blood could get us high enough. And we did so want to fly. Wings nearly sprouted from our backs when teeth and sharp little knives marked us out for each other. Allowed us to feel.

I saw myself in the mirror as I scraped together neat lines of snow with shaking hands, and I felt very beautiful and invulnerable. I looked up at Creepy. He was sitting watching me in the twilight like a black shadow with his smooth shaven head cocked to one side. He smiled at me. I was really pretty crazy about him.

Winter was starting to break up, melting snow dripped off the roof, the first buds swelled longingly on the bare branches of the trees. Under Creepy's heaven the purple stars winked enchantingly, and exploded in a sea of light which filled the entire coffin. 'You look like a Barbie doll who wants to die', Creepy whispered hoarsely, moaning as he grabbed my nipples between his nails in a long excruciating grip. I laughed aloud, rocking on the padded satin. I thought the bird was flapping its wings in its formaldehyde.

No one could deny the winter had been long, we were so lacerated by all the cold.

*

She said she was on a good trip. One that lasted. She said I should mind my own business and leave her alone. Her laughter was soft and full of contempt and derision. She did laugh a lot that winter, more than normal, shrill and bright, while her hands flew nervously all over her arms and her chest. She rubbed her skin, smoothed and stroked and scratched her white skin, and she tossed her head so her long hair was in constant movement. From under her hair her eyes flickered, she snuffled and moistened her lips with her tongue.

Our mother had long since given up. Only when she dug out old polaroid photos of us from when we were little girls with our hair in plaits and our party dresses on did she cry. Her tears put out the fag-end of her Cecil dangling from the corner of her mouth. Otherwise nothing. As though Sisse was already dead. Yet she was very alive that winter, very restless and alive. For fuck's sake Sisse, I said, trying to pin her gaze. She just laughed.

Soon I gave up saying anything much, and did no more than open the door to her when she rang my bell at all hours of the day. Of course she wanted money. And of course I couldn't stop myself giving it to her. She begged as though it was sweets she wanted, as though we were children and she'd emptied her sweetie bag much too fast, while I had saved up a whole supply in the desk drawer—anxious as I am.

She was a greedy child, my little sister, and very charming. That winter too. Terribly charming, with the most seductive peals of laughter imaginable. She had no idea how tired she had got. I put her to bed and slept with my arms round her to be sure she didn't disappear while I was dreaming. But she always disappeared. When I woke she would be gone, only the crumpled bedclothes and her smell in the room showed she had been there. For a long time I didn't know where she went to so early in the morning, and I felt lonely when she took off like that without saying goodbye. But at Christmas she came home.

Our mum and her fellow Kaj and I tripped rather than danced round the small over-decorated Christmas tree in the flat they shared on Gammel Køge Landevej. It was a pretty sorry show, three grown-up people and the whole Christmas spiel. Our mum had hidden two cases of beer under the kitchen sink. I'm always discovering these things. Kaj was already plastered when he arrived, though we pretended not to notice. And we were in the middle of coffee when suddenly she stood in the doorway. With stars in her eyes and far too few clothes on.

'No presents for me?' she asked in a little baby voice, dropping into an arm chair.

Our mum lit a Cecil and glanced nervously at Kaj. But he didn't care. He started a game of solitaire on the coffee table. She got a plateful of lukewarm roast duck and one of my presents. I had removed the 'to' and 'from' label in the kitchen. Then she flung her hair back and rubbed her bare arms. Got up quickly and put her jacket on.

'I've got to go now,' she said and kissed us both on the cheek. Her bracelets jingled, her feet hardly touched the stairs as she ran down. As though she was flying.

Then our mum got quite openly drunk, fetched the photo album and started snivelling. I stroked her dry permed hair and turned off the lights on the Christmas tree. Kaj went to the pub. And that was that Christmas.

'Don't say anything to Kaj', our mum said before she fell asleep on the pull-out bed, 'but I slipped her a five-hundred kroner note. Seeing there were no presents for her . . .'

I took a taxi home; Christmas night was foggy, with a bit of sparse wet snow falling which melted almost before it reached the ground.

It was soon after New Year when one day I felt I had to find Sisse. Or was it the beginning of February? I rang round some of her girlfriends; it was the usual charade with them covering for her and not wanting to say anything and acting all innocent. I had a huge desire to punch Sisse, really beat her up, wipe the smile off her lips, stop the sound of her bell-like laughter that haunted me in my most confused dreams. One day a girl phoned and told the clinic her name was Tina (I have an uneventful steady job as receptionist in a dental practice). Was I looking for Sisse? Did I want to know where she was? A house in the inner city, she said she didn't have the exact address, and hung up.

I trudged around in the rain after work, through the dark afternoons. I was looking for my unmanageable sister who is always hungry and is never satisfied.

It was quite a big building, old and dilapidated, with rain streaming from countless holes in the gutter and downpipe. I spotted the house around six in the evening, and knew straightaway it was the one. The atmosphere about the house was precisely as gloomy and despairing and hermetically sealed as I had imagined it when the girl

Tina phoned. I went in through a large door. It wasn't locked, a dusty staircase greeted me.

I got a shock when an insane bellow drowned out the noise of the rain dripping outside and the sound of my clothes as I moved. I could tell how scared I was, I started to sweat. I could so easily have turned round and walked back, I've walked away from so much over the years, but something made me stay and keep on going in the direction of the sound. I opened several doors and walked through several wrecked rooms. Old engine rooms or something of the sort.

The noise of people shouting and talking, and bangs and crashes of varying strength mingled with that bellow which at times filled the whole house and gave me goose bumps on my arms. No one took any notice of me when I suddenly appeared in the doorway and was in amongst them. There were probably seven or eight of them, maybe more, and an upturned table in the middle of the room, and milk and juice and yoghurt in puddles on the floor. They must have just had breakfast. There was a sour smell, tobacco hung in the air, and faces glowed white in the half-light. I looked for Sisse's face. She was almost unrecognizable. She was squatting against a wall smoking a joint.

'Crap weed', I heard her snuffle to no one in particular.

I wanted to jump over to her and grab her. I wanted to pop her into the pocket of my warm quilted jacket, carry her off from that place and put her in a doll's bed, rock her to sleep away from all that racket. But I couldn't move.

A crazy guy naked to the waist with a live snake round his neck suddenly smashed a guitar against the stone wall. His long hair was drenched in sweat, and sweat ran down his chest. He bellowed, he was the one who had been bellowing. The snake lifted its head stiffly away from his body every time the sound swelled in his throat deafening everything else.

Including my beating heart, my pinched breath.

Someone casually righted one or two fallen chairs. Another lay down to sleep under a window. A young girl with a skull tattoo on her bare shoulder began kissing a little bald-headed fellow with great passion. He was utterly hairless, even his eyelashes were gone. He grabbed her breasts and squeezed. She put her head back and closed her eyes. Sisse passed the joint to another girl.

'Crap weed', said Sisse.

The girl nodded a long while, inhaling deeply.

The crazy guy with the snake tossed the guitar into a corner, it landed with a hollow thud. The one who had lain down to sleep picked it up and started playing. Bent over the fingerboard, his long hair hid both his face and the guitar.

'Great box this . . . ', he mumbled, 'great box—is it Joe's or what?'

'It's bleeding well not Joe's, you impotent little tosser', shrieked the nutter with the snake, moving threateningly towards him.

'Crap weed', said the girl who now had the joint, and stubbed it out on the floor. Sisse nodded long and thought-fully. While this was happening the bald man pulled away from the kiss and shouted at the crazy one:

'Give me Plexus, dammit Steen! It'll flip if you don't let it go now, let go of that snake, man . . . you're fucking sick in the head!'

He ran across the floor to Steen who was just reaching out to grab hold of the long-haired guy with the guitar. He stopped in his tracks, hesitated, turned to the bald man, and with both hands round the snake tried to pry off its body which was looped round his neck. The bald man quickly pulled the animal free while murmuring to it in a monotonous but surprisingly gentle voice. With the snake in his arms he swept past me and out of the door, which banged shut behind him.

I stood rooted to the spot, freezing in my winter clothes, and still no one noticed me. Sisse glanced my way, and for the fraction of a second her eyes met mine, then slid away. She hadn't recognized me. And then he started his bellowing again, the one called Steen, and lifted the guy with the guitar high in the air on the ends of his arms.

'You lousy little swine, you haven't understood shit, and for that I'm going to bloody smash your filthy little poofy face in...', he shrieked and dashed him to the floor.

He grabbed the guitar and hit him. Hit and hit and hit, it seemed never-ending as he just went on thrashing the other guy who resembled most of all a skinny dog, not once did he try to defend himself, blood spilling in a thin stream out of his head all over the dusty wood floor. No one so much as raised an eyebrow.

Finally he stopped. The man lay unconscious on the floor, his face smeared with blood.

'Chill out, man', said the girl with the skull on her shoulder, picking a carton of orange juice off the floor. 'What the heck, no more juice?' She shook the carton up and down. 'You go over the top...'

Steen took deep gulps of air and wiped the sweat from his forehead. He walked with echoing steps in pointy boots over to the door. I could smell his skin and hear the panting of his breath at my ear. I thought I was about to die. From fear; like in a nightmare where you think, Now my end has come...

Sisse sat with her eyes closed. I thought she was asleep. But then the little bald fellow came back in, with the snake hanging long and yellow over his stomach. He took Sisse by the arm and shook her.

'You coming upstairs?' he said. 'Hello! Coming up to see the stars?'

She got up with difficulty, and before I could react they were out of the door.

'Over the top, man...', said a dull voice, as very carefully and with knees like jelly I started moving towards the banging door. I could hardly breathe.

Out in the street I burst into tears. Night had fallen. Weeks could have passed since I'd entered that house, it could just as well have been a different day, another evening. But I looked at my digital watch, and it showed 18.32. I was tired as never before and dragged myself home, where I went straight to bed without undressing or putting on the light, and at once fell into a deep and troubled sleep.

After that day I never again tried to call on Sisse. She didn't call on me either. And spring came, the way it always does, and we were into April before I was reminded of my sister again.

And by then she had already flown.

*

Lacerated. I guess we were all lacerated. Whatever our names were. But Creepy looked after me so well. I was his favourite doll, he said, because I jerked him off at incredible speed under the starry sky. I didn't lack for anything and was even allowed to hold Plexus once in a while, he said we looked great together when he let it coil round my bare body. It felt a bit cold, or rather neither cold nor warm, just curiously nothing. But that didn't matter. Because I wasn't freezing anymore. Creepy picked bags out of the shrine many times a day, and at night too.

I felt flattered too when he asked me if I wanted to take part in that film. I wasn't the least bit scared.

'It's top notch stuff, an American order, I'll be breaking the bank if you agree.'

'Yeah', I said, 'that's okay with me.'

He smiled and prepared a sumptuous fix for me.

'Nothing's too good for you', he said.

He made me a present of his best cross, handmade and solid silver, and said it would bring me luck with my scenes. We left shortly after. The butterflies in my stomach were just incredible because of all the coke.

It's very hot in California, I remember that, hot and dry, my skin wasn't used to the light. Plexus came along, Creepy smuggled him in a suitcase. Of course Plexus came along.

And my scenes. Or scene, because there was really only the one. Out in the desert, masses of sand and sun, masses of light and many voices all moving about. They spoke Spanish and English, I didn't understand what they were saying. Creepy was proud of his masks, there were two, for the men; mad twisted monster masks. Not that they bothered me. Not that anything bothered me. I wasn't scared at all, just let the yellow sand run through my fingers, shut my eyes against the sharp light and waited until my turn came. My turn came. Plexus looked at me with his snake eyes and flicked his tongue through the bars of his cage.

And then it started. The cameras were rolling, I was well doped, Creepy had jabbed something into my arm whispering that it was the best, the best of the best. 'You're on Barbie doll, ready for take-off.' He gave me a lopsided smile. He kissed me. He had never kissed me before.

The men in the masks took turns to fuck me, tied my hands and feet and whipped me with a short-handled whip. They cut me in my breasts and around my crotch, small bloody gashes in the flesh. I was mostly aware of the sand, that kind of sand gives a special sensation. It's everywhere and gets into everything. Dry dusty taste of sand, crunchy between the teeth, little grains in my eyes ...

And then. And then they started stabbing. I could see how they raised their knives. Did I scream? I don't think so. I already knew. And it happened so fast. So incredibly fast. Until I took off, took off and flew. Up above the yellow desert and the lifeless, perforated body. The snake in the cage, Creepy bent over the body, the men stripping off their masks and lighting a cigarette. Wings grew out of my invisible body, I could feel myself. As a light, light creature, weightless and filled with happiness. I had become an angel, I who had always dreamed of flying. Soon all became all bright and fantastic, and here I am, and it has been like this a long time. I just fly and fly through the most brilliantly coloured spaces. There's nothing to stop me anymore.

*

'She's dead!' my mother screamed down the phone, and the waiting room was full of people.

I took a taxi to Gammel Køge Landevej and stroked her dry permed hair. She screamed like a newborn baby. Kaj made coffee and lit her a Cecil. Then I called up the duty doctor who came and gave her a tranquillizer.

She was dead. She was dead. The police said so. When my mother had dozed off I called them up, and they went over it again. That she was dead. That some guy or other had brought her home in a coffin. An accident, he claimed. An assault, said the police in San Diego, it was there in the report.

'But we aren't so sure', said the man at the other end of the line, 'we mean to get to the bottom of this case.'

His voice was from Jutland and soft and I didn't cry. I just felt stiff all over and very tired.

They'd closed her eyes when I had to go and identify her, and I was glad of that, I didn't want to see her starry green eyes gazing greedily at me. She wasn't laughing. But there were ugly cuts almost everywhere on her body, and there was sand in her hair, coarse yellow sand, and in her ears; she didn't actually look scared or anything, her mouth just had nothing left to say.

It is summer now. I am sitting here behind my counter, and my coat is white and clean. We gave her a decent burial. My mother has been taking sedatives and worse since then. And Kaj has moved out. Otherwise nothing much has happened.

We sometimes look at the faded Polaroids from the time Sisse and I were small. 'She was such an angel when she was little', my mother always says, 'such a real little angel child. Oh, she truly was...'

There simply weren't enough sweeties in this world for Sisse. That's how I look at it. That's how I can sit here today smoothing my cool white gown. With tight lips and not a hair out of place. Without shedding even a single tear. For all I really did love her, the little devil. But lonely, it does get lonely at times.

The Trousers

Benny Andersen

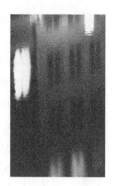

Yes, yes, I'll get to the point, after all I'm in a minority of one so I don't have much choice. The majority never have to explain themselves, it's enough that they're the majority. Not so many details, you say, but on the spur of the moment it's not so easy to tell what's important and what's not, I mean my grocer for instance has a glass eye, what's that got to do with it, and yet not long ago I bought a half-pound of butter off him, and when I'm about to butter my sandwiches for the day all at once the butter lump starts glaring right at me. He's got a bigger size eye now, but it was such a shock I switched to margarine, and that's how I retrieved a taste from childhood, margarine on black bread, and a whole lot more came back to me, and I think that's what made me buy the trousers.

You see, as a boy I was sold short as far as clothes go, I got my brother's cast-off gumboots, jumpers, socks with knobbly darning, coats, books, toys, I made an unholy fuss every time, but there was no way out, I had to be good and accept my place in the pecking order. But now I'm getting on and live alone and can buy my own clothes, now I go rummaging through boxes of second-hand clothes, I feel naked in a tailored suit. At junk dealers and auctions I buy shoes and clothes which belonged to other people, watches, braces, trousers, hats, it's a big relief to slip into a pair of trousers worn into shape, sat into shape, sometimes also pissed into shape. It calms me down. All my worries settle in the turn-ups, easy to tip out once in a while along with the grit and other rubbish that normally collects there. Yes, I've noticed, nobody wants turn-ups these days. Why don't they abolish gutters as well, let all the dirt fly all over the place? With turn-ups you know where the dirt is.

So what with this taste of margarine in my mouth I realized I had to get me some cast-off trousers, I needed to recapture the feeling. Then yesterday I found a pair in a little shop where I often go. They were dark brown with the makings of a saggy seat and the knees bulged like they'd been sitting on a horse, but I'm not really looking to see whether they fit or look nice, I'm looking to see if they have some personality, if they've got a bit of atmosphere about them. Naturally they'd been cleaned after the previous occupant, but I could still detect their own special whiff of something sad and loyal which greatly appealed to me, and excited me too, I could hardly wait to get home before putting them on. I tell you, every time I pull on a pair of old togs like that their atmosphere seeps into me and makes me behave different to how I normally do, it takes me to parts of town I've never been before, makes me speak to total strangers who the clothes presumably know.

These particular trousers took me off to the port, but not the end of the port where I normally go, they walked me out along the harbour road, the smart shops finished, little dives appeared, but the trousers kept on going right to the very last one. You couldn't tell what it was like, the curtains were drawn so it looked pretty drab and dreary from outside, and so who'd want to go in? But there was nothing for it, that was the place the trousers had settled on.

Well, it wasn't so bad inside, even though there weren't exactly tablecloths on the tables, it was special green lino for rolling dice. Nice people, bit loud-mouthed but not specially drunk, coats on and their hats beside them so they had to shift them every time the dice looked like rolling into them, they should have put them on the floor, there was a right old to and fro of hats and bottles. I kept my coat on and ordered a lager and a stout. I was well pleased with the trousers. I was a bit on edge at the start, but now I patted them and enjoyed being able to sit down without them getting tight over my knees the way new ones do.

Now there was a lady sitting on her own in a corner, attractive woman, in her thirties I'd say, dark coat and a fur hat, like a Russian hat, bit full in the face, dark eyes, dark as stout, and a mouth looking like it wanted to wail, but I wasn't sitting there watching her, mind, that chapter is over and done with. The last one I had was called Ruth, and one day at my place when we were lying on the sofa doing it, she came out with the perfect words for the occasion: 'Your ceiling needs painting, Karl.' So that fizzled out of its own accord, because it was not Ruth or anyone else I was interested in, it was a frightened little girl from long ago, something about wet trees and wet benches, small hands in big pockets and big hands in small ones and a treat of gob stoppers and toffee bars, that's what I couldn't forget, all the rest was just padding on an old sore. Naturally I sent Ruth packing, though I should be bloody grateful to her for that remark, it couldn't have been put more clearly. After that I started going for my beers in different places, consumption grew, and I don't much care to be noticed. Stouts and schnapps, the spirits to wash the slimy thoughts down. Yes, I'm coming to the point, but it all has a part to play in what happened. You should be a damn sight more worried about whether I might have missed something out—I am. How it went with the lady, that was all to do with the trousers, either they sighted her or she sighted them. She looked across at me, but I think she looked at the trousers too, and then she came over all nervous, set about rummaging in her bag for a lipstick, put it away again, lifted her glass, put it down again, looked round for the waiter, but looked at me—or the trousers—once she'd caught his eye. I can only see one explanation for her nervousness: there was something between her and the trousers, maybe she'd been expecting the trousers, but not with me inside. And then the strangest thing happened—promise not to interrupt me now—the trousers started to get all tight at the knees, they made me get up and go over to her. I know, probably you don't think it so very strange, you're thinking 'the old tomcat', but that's because you haven't been listening to the details, they're what matter. It was the trousers that wanted to go over to her, and for reasons of public decency I had to go too. And so there I sat. The trousers couldn't speak, I had to put their case for them, and I sat there trying to decipher what they wanted.

Yes, naturally the first thing I said was: 'What's yours?' Idiotic really, she was sitting with a glass of liqueur.

'Thank you, I have something already', she said. Now here's the thing, I mean I take it as a sure sign. She could either have said, 'Leave me alone, how dare you', or else

'Thanks honey, what can you afford?'—but she said what I've just said, and I reckon that must be proof she knew those trousers very well. As soon as I sat down she put her hands on the table and kept them lying there all quiet. Now let's see if we can figure out what's going on here, I thought, but take your time—if these trousers are after something they'll soon let you know. And so I sat quiet as a mouse feeling something stealing over me. Something was wrong somewhere. Someone had got hurt, her perhaps, or the bloke in the trousers, or both. A clamminess was coming off the trousers which gave me goose pimples all along my thighs.

I stared at her hands which were lying just opposite mine. The finger tips lightly touched the green table top. My own clumsy parsnips were lying the same way, and their square yellow cracked nails were staring right into hers, and they were delicate and transparent like the petals of a flower when you hold it up to the light. Then she pulled her fingers in, and that made my own fingers go utterly crazy, they stretched out for hers, crept across the table and reached in under hers to open them again, but it was still those trousers behind it all, and she didn't take her hands away, didn't open them either, though she let my fingers stay there, half inside hers—and not until then did I look up. Her eyes were round and black now, I thought at first she was looking at me, instead it was at something just behind me.

'What's going on here?' It was a shrill jarring voice like a little lad trying to sound grown-up, so you could have knocked me down with a feather when I saw a giant of a man step up to the table. I retrieved my two fists. Her hands hopped into her handbag and hid there.

'Nothing at all, it was just—' She tried to smile, presumably she wanted to say, 'It was just those trousers', but doubtless he wouldn't have taken it in the right spirit. I kept my own mouth shut, I got no instructions from the trousers.

From the very first I couldn't stand his face, but that has to be taken in the right spirit too, because I have friends who look at least as obnoxious without it vexing me, the same suspicious little foxy eyes in a great big stinking mug, the same smug crooked mouth, I've never understood what pleasure women can get from a noodle like that, and yet they've been good mates of mine, and I do believe he and I could likewise have enjoyed a few jars together if we'd just met up and I hadn't been wearing those trousers.

'Has he been bothering you?'

'No, not at all, we were having a chat, it doesn't mean a thing.'

Chat? We'd barely said a word. Quite honestly I was touched at the way she was covering up for me, even if it was the trousers she was concerned for, though equally she'd said it didn't mean a thing. I was touched and relieved and at the same time bloody sorry for the way women humiliate themselves before men and get scared of them because they're big and cocksure and jealous. I stood up. He barred my way.

'Off already?—and just as I arrive, how strange is that', he said sweetly.

It helped a bit to be on my feet, even though he was still a head taller than me. But over the course of time I've discovered that the worst thing you can do when faced with tall people is to tip your head back and address their nostrils, they just love it, and then they adjust their nose, sniff in blissfully, and slap you on the back like they're letting you off some old debt. I just eyed the knot in his tie which was positively plump, the exact opposite to mine which looked like a strangled intestine, and I said:

'Yes, now you say it, it is rather strange. I'll go away and have a little think about it.'

So then he stepped aside. The dice players had gone quiet, all I could hear was her trying to smooth things over behind me:

'I promise you, he was ever so polite.'

'Yes, he even gave you his hand, I noticed.'

I waded out into the cold. The wind was up, the trousers flapped around me. I hurried away from the place.

Somehow autumn had suddenly come. Before, when I was plodding along out there I hadn't bothered my head too much about it, I was more excited about where we were going, me and the trousers. But now I noticed. You know how it goes, how it can be autumn for a long time without you paying attention to the fact—yeah, even though you know it full well, and in fact if anyone happened to ask you, 'What's the season right now?' you'd straight off say 'Autumn, of course.' But suddenly one day you actually see it, the leaves trampled flat on the wet paving stones, the wind up your trouser legs, you get a peculiar sinking feeling in your heart, oh no, autumn's here, and you wonder how come it's only struck you now though you've known it for weeks, only in a distracted sort of way, but now you too are riding along with it and you can't so to speak hop off while it's moving, even if you'd like to. You're one of those slippery leaves yourself, trampled shapeless, and there's not a damn thing you can do about it. Incidentally it's much the same with spring, now I think about it—okay then, we'll stick to autumn. As I said, I was walking along gawping at the fallen leaves, I must have been feeling pretty low, because all I remember is cobbles and paving stones, fag ends, dog shit, silver paper, an incredible amount of silver paper there was, the sort you find wrapped round chocolate, toffee bars and such, it's one of the saddest sights you can ever get to see, all that discarded crumpled silver paper trampled on by wet shoes. I was walking along there, feeling pissed off about that whole business, and then I thought what's the bloody use, best not get involved, they'll work it out those two, forget it, it's not like you to go on like this and go to pieces, stick to your own worries, that might cheer you up some. Which is what I did, thank you very much, and it was easy, all too easy, sliding around in dead silver paper. She was scared of me you know, the little thing. I didn't want her to get hurt, but the only thing that could calm her down was toffee bars, I force-fed her with toffee bars, but there weren't enough toffee bars in the land to calm her down, poor mite. How old was she, about seventeen, and I was twenty-odd. I'd known a good few others, but never in that way, there was none of that, I wanted to make her happy, she was like a little sister, I only ever had brothers, a sister to look out for, buy some nice clothes for, be nice and polite to, take along to the pictures when there's something worth seeing, make her smile once in a while—and stop interrupting me, or I'd rather shut up.

Well, it didn't work out. And the worst about is I saw her later. It was enough to drive a man to drink, if he wasn't there already. I was out to pick something up myself, on my way in to one of those places with a red neon sign over the door and a smart-arse obnoxious doorman just inside, and then I step aside for a couple on their way out, a fat slob with a girl, it was her, thank God she didn't see me. She was laughing at the top of her voice about something or other, but I could have done without that laugh. It was no longer a case of toffee bars, it was no longer a case of anything at all. There just aren't enough toffee bars in the world.

Well, so here's me walking along pondering this and that with my hands in my pockets and my chin in my collar-ends. I wasn't looking where I was going, because I all at once came to a stop right on the edge of the quay. The wind was going full blast, the water was spraying up at me. It was cold standing so near the edge, but I stayed there anyhow, I'm not sure why, the whole thing was a bit strange. Your ceiling needs painting. And then what, when it's been painted?

I'd come a good way along the quay. No one lived here, just locked warehouses and the bare scaffolding of cranes with the wind whistling in them. A single darkened coal freighter lay creaking at its moorings, otherwise all ships were lying safe and sound deeper inside the harbour, where there were lights and people and bars. Those two would be home by now, and they'd be rowing about me, or about the bloke who was in the trousers originally. Most likely he was beating her, he looked the type, the big oaf, because he couldn't get at me. And most likely she was wailing, trying to make herself small, warding off his blows with the fur hat and her bag. Though possibly she also felt she deserved it for what she'd done to the other bloke, not letting him near her, so he took off and stayed away for several days. No doubt that had happened many a time, and each time he had come back, but women want to see how far they can push it, it's like they need to make some kind of calculation, how beautiful they are, how indispensable. But finally she miscalculated and went a step too far, and so then he walked out here like me, and presumably hopped into the drink.

But that was all stuff I didn't want to think about any more just now, and I had no desire to ponder my own fate either, so how was I going to entertain myself, try to think ahead maybe—think of new margarine sandwiches, new drinking companions who have so many of their own troubles you don't fancy coming out with your own—or there might just be something worth seeing at the pictures, except that's another thing I've quit doing. I can't focus on what's happening up on the screen anymore. It's down among the audience things happen. There are so many people round me who've got each other to sit with, a big hand and a small hand meet in a bag of liquorice all-sorts so it splits and the sweets go rolling under the seats like dice, a toffee bar is broken in half and gallantly he leaves her the bit with the silver paper on—no, I don't get much out of the film, and much too much out of the other stuff, so far better stop at home with a coloured bottle or two, and sit and stare at the ceiling. It needs painting. And then what when it's painted? Why were you so scared of me, you poor little sod, I only wanted the best by you. Oh shut up, better to stop thinking altogether.

There was a sort of jetty right down by the water, like a drawer pulled out. I went down the stone steps and tried to stop thinking. The water lapped right over. I shuffled back and forth for a time and was about to go back up the steps when suddenly one of my shoes took a powerful gulp, got a terrific wetting, but never mind, it was a fair while since I'd given my feet a wash, so I stayed put and let the water splash over my shoelaces. Just stop bothering your head about anything. You've stopped so many things, why not stop that too, why not stop altogether—take a holiday, hop off—hand on heart, would any one miss you? I stood there freezing, with my hands in my pockets, found my lighter there, and away with it. It didn't even make a plop, at any rate you couldn't make it out among the other plops and sounds. One plop among many. A little foretaste. My pipe was in the left-hand pocket, away with that too, so now we've stopped smoking as well. And off with my coat. It floated a while with outstretched sleeves like trying to hold onto the waves, comfort them a bit. One coat-tail sank, but it still kept afloat, there must have been a bit of air left in the pockets. That annoyed me. My shoes were already wet anyhow. I couldn't undo the laces, so I tore them off. One went too far out, the other landed right on top of the coat, so finally it began to sink. Now I stood there freezing for real, but that didn't matter, it was one more thing I intended to give up. I bent my knees and put my arms out, but that was too much like the starting position in swimming races, and here the whole point was to quit swimming. Probably it was best to step over the edge and just let myself sink. Then it occurred to me I've never been able to stand getting water in my ears. I went through my jacket pockets, there was all sorts there, only not cotton wool. But my tobacco was sitting in the inside pocket, and I stuck a good plug of it in each ear. So then I was just about ready. But which leg goes first? I tried to remember which leg I normally start with, but that's one of those things you never manage to quite sort out, and so when the time comes you're left just standing there. You're simply not trained for the situation. I could go out sideways, or backwards, or I could lie down and let myself roll over the edge. The longer I stood there the more muddled I got by the many possibilities. The trouser bottoms were meantime soaked right through and stuck to my shins, the trousers should have been able to give me a tip, after all they started it. I looked down at them, and then my knees started knocking together, but it wasn't with cold now. It was the trousers that had wanted to come down here, it was the trousers that had me doing knee bends at the water's edge, for even though I've never claimed existence is marvellous, quite the contrary, life's a headache, though it does have certain advantages such as stout, no, it was the damned trousers that were hell bent on getting down to the bloke in the watery grave. Probably he'd put on a pair of harmless new trousers that day and left the old ones in the lurch, and now they wanted to get back to him, only it was going to be without me. In a trice I pulled them off and chucked them in. First one leg sank and flipped to and fro under the water like it was hunting for something, then the other one joined it, and then they were in complete agreement that was the right route for them, and in the twinkling of an eye they'd dragged down the saggy seat and everything else with them. I turned my jacket collar up to my ears, scrambled up the steps and made for home.

I can well understand it must have given you food for thought, seeing me going full gallop down the street in my jacket, underpants and wet socks, but that's the pure and simple explanation, and the reason I didn't stop the first time you yelled at me was likely on account of the tobacco in my ears, it was well nigh impossible to get out. I've no objection to spending the night here in the police station, inspector, I'm perfectly aware it won't do me any good to

insist I'm more sober than I've been for a very long time—
but if you would just be so very kind as to lend me a pair of
trousers to go home in tomorrow morning. Though promise me one thing: I'd very much like to know a little bit
about the trousers first. Whether they belonged to an old
soak, a pimp, or maybe a rent boy. You can appreciate that
I've grown a little more choosy after this business.

Nightingale

Meïr Goldschmidt

This is an account of a poor old or ageing Jew who hanged himself for love, but was cut down in time and yet remained caught in a noose.

Such matters are best recounted in some detail and beginning from the beginning, which is to say with Leizer Suss.

Very few will still remember Leizer Suss, partly because he died many years ago, but also because to the public he was not known by the name of Suss but Lazarus, which is a direct translation of Leizer. The surname Suss he had either inherited or acquired by accident, for it means horse in Yiddish, yet he was no dumb animal. He was in many respects well esteemed within the community, in particular for his piety, that is to say his orthodox observance of ritual, and for this reason, and also because he was poor, he had been entrusted with the job of *schauchet*, namely butcher and dealer in meat which the community can confidently eat. Otherwise there is little to say about him. He passed all but unnoticed out of this world, leaving a widow no longer young, and six children, a daughter and five sons, having made good provision for all the latter, raising them according to custom until the age of thirteen and then sending them out to make their way in the world, one with a merchant in Altona, the rest with traders in this city.

The years went by and the family lived happily according to the Latin precept *bene vixit qui bene latuit*: whoever lives in obscurity lives well. The mother grew old, about sixty, but still hale and hearty and somewhat imperious; the daughter, Gitte, was approaching forty and still unmarried, either because she was without private means and merely a *schauchet*'s daughter—failings which not even her beautiful brown eyes could make up for—or because she was not 'active enough in the pursuit of her own happiness'. In short, there were reasons enough, and together they were called God's will. The brothers sought to make up for it with quiet affection, at times with a jest, more often with presents. Through their own diligence and thrift, their rising income or wages, they were in a position to make a growing contribution towards their mother and sister's keep. All four who were here in the city would gather at their mother's on a Friday night, just as surely and regularly as she would light and bless the Sabbath candles.

Aside from its slowly but steadily increasing affluence, the only change which had occurred since the father's death was that the family slightly altered its name, and the reason for this went back to Altona, where, as already mentioned, the eldest son, Michael, had been placed. It happened he was due to be promoted to partner in the 'firm'—it was an outfitter's shop—and to this end the firm's 'chief', whose name was likewise Lazarus, said to him one day: 'You are called Lazarus. Well, it's a good name—*I* won't pretend otherwise. But there can be too much of a good thing! Lazarus & Lazarus: say what you like, it won't look good on a signboard.'

'Then Lazarus & Co.', said the prospective partner modestly.

'Lazarus & Co. And when people ask who is Co? Lazarus! Whichever way you look at it: Lazarus & Lazarus!'

'Well, then', said Michael, not daring to complete his meaning, which was 'So won't I become a partner?'

After a moment's pause the chief continued: 'Tell me, did your father not have another name than Leizer?'

Michael reddened and failed to answer.

'No matter, that's between you and me and need not disturb your blessed father in his grave. But was he not sometimes called Leizer Suss?'

'That is possible', answered Michael.

'Well, that's it then! Who says you have to hold on to every letter in your father's name, when he himself never willingly used it! We'll put an A instead of a U. Sass is a good name. Lazarus & Sass—it has a ring to it, and will do nicely!'

So that was that; and since Michael, who was now head of the family, called himself Sass, one after the other the brothers followed suit, and last of all, with some trepidation at first, but finally, as no one appeared to object, their mother likewise boldly assumed the name of Sass. It is possible, indeed probable, that the name change prompted a little raillery within the community, but as we have said, no one protested.

The only person who disliked the change was Avromche Nattergal. From boyhood he had been almost one of the family; on a Friday night he was present as surely as any of the sons; he had watched them all grow up—he was eight years older than the eldest son—had played with them, shared sorrows and joys with them all. There had once been some talk about his having Gitte, but that had blown over without leaving any bad feelings. But now, since the new name also came with various new items of furniture and a certain new 'air', greater expectations or pretentions, vaguely, obscurely, it seemed to him he was being put aside, no longer belonged as fully as before, that his lowly occupation was more noted than before. Yet he couldn't quite explain it; it was an uncertain feeling, there one moment and gone the next. That was why he disliked the name of Sass, though he took good care not to say so.

So what was his occupation, I am bound to be asked. Permit me not to act like a bull in a china shop, but to prepare the reader by relating how he happened to come by it.

He was the son of a man known to the community as Reb Schaie, surnamed Pollok, one of the very last here to go about in a caftan and a fur hat and a long beard. But although on the outside Reb Schaie resembled some vagrant Polack, he was an intelligent and active man in society who ran a not inconsiderable skin-and-fur business. He kept account books—something virtually unknown in trade at the time—and was altogether an exceedingly precise, serious, and strict fellow. Naturally he wanted his son to join the business; however, his Abraham (Avrohom: diminutive Avromche) came to develop an ever growing passion for music and song. Not only did he never miss a chance to hear music, remarks at times escaped him which indicated he wished, nay, dearly hoped, to make his own voice heard—by taking to the stage. For a good while his father treated this as childishness, a daydream which would soon evaporate in 'the business', and against his wont would even jest about the matter, sarcastically remarking, 'Avromche will yet get to be *hrasan*', that is, cantor in the synagogue. But then one evening, when chance happened to bring him up to his son's attic room, he surprised Avromche dressed in tights with a beret on his head performing a bravura aria, while the old music teacher Leibche Schwein, also known as Levin Snus, accompanied him on guitar. Reb Schaie chased Leibche Schwein down the stairs, and said to his son: 'Knitted drawers and a hat with a feather! Why not with the grand cross on the national flag? Nah! What *meschuggàs*, what madness do my eyes have to see! Do you even know how crazy you are? I have but one thing to say to you, so listen: Anyone in the theatre not whistling at your long nose and crooked mouth, do you know what they'll whistle at? Do you?' 'No, father.' 'At your crooked legs!'

These cruel but not wholly unjust words extinguished an ideal, a hope and a lifetime's ambition in Avromche's heart. He was barely nineteen, yet from that moment on he was no longer young. He did not show his despair, complained to no one, in fact from the moment a mainspring had been snapped inside him it seemed that even the memory of ever having had such a drive had been quenched, yet at the same time something of life itself had been quenched. Even so, a profound unspoken passion remained with him: the longing to hear music; and seeing that his father now kept him on an even tighter leash so he could not afford a music teacher, Avromche hit on the idea of renting a box in the theatre and selling tickets for it so as to get in for free. For a while he even struck lucky, but just as a plant necessarily requires a modicum of warmth in order to flower and fruit, in the long run any business, no matter how modest, similarly requires a modicum of time and care. Not all box tickets always sell like hot cakes; one needs to look sharp; there are competitors, opportunities, and market trends in that business too, and Avromche was often most cruelly torn between his duties towards his father's business and those towards his box, with the result that both fared badly. Without knowing the true reason, his father had ever more cause to be dissatisfied; and then finally all came to light: Avromche had incurred debts far greater than the cost of a regular seat in the theatre, and his father was contacted for payment. Reb Schaie paid off the debt, gave Avromche a sum of money, and said to him between his teeth, in Yiddish, which with its cryptic ring pregnant with curses had a force no words in Danish could ever express: 'Leave my house! On account of the theatre you will yet seek a nail from which to hang yourself! You are useless and unnecessary on this earth! Go!'

It was at this juncture that Leizer Suss and his wife proved to be Avromche's best and perhaps only friends. It even happened that Leizer Suss did something quite exceptional: he went straight round to Reb Schaie to impress upon him his harshness towards his son and to persuade him to make amends; but he came back most crestfallen and never spoke of what had transpired. But to Avromche he said: 'No matter what, you shall never go wanting so long as I have meat on the table.' Both he and his wife next attempted to the best of their ability to help Avromche plan his future. As there was no hope that he would ever give up his passion, it was found to be quite in order for him to devote himself wholly to the theatre, not to the stage itself, but to one or more boxes and the ticket sellers' beat between the theatre and Lille Kongensgade. With all his experience plus some perseverance there was a livelihood to be had, and—in short—he became a ticket tout. There, we've said it now, and after this preamble it shouldn't look so bad, and won't lessen the reader's sympathy for Avromche 'Nattergal'. Ah yes, whence came the nightingale nickname? It was all down to his failed singing career. The Jews have a quite uncanny gift for bestowing suchlike ironic nicknames. Madame Sass herself would on occasion adapt and expand the soubriquet with a degree of malice which did not imply any actual evil intent, but merely went to show that friendship did not blind her to her friend's imperfections. *Natten gal,* she would say, *dagen ikke klog.* Crazy at night, not too clever in the day.

Leizer Suss died, and a while later Reb Schaie died too, leaving his son a small capital, less than anticipated but large enough to have enabled him, with his modest requirements, to retire from active life and live off the interest. But art, even in its obscurest antechambers, has an allure which few who have once succumbed can ever escape, not to mention that it is by no means easy for a man to give up his habits and his occupation. There is excitement even in gambling with theatre boxes; there are triumphs which though small still quicken the heart; and there are evenings when a person feels a certain importance, partakes in the life throbbing so strongly on the stage, whose blaze is reflected in the glow on his face. And access to all else may be denied, or one has neither the desire nor the power to explore new paths. Thus Avromche Nattergal continued working as a ticket tout.

There was perhaps one moment when he might have given up his occupation, and that was shortly after his father's death, when in return for all the kindness shown towards him he felt obliged to see Gitte married by offering her his hand and his fortune. But Gitte was not willing, and her mother did not force her, no doubt because she still had hopes for her daughter elsewhere: offer and rejection were amicably exchanged, and Avromche's relations with the household remained unaltered.

He lived in Pilestræde on the third floor of a backyard building where he lodged with a joiner's family, or to be more precise, right next to the joiner's workshop, which was why his clothes always smelled a little of wood shavings, and why his rivals at the theatre called his box the coffin. He got his revenge, and not without malice and wit when the occasion arose, though he preferred to murmur his apt remarks to himself with a little smile rather than utter them out loud. It was sufficient for him to know he could retaliate, and besides he felt that as a pious Jew and someone who had not become a ticket tout out of necessity he possessed an inner dignity which enabled him to rise above the twitting and even the job itself.

At the time we are now approaching, that is around his fiftieth year, anyone coming across him—in a long coat, or in winter a greatcoat just as long, somewhat stooped, pale, with a mild fixed slight smile, hands clasped inside his sleeves, and with a quaint little sideways bob of the head as though constantly and surreptitiously beating time, and one eye or eyelid batting to the same beat—would instinctively have gained the impression that here was a man whose destiny was accomplished, who was peacefully and quietly tottering the shorter or longer path to his grave.

Far from it! The storm in Avromche's life was still to come, and it was prompted by one single careless word, or by the careless use of one single word: Suss.

One evening when he arrived at the Sass home they had changed their maid, and the moment Avromche saw the new face in the doorway he quickly grasped what had happened, and just as quickly, due to his old grudge against what was for him the still new name of Sass, he conceived the mischievous whim of asking: 'Is madam Suss at home?' The words just slipped out like that. He hadn't really meant to inform the maid that her employers' rightful name was Suss, though possibly he did half intend her to overhear it, needing in that demonic moment a confidant, just like king Midas's barber who simply had to reveal, if only to a little hillock in a field, that his master possessed ass's ears. It was a joy for him to utter the word, he got it off his chest; but the very next moment, when the maid softly rejoined, 'Yes, Madame Sass is at home,' he regretted it because he felt her answer to be a well-earned rebuke and also feared she might inform her mistress. But it was too late now. It would only make matters worse to implore the maid not to say anything, and in any case there was no time for that, for next moment he was in the drawing room. All that evening and the next days he was miserable. He said to himself: 'Next time I call I know how I shall be received. She'll pretend she can't see me, and if I sneeze she'll ask "Who's that? Oh, it's Pollok!"—because now she'll no longer be saying Avromche. And later in the evening when she cuts up an orange she'll pass round the pieces to the side where I'm not sitting, and there'll be nothing for me. What do I care about the orange? It's her look! It's her face! My stomach is already in knots with panic. And she'll keep me in this state for a week, a fortnight, possibly longer, until a good play comes along and I beg and beg her to go. And then she'll most likely say "Oh yes, let Madame Suss take a nice trip to the theatre again!" And then she'll dart me such a glance—two needles in my heart! And all that for my damned mouth.'

He didn't dare call round and didn't dare stay away, but in the end he put a brave face on it. He received the usual simple almost casual welcome, and at first presumed it was the calm before the storm, that they had carefully prepared things so that when lightning struck it would be that much more startling and devastating; but very soon it became plain to him the barometer was set on fair weather, and then he felt an enormous sense of relief and gratitude, gratitude towards heaven and the maid, who had clearly kept her mouth shut. One of the very next evenings he found a pretext for calling again, and brought the maid a present of a four shilling Christmas cake. At that time both maids and Christmas cakes must have been better than they are now, for the maid accepted the cake with thanks, and when the time came for her to light Avromche downstairs and see him out by the front door, she thanked him yet again.

'Don't mention it', said Avromche. 'You are a good girl. I won't say why you are a good girl. You *are* a good girl. What is your name?'

'Emilie.'

'Emilie. That's a good name. How old are you?'

'Nineteen.'

'Nineteen years old', said Avromche, for the first time taking a close look at her sweet, young, fresh face. He added with naive satisfaction, 'You look like a good girl too. Very much so! Where are you from? Are you from this city of ours?'

'No, I'm from Nakskov.'

'From Nakskov? What did your father do?'

'He is a tanner.'

'He's still alive? So why are you not at home?'

'Father married again, and my stepmother wanted me out.'

'Poor girl! You're a good girl. Keep on being a good girl.'

'I certainly shall', she replied. But whether both meant the same by this exchange is doubtful. Avromche's meaning was that she should continue to keep mum about the word Suss.

Without really being able to account for it, that night and all the following days Avromche had the feeling he had experienced something—something momentous.

True, he had been rescued from great fear and danger, but it was not just that. No matter how very unremarkable had been his conversation with the maid it was still something wholly novel in his life. When did he ever converse with anyone about anything other than tickets, or the desultory trivialities which constituted the entertainment at Madame Sass's? When had he ever asked about something with so much interest, when had an answer to a question aroused in him a state of such tender animation as this girl's, whose youth made her at once so delighted and delightful? There comes a time in every man's life when youth exerts a power over him he had no notion of in his own youth, yet this power affected Avromche all the more strongly for his being so wholly unaccustomed to anyone looking at him and speaking to him with such good will, in addition to being so pretty. The ageing man's soul lit up, as if in some curious way he had met a sister he did not dare acknowledge—and moreover would not wish to acknowledge; for it was so infinitely far from his thinking that there could ever be anything closer between himself and a Christian maidservant, or woman, let alone an affair of the heart.

And yet he felt reinvigorated every time it happened that the maid lit his way downstairs on his own and he could conduct a conversation consisting of almost the selfsame words as on that first evening. For him, who merely longed to hear her voice and once in a while steal a glance at her fresh face, it scarcely mattered what he asked her or what she answered, and he failed to notice how he made himself ridiculous by always repeating the same words. 'You are from Nakskov?' 'Yes.' 'And your father is a tanner?' 'Yes.' 'And you have a stepmother who won't have you at home?' 'Yes.' 'You are a good girl. Good night!' And when in her laughing clear voice she replied 'Good night', he rejoiced to carry the sound away with him.

He now had something beyond his usual humdrum life to think of and long for, and the years dropped off him. He walked with less of a stoop, returned people's gaze with greater openness, and shed a crustiness which had begun to plague him with the onset of old age, and which had already lost him customers. He went to the expense of a new coat, and although there was a good and very natural reason for this—the old one was so very old!—it attracted notice, both on the corner of Lille Kongensgade and in Kompagnistraede where Madame Sass lived. 'What's up with Nattergal?' people started asking. About anyone else, even a ninety year old who had similarly altered, they would have said, at least in jest, 'He's in love, he must be courting'; but not once did any such jest occur to anyone where Avromche was concerned, for all it was in earnest, though Avromche himself had not the remotest inkling. All he felt, for the first time in his life, was the joy of living, or rather for the first time since boyhood a pleasurable longing inhabited his soul. The mainspring which his father had snapped had, albeit in its own strange way, recovered its tension. And it had come about in such a gentle and gradual fashion, was so nearly trouble-free, so naive that he himself was aware of it only to the extent that he felt happy. Thus might a wood perhaps feel on a November day when the sun shines as in spring.

At that time 'Svend Dyring's House' had its first performances, and was not only a great success, as is well known, but aroused much emotional turmoil, especially among the female section of the audience. Several ladies, it was said, had fainted away from sentiment. The following Friday night when the sons gathered at Madame Sass's all had seen the play and were enraptured with it, or in the grip of the general rapture; even so they were agreed their mother must on no account go and see it: she would not be able to stand the emotion. Avromche was no great fan of the play; it filled, indeed overfilled the boxes, and was from that point of view a good thing, but from another, as far as his own aesthetic preferences went, it was poor because it was not an opera, and because what music it did contain was lost on him; his heart, artistically speaking, was fully taken up with 'La Muette', which was also playing at the time, and above all by the 'Slumber Aria', and he regarded the public's enthusiasm for 'Svend Dyring's House' as a fad.

All the same, he wanted Madame Sass to visit his box and see it and to be gripped by the same fad as everyone else, partly because to him it was now dearer than ever to bring some joy into this household, and partly also because by treating Madame Sass and her daughter to tickets and bringing them to and from the theatre he would at least for a moment come across as a man of some importance to the family. He was therefore unusually keen to contradict the sons' opinion that their mother would be unable to stand the emotion.

'Not stand it?' he said. 'What is there to stand? What's there to faint about? It's beyond me! A woman fainted in the next door box, that's very true. But why did she faint? Because she was a fat brewer's wife, and because Henriksen packed too many in. Henriksen is a *retseiach*. But will I be packing too many in when a good friend is to be there, and in my box will Madame Sass not get a good front bench seat and no crowding in front or behind or from either side? Not stand it? Nonsense!'

However, one of the sons repeated his assertion, and backed it up by referring to the play's content. He cited fairly accurately:

> Every mother knows for herself, 'tis true,
> What the milk of my breasts may do for you.

---

retseiach: ruthless fellow.

'How could Mother bear to hear and see that?' he added.

'Why not?' cried Avromche. 'Does a person in the box have to be female just to know that? Am I a woman, yet don't I know that somebody dead and gone and buried and no more than a ghost cannot have milk in her breast? If I know that then your mother knows it too, and she won't faint.'

Another of the sons said with quiet gravity: 'Mother will think of our blessed father, *olaum ve scholaum*. That moment where the deceased walks off and Mr. Dyring reaches out after her imploring her to stay, that's when Mother will think of our blessed father as he lay in his funeral best.'

'God forbid!' cried Avromche. 'That must never happen! Never on my *neschommo*. But is your mother not a reasonable lady? Will she not be sensible and say to herself "One of the wives *has* to go, otherwise the man will have two wives—so which shall it be?" Who else but the one who is dead and buried?'

All Avromche's eloquence might have been to no avail had not the sons chosen a line of argument which led to precisely the opposite conclusion to the one anticipated; for women do in fact relish emotion, though they are loath

---

olaum ve scholaum: God rest his soul.
neschommo: soul.

to admit to it. Madame Sass said, with dignity: 'I'll not think about your father, *olaum ve scholaum*. Why should I? It's some other man's wife who died and walks onto the stage—what's that got to do with me? I want to go!'

During this conversation the maid had been coming and going, and never having been to the theatre she gained an even more colourful notion of plays in general, and 'Svend Dyring's House' in particular, than any other mortal from the provinces. The mysteriously bloodcurdling and infinitely enticing prospect increased, if that were possible, when Madame Sass returned home accompanied by Gitte and Avromche, while the sons were gathered to receive her as if after a journey. As she came through the door she called out proudly: 'Did I faint? Did I feel unwell? Tell them Gitte! Not once did I cry—what was there to cry about? Though just for the sake of appearances I dried my eyes and blew my nose when the others wept. Ah, but it was wonderful—though to be in love the way she is—well, I suppose they were in those days—but that bit about the roast apple I didn't get ... '*

'Roast apple?' exclaimed Avromche.

---

* Danish *riste* means both 'to roast' and 'to engrave/carve'. The hero engraves magic runes on an apple intended for his beloved.

'Well, *mahnschten* roasted, *mahnschten* toasted! Does he not bake an apple? What happened to it? That never came out...'

From her sons' awkward expressions and Avromche's twitching face she understood she had said something silly; but she had no idea what it was, and her dignity as a mother did not permit any dwelling on the fact that when she was with her children she had her intelligence enriched at the cost of her self-esteem, so the discussion moved on to other things, the play, the costumes, the knights, the poor little children, the wicked Guldborg, and the rest of it.

To the maid it seemed worth giving years of one's life to see something so wonderful; but how could that possibly happen, how would she ever get in there? Just because Avromche Natttergal had presented her with a Christmas cake didn't mean he owed her a ticket to the theatre. True, she was in possession of his perilous secret, but she herself was unaware of it; she had not heard or at least not understood the deep significance of the difference between Suss and Sass, and even had she known the secret she would hardly have thought of using it, even to obtain a ticket. But in Avromche the sense of his debt was not only undiminished but had multiplied; mixed with the silver of gratitude was the gold of love, though he did not know it,

mahnschten: never mind.

and so some nights later when again he was fortunate enough to be alone with her as she lighted his way out, he said: 'Do you know what engraving is? Do you know what it is to engrave runes? To *riste* them?'

'Yes, it is to carve them.'

'Not roast them, is it? Then you too can go and see the play. Would you like a ticket?'

'Oh, Mr. Nattergal!' she cried, nearly dropping the candle when she instinctively wanted to clap her hands.'

'In actual fact my name is not really Nattergal. It's Pollok. But never mind. If you want to say Nattergal then say Nattergal, though in fact it's Pollok.'

Doubtless without realizing this represented a change for the better, the girl said: 'Forgive me! Oh Mr. Pollok, how very good you are!'

And she said this with such fervour in her voice and with such a look that had Avromche been a young man and not developed according to the portrait his father once painted of him, there might well have been cause to believe that in her too the silver of gratitude was mixed with a weightier metal. Avromche had no eyes for himself but only for her, and with the words 'We'll talk about it further!' he hurried away happily.

The matter proved fraught with difficulties, but the very difficulties delighted Avromche more than can be imagined. There was much to plan, more talks to be had.

Emilie could only come out every other Sunday, and she barely knew where the theatre was, let alone the box. It therefore fell out quite naturally that Avromche offered to fetch her, to wait for her by the front door, and accompany her both to and from the theatre. Her own mother, had she lived, could not have wished her a more innocent escort— and for Avromche it was a belated yet genuine assignation with all its attendant secrecy and longing—he too was at last young and happy!

Emilie had dressed as though for a ball, in a low-cut dress made of fine lawn, though with a little silk necker-chief knotted chastely about her neck. She looked so pretty, almost lady-like, that Avromche glowed with pride when he showed her into his box; but so that she should not be too much in the public eye he placed her on the second row bench whilst he remained standing behind the third, bending down to her to explain the action and preparing her for what was to come. Out of politeness or gratitude for his attention, however wearisome, she turned round to him as often as possible, and this movement frequently caused the little silk neckerchief to slip to one side, without her noticing in the heat of the moment. Avromche, who felt that thereby something was exposed to his eyes that for decency's sake they had no business to see, constantly and conscientiously and very gently set the neckerchief back in its rightful place. This manoeuvre very soon came to the attention of a young person, or gentleman, who was sitting in the neighbouring box right beside Emilie and whose eyes were not as conscientious as Avromche's. At first he thought it was a jealous elderly husband who had brought his young wife to the theatre; but soon he recognized Nattergal, and the matter struck him as incomprehensible, not to say piquant; she appeared to be a pretty little flirt of a girl whom the ticket tout kept covering up in uncalled-for fashion. When the curtain fell he struck up a conversation with Emilie, and not wanting to reveal that she did not belong among all these nice people who looked like a grand company of friends and acquaintances, she answered in a friendly and grateful, even cordial fashion, which in turn was thoroughly misunderstood by the young person. Avromche could not forbid her to answer, no more than he could give her advice or a signal, and besides he suffered all the agony of jealousy over what the young person might be talking about with her, or gazing at. Fervently he wished for the strength of ten men and the courage to strangle him, or at the very least to throw him out.

The curtain rose again, and as the play progressed it touched Avromche's heart in a way that he had never before suspected. Deep within him, a painful, abruptly awoken poetic sensibility revealed to him the fact that down there thrived, stirred, a sensitive and expansive spirit or mood—

we call it romantic—which he had long grown out of, or rather in which rightly or wrongly his soul had been denied the right to share, and to which in the eyes of the world Emilie and even the revolting young person belonged. He felt this with inexpressible anguish, as though present at a death sentence pronounced upon him, or at his own funeral. Never had the stage acted upon him as it did now.

All the small pictures turned to the wall*

The knights and ladies and young lovers all suddenly recalled his father's words and said to him: 'Why will you be hissed off stage? Because of your hook nose and your crooked mouth and your crooked legs!' And how they described him was how he saw himself, abhorrent and alien in their midst, miserably repudiated. And yet the very music he had scorned because it was not like 'La Muette' now possessed his whole being, lent him an artificial youth, frolicked with him as though he belonged, though he did not belong. Why should he not be happy? He could marry the girl—yes, he would propose to the tanner's daughter! The community would repudiate him, but in his soul he would not cease to be a Jew—and so what! What had he ever had in his life other than clammy fog?

* A haunting line from the ancient ballad *Agnete og Havmanden* (Agnete and the Merman): all the holy images shun Agnete's merman lover when he appears in church.

Whom did he have to thank for anything? If she who as a blessing or a curse was after all the sole patch of sunlight in his existence were to be torn from him now—the very thought drove him to distraction. He would not need to remain in Copenhagen, he could move to the country and live with her in some suitable quiet out-of-the-way place. He was after all a man of substance—what was that windbag compared to him? He could be happy, he *would* be! His resolution had only to be spoken to be irrevocable— and then the curtain fell.

Where was reality—in the box with the girl and the tenderness and jealousy she aroused, and where though now so close to her he could not find one right word to say to her but with disgust heard his own voice saying 'Is it good? Are you enjoying yourself? Do you like it?' when all he wanted to say was 'Speak to no one! Look at no one! Be my wife!'—or was it on the stage, where again the curtain had risen, and again he suffered from old age and again became young, and once more renewed his resolution? The storm had truly engulfed Avromche Pollok! Ah, all ye sympathetic hearts, you would have wept to see inside him, and laughed to look at him.

After the play finished, bewildered by so many unfamiliar emotions, he guided Emilie downstairs as though into a safe harbour from tumultuous seas. But the young person stuck close to them, and in the dense throng on the last flight of stairs into the foyer where it clashed with those streaming out of the rear stalls, that same person cut in between Avromche and Emilie and offered her his arm. Avromche uttered a shriek, a cry whose content can only be explained by all he had so recently experienced in the depths of his soul, though no doubt also he hoped to gain sympathy thereby, proclaim his rights. He shouted: 'Stop! Help! He's taking my wife!' The young person slipped away like an eel, but at the same instant several hundred pairs of eyes in the foyer were now riveted on the familiar figure of Pollok, or Avromche Nattergal: in that fleeting second of silence he became a little story to take back to the supper table, or elsewhere.

Moments later they were outside. Avromche kept silent as they crossed the square: the moment had come, he had to speak, and yet there were still so many people about; he wanted to reach Vingårdsstræde and there obtain her signature to the document to which he had already set his seal. At the moment he chose to do so, and turned right round to face her, he saw that she was crying.

'What is it?' he exclaimed, startled, 'Why are you crying?'

'Because you shamed me by calling me your wife.'

He failed to understand that any young girl publicly and against her will represented as married might feel humiliated, and that the small-town girl felt keenly she had been dragged into a minor scandal. He took it instead as a declaration that she considered marriage to him, the Jew, to be something shameful, and all at once, if not cured, he was at least pitched right out of his private heaven. He said not another word, not even goodnight when they parted.

He did not wish her goodnight, nor did he wish good evening to the carpenter's journeyman who, as was his wont, appeared on the stairs and handed him the little lamp—for according to ancient and strict custom no one was permitted a naked light in or near the workshop, and a journeyman had to be lodged up there as night watchman. The moment Avromche was in his room he gave vent to his feelings:

'*Ausgefallene Schtrof*'! I must have sinned in my mother's womb to end up not only *meschugge* but *meschugge metorf!* To go and shout it out to all and sundry! Where was my *seichel*? Have I ever had any? Was I born blind, deaf and crazy? *Schema Jisroel!* This will be the death of me! How can a person carry on living after behaving like such a *verschwärzter* idiot? How can he? *Oy! Oy! Oy!* They all heard it, and they'll hear even more! By tomorrow I'll have also fathered children all over town! And how can I prove

---

Ausgefallene Schtrof: a punishment or misfortune falling like a bolt from the blue; *meschugge*: mad; crazy; *meschugge metorf*: stark staring mad; *seichel*: reason; *Schema Jisroel*: Hear O Israel; *verschwärzter* idiot: damned idiot.

it's lies and *schkorum*, when I lied too? Fetch her out and have her say all over again... *sau m'hrulle, und sau m'hrulle!* No, one *m'hrulle* is even worse than the other... If only she'd been willing! But I was the only willing one, *hramor* that I am, *posche Jisroel* that I am! And I must own up to it? I can't own up to it!—Avromche, Avromche, one minute has made you an unhappy man! *Oy! Oy! Oy und Weh!'*

At this point something remarkable happened: he could feel his unhappiness and still not truly fathom it; something in his head came close to breaking every time he tried to conceive and grasp the full extent of the trick fate had played on him: how happiness could have led him to compromise himself before both the public and his own community, how happiness had turned to unhappiness and mortification, until all that remained was the spectacle he had made of himself, which moreover grew and grew. His thoughts tore in a circle about the deception, sought out its centre, but shrieked in pain before penetrating so deep, and fled to the circumference again. All this did not take place in silence; through the thin wall the journeyman could hear him storming up and down, talking at the top of his voice, moaning and wailing, and since on the stairs he had already noticed Nattergal's look of suffering, he

---

schkorum: untruth; *sau m'hrulle und sau m'hrulle*: ruined one way or the other; *hramor*: ass; *posche Jisroel*: insulter of Israel; *Oy und Weh*: woe is me.

went in to him. 'Is something the matter, Mr. Polack?' he asked, as he stuck his head round the door.

Avromche clutched his head and replied: 'Toothache— yes, toothache! Dreadful!'

'Is it a molar?' the journeyman asked as he came closer.

'A molar? It's worse than a molar! It's a *schikse*!'* Avromche retorted, relieved to be able to unburden himself to another human being without giving himself away.

'So it's a canine?'

'Well, I wouldn't know. But I'm as bad as a dog myself, and suffering like a dog, oh, oh!'

'But where does it hurt?' asked the journeyman as he lifted the lamp up to Avromche's face.

'It's gout. We get older. I'm an old horse, a great ass, and like every other old ass I should be hauled out to Amager and slaughtered. And they really will haul me out—just you wait and see!'

'Yes, you do need to have it out; but you won't be able to have it done before tomorrow.'

'Tomorrow! Would that tomorrow would never come!' replied Avromche with a shiver.

'Now, now, Mr.Polack! Won't you take something?'

'Take something? Is there anything to take? What do you know about such things? A young man, and a good-

---

* *schikse*: Christian girl.

looking man, how happy you must be...I mean', he added, struggling to pull himself together a bit, 'a young man with such good sound teeth.'

'As a matter of fact I have experienced it too.'

'Have you? What did you do? I'm telling you—you've experienced nothing like this.'

'Oh yes, I held some brandy against the tooth.'

'Brandy against the tooth,' repeated Avromche slowly. Instinctively he felt in need of warmth and resuscitation, and suddenly it struck him as good advice. 'Where can we get brandy? Have you got some?'

With the quiet satisfaction laymen feel when their proffered advice about an illness is accepted, the journeyman went next door and brought back a blue flask and a heavy broad-based quarter-pint glass.

As Avromche took the glass he wanted to say the Jewish prayer but had the dreadful feeling he must not presume to, that in thought and deed he had betrayed his God and his people, and in desperation he emptied the glass without preliminaries. Once over the first shock of the unaccustomed drink, and feeling the warmth spread through his veins, he said: 'That did me good, after all.'

'Not much got to the tooth,' said the journeyman.

Avromche answered with a queer laugh: 'It didn't get to the tooth, and yet it did get to the tooth!'

'Yes, it does one good all the same,' the journeyman said as he poured himself a glass too, and emptied it.

'How would it get to the right tooth?' continued Avromche. 'If it could get to the right tooth I wouldn't be here and you wouldn't be here, and so then it would not be needed.'

The journeyman could make no sense of this dark Talmudic speech and contented himself with replying: 'Try another small one.'

'Yes, but just a very small one.'

Avromche took another deep draught, and with thanks to the journeyman declared he was much better now, whereupon the journeyman wished him good night and went back to his room.

But once the journeyman had gone so had the human sympathy and the momentary distraction, and the fearful reality broke with fresh and feverish power into Avromche's now drink-fuelled consciousness. It seemed impossible things could be as they were, and yet it was impossible to deny. It was as though some creature were with him in the room, one moment lurking in a corner and next moment hurling itself at him to grab him by the throat and dash him to the floor. And all the while thoughts and memories whirled past him in a frenzied ring dance, and he saw the most diverse things at one and the same time: Emilie in the square gliding away like a shadow, the young person in the box laughing in his face, the crowd in the lobby infinitely far below, and their muttering and their laughter, and the shrilling of the music from 'Svend Dyring's House' together with the revolution scene from 'La Muette'; and in the middle of it all his father arose, swaying in the air, deathly pale, saying to him: 'On account of the theatre you will yet seek a nail from which to hang yourself! You are useless and unnecessary on this earth!' And whenever all began to fade for a moment, then horror at the thought of the following day loomed in the shape of another ghost leaping on him from the corner.

It was impossible to endure, and impossible to shake off. He could not even summon the strength to let out a scream, but as in a nightmare stood wavering in the middle of the dim room, with one sole half-formed wish: to get away from this life which offered no place to hide.

What brings on the thought of suicide? The doctors say it is a sickness, a sort of insanity. But how and at what moment does our private innermost being pass from its intrinsic unity to the discord which is insanity, and which prompts the urge? And how of itself can insanity persuade a person to hang himself, an undertaking which in sane people's eyes is demanding and requires considerable practical sense? With all other methods of doing away with oneself we have some sort of training. Everyone has tried to prick or cut himself, drink something that makes him sick and so forth, and people who shoot themselves have previously fired a gun or a pistol; but to hang oneself by the neck from a nail or a hook lies beyond all possibility of rehearsal, and yet people carry it out at the crucial moment with assurance and a sort of uncanny ingenuity, in the hour of madness.

How did Avromche come to hang himself? He stood on the very brink of madness, but had yet to go over the precipice. His dead father pointed to a nail from which to hang himself, but hardly ever had Avromche taken it for anything more than a figure of speech. He wished himself out of life, but still had not lost all sense of self-preservation, that instinctual love of the self as a person alive. An apparent trifle tipped the balance. He saw—as the horrifying ring dance still whirled about him—something on the wall, something solid resembling a human figure. It was his own old coat hanging there, but at once it seemed to him he had company, that something human was in there with him, and he formed but one great wish: to get to it. After an age which to him seemed endless, by exerting all his strength he managed one step towards his salvation and felt inside it—and it was empty, just the husk of a human, perhaps his own father. Through his dismayed and terrified fingertips a sensation mounted to his brain and unleashed the madness. With extraordinary speed and assurance he remembered the maidservant had recently run up new clothes lines outside the window, and with equal certainty he recalled there was a great nail in the ceiling. In a trice he had seized the clothes line and—hanged himself. But this time too he had made more noise than he knew, and he was barely strung up before the journeyman was inside the room and had cut him down.

So Avromche did not die by the noose, though he was still more dead than alive. The journeyman raised the alarm, and had him taken to hospital.

The townspeople received the mysterious news of his marriage almost at the same time as they heard that he had been taken to hospital in either a state of madness or a fever. The latter swallowed up the former, for when someone is struck low by an everyday mishap he ceases to be of interest. With the Sass family this was not quite the case. Sympathy for him in his illness did indeed have to battle hard against their resentment at the fact he had so craftily got married on the sly, for all that there was something mightily surprising and hard to credit about the marriage itself. They obtained the most impeccable information from town, and were none the wiser. At his lodgings they were told he had been raving and had tried to take his own life, but both the journeyman and his master and the entire family were much astonished when asked about his wife. In the foyer, too, they confirmed they had seen

Nattergal and had heard his declaration, but no one had sighted his wife in the throng. Even had someone picked out Emilie amongst other female figures near him, she would have seemed the person least likely to be his partner through life. One or two people remarked offhandedly that it was probably none other than Gitte Sass whom Avromche had married, and the Sass family, who had gone hunting for his wife all over town, were to their amazement redirected to their own house. That in a sense she was indeed at home, in the kitchen, and that one little question there might have put them on the right track, occurred to none of them.

Meantime, the one person who could have best solved everything, had he so wished, was lying in hospital; and since at first no one really knew how things stood with his head, no visits were allowed. There he lay, shielded from the world by his very illness, the hospital his sanctuary, and in the rapidly ensuing state of bliss, that feeling of both powerlessness and new life which as a rule accompanies recuperation, recent events appeared to him to have no blame attached, shrouded in a veil of mystery. He realized, to his delight, that he was not married and had not abandoned the community; anyone could come and enquire for themselves: though he himself had said so, it was still untrue. So why had he said it? Here his head started to spin. He hoped Emilie would keep quiet about his love, just as she had kept quiet about the word Suss; nonetheless this was the point which troubled him most: he had no idea whether he had betrayed his love to her or to anyone else.

Madame Sass, on the other hand, had had time enough to recover, and to get over her initial resentment at his craftiness, and time to begin to doubt it, and to ponder many possibilities. If he was not yet married he still could be; such things had been known to happen; there were enough widows and spinsters a *schathren* could recommend to him.* All the town knew he was a man of means. How could she have forgotten, walked about with her eyes wide open and overlooked the fact? His new coat! If it wasn't a sign he had already celebrated marriage—and all things considered that was unlikely—then it was a sure sign he could 'change his ways'. She just could not believe herself. It would serve her right if he really was married, she fully deserved the mortification of seeing both him and his money borne off by another family who had never looked after him, who wouldn't have opened their door to him that time he was rejected by his own father. But was he in fact married now, or was he not married? For the present all depended on that. At last came the moment

schathren: marriage broker.

when she could ask. She was sitting at his bedside, and did ask, or rather did not, but said:

"Avromche, everybody's saying your illness is because you let yourself run to seed, and you have no one to look after you."

'Who'd look after me?' answered Avromche with immense weariness and a feigned immense innocence. But immediately he grew dreadfully scared, for she could answer: What about our maid Emilie? Terror made him so deathly pale and grey-blue that Madame Sass did not press the matter for fear his illness had overcome him. But once she was home she said to herself: 'He's no more married than the back of my hand!'

On her next visit, she said: 'Avromche, could you bear it if I were to discuss your future with you?'

He had no objection to the future so long as the past was left in peace. He answered: 'My future is the celebration of my *levaie*.'

'Fiddlesticks! There's nothing wrong with you! Never have you looked better than now.'

Avromche didn't worry his head about fathoming what this two-edged compliment portended, but lay curled like a snail, listening.

She went on: 'We have spoken about your future before—do you remember? When my dear husband was alive?'

levaie: funeral.

'*Gebenscht soll er sein!* If anyone is in *Gan Eiden* he is.'

'If God is merciful he will be. Do you know what he would say if he was alive now?'

Again Avromche was overcome with terror, for he expected the answer: 'Leizer, God rest his soul, would say you should not make a fool of yourself with our maid.' All he managed to say was: 'He would speak gently'.

She answered with a grave and portentous nod: 'He would speak gently. He would say: "Avromche, you are too good to have to go out in the rain and cold every night, and fall ill and die in hospital. You need someone to be there for you and look after you, and be good to you in a home of your own. You need to get married, Avromche."'

Now it was edging closer, now it was only a hair's breadth away, now it would come, scornfully, crushingly: To our maid! He groaned: 'It is all up with me', and shut his eyes before the thunderbolt.

'Nonsense, Avromche! It's never all up. Do you believe my son Isak is an honest and worthy and decent hardworking man?'

What was this? She was speaking of her son! Her mind was not on the dread subject! Avromche opened his eyes.

'Is that what you believe?' she asked.

Genbenscht soll er sein: Blessings upon him; *Gan Eiden*: the Garden of Eden.

'*Und wie* do I believe it!'

'And do you think he is proficient in his *geschaeft*?'

'*Kol Jisroel* should have a son like Isak! What more can I say?'

'Well now. Isak wants to set himself up. You put in your little bit of capital and go into partnership with him, and our Lord will see to the rest.'

Now Avromche fully understood. He understood he was saved, he felt it to be a miracle, and in return for so unexpectedly finding his indiscretion undiscovered he found marrying Gitte a small price to pay. He hastened to address a silent blessing to God, and asked, almost without thinking: 'What will Gitte say?'

'Gitte', replied Madame Sass, 'is a sensible girl and has long reached the age of discretion. So what do *I* matter?'

The next day Gitte came on her own.

She said, without preamble: 'Pollok, Mother says the two of us are to marry.'

Avromche replied: 'She said the same to me.'

She went on: 'We are children no longer, Pollok. You're getting a poor spinster past her prime. Well, you know that. But there is something I must ask you.'

'If I can answer, then ask, Gitte.'

---

und wie: And how!; *geschaeft*: business; *Kol Jisroel*: all Israel.

'You can answer. You are the only one who can, and the only one who must. Is it a sin to be fond of a Christian—I mean really fond, in love with a Christian?'

Avromche had thought they were entirely on safe ground; now the question so knocked him back he nearly fainted. But managing to pull himself together he mounted a modest defence: 'A sin?' he replied. 'There are greater sins.'

'But if I'd been in love with a Christian, then what?'

'You!' exclaimed Avromche, and a novel prospect arose before his eyes: he was a man, he was woman's master and judge. And then just as quickly he grew uneasy: was it not a trap? Otherwise what kind of story was this? He dared not utter a word.

She paid him no heed, but went on: 'It would be to sin against God if I were to hide something from the husband He intends to give me.'

So she meant it in all seriousness, and the thought incited Avromche.

'Who is this man?' he cried 'What kind of a man is he? How did you meet the man?'

'He was an officer.'

'An officer!'—Soldiers were created for our sins, and officers for our greater sins!—'An officer! How did you come to meet him?'

'I don't know, Pollok. It must have been *k'sof*. I was just walking down the street, and all at once his eyes were looking right into my eyes! I had never seen him before. It was something quite new. It was as though he'd been created that very moment, and I was created that moment too.'

'One walks straight past a creature like that—an officer!'

'And did I not walk past? I made so much room for him it was like I'd be swallowed up by the house walls. I became nothing, I became air, and I got past.'

'Well, past is past. And now it's all past—no?'

'No. One day when I happened to be sitting minding my own business, he was standing in the street and looked up. I thought I'd fall out of the window. I couldn't help it.'

'*Ausgefallene Schtrof*!' cried Avromche with a bitterly ironic play on words. 'Now I see—so you did see him again in the street?'

'I saw him again in the street.'

'And what did he say?'

'*Um Gottes Willen*, Pollok! How could he have spoken to me? I would have screamed! I would have died! Speak to an officer there in the street! ... I never saw him again.'

'Well,' said Avromche with a faint smile, 'if you didn't speak to him, and haven't seen him—'

---

k'sof: preordained; *Um Gottes Willen*: for God's sake.

'Pollok, I am going to tell you the truth, that's why I came. I didn't speak to him, but I thought about him, and then when I saw him there I could feel that he knew.'

'And you say you didn't look at him!'

'I didn't look at him.'

'*Schkorum!*' muttered Avromche, half turning to the wall.

'I didn't look at him, and I stayed at home, and I never went out on my own.'

'Very good. That's very good.'

'But he wrote to me.'

'He didn't speak, but he wrote! What am I hearing, Gitte? Why put *hei* before *vof*? Just tell me everything straight out!'*

'But I did tell you: he wrote to me!'

'What did he write?'

'He wrote—well, what do you write to a young girl? He wanted to see me, he wanted to speak to me, he wished to meet me.'

'That's how they write to all girls. And people pay no heed.'

'And people pay no heed. Pollok, that time you took me and Mother to the theatre to see "Svend Dyring's House", and the theatre people down there talked about

---

* *schkorum:* a lie; put *hei* before *vof:* beat about the bush.

runes, I understood what was meant by runes; but you didn't understand, Pollok.'

'*Sie wasz viel!*' Pollok muttered to himself, and went on after a moment's silence: 'Runes. She runs after him in the play.'

'I didn't run after him. How could I? How could I leave Mother and my brothers?'

'That's very true. You're a good girl, Gitte. You stayed at home. So then it really was finally over, in *emmes* over?'

'Then one Friday afternoon I got a letter from him saying he was leaving on Sunday morning, and now he had but one last wish, like a man facing death, to see me just once, and it was for me to decide what time I wanted to come on Saturday evening. And I could too, for that evening Mother was going to the theatre, and my brothers were not coming to the house. And he begged like a man facing death.'

'Runes!' said Avromche. 'That *verschwärtzter* writing! The damned runes! The Lord curse whoever first invented them. *Omein!* Well, so then did you go?'

'No, because when I was about to write to decree the time and place it was *nacht*, and Mother had lit the Sabbath candles, and then no one would dare to write.'

Sie wasz viel: Fat lot she knows; *emmes*: truth; *verschwärtzter*: damned; *Omein*: Amen; *nacht*: Sabbath Eve.

'And so you didn't write, you really didn't?' asked Pollok, though he found it perfectly natural.

'I had the pen in my hand, but as I was setting it to paper and for the first time in my life about to be *mekhalle schabbas*, my father rose up in his burial clothes.'

'Really?'

'Really. And Saturday night when I was tempted to write it was too late to write, and it was all over, and I thanked God.'

'When did this happen? How long ago was it?'

'It was when you proposed to me the first time, twenty years ago.'

'Twenty years!' cried Avromche, and sat bolt upright in bed. 'Gitte! In the name of God almighty! I was in love with a Christian girl, and that wasn't even twenty days ago!'

'You, Pollok? Poor Avromche!'

'Can you forgive me, Gitte? It was on account of her I wanted to hang myself. I was crazy, stark raving mad, but it's true—that's why I'm lying here! But it is all over now, Gitte. Can you make allowances and forgive me?'

'Poor Avromche, my husband before God! Let us remember the dead and keep together until *Bal Hamoves* comes.'

---

mekhalle schabbas: breaker of the Sabbath; *Bal Hammoves*: the Angel of Death.

Some time after this Avromche called at his old lodgings in order to move a lot of things into the new residence
which had been made ready for him. He looked much as
he had in the time before the great events, only still paler,
but more agreeably pale. The journeyman looked in to
wish him goodbye, and very nearly voiced his private
impression that he looked like he had been whitewashed
inside, but was too embarrassed, and Avromche felt just as
awkward. But in the end Avromche took the bull by the
horns, and said:

'Well, I was crazy, utterly crazy, and wanted to do
myself in, and you saved me and cut me down—and yet
I'm still caught in a noose! Only now it's the right noose!'

Amelie's Eyes

Anders Bodelsen

While Jytte was lighting the candles on the dining table,
the two visitors carried their welcome drinks round the
living room. Leif followed them with an ashtray. The
guests stopped by the little portrait which hung so low
above the sewing table that they had to stoop to see it.

The guests were the newly appointed junior partner
Knut and his wife. She had introduced herself in the
hallway, but so softly that Jytte hadn't caught her name.
But sooner or later it was bound to be said again.

Jytte cast an eye over the dinner table, then looked
across at the guests again. They were still standing side
by side, heads bowed studying the portrait.

'Yes', Leif was saying, 'that's actually quite an elderly
lady. In fact she's Jytte's great-grandmother.'

'Great-great-grandmother', Jytte corrected him quietly.

'Could we have a bit more light on it?' asked the junior partner's wife.

Jytte went over to the three of them, but stopped a couple of steps behind them. Leif redirected the work lamp, which was clipped to the window sill, training it like a spotlight on the little portrait.

'Oh, that's just so beautifully painted', said the woman. She turned round to Jytte. 'Your great-great-grandmother? Do you know who the painter was?'

Jytte shook her head.

'Could I take it down?'

Jytte nodded just as the woman very carefully took the picture off the nail and proceeded to turn it over. Her husband moved behind her to peer over her shoulder.

'Can you date it?'

'I can try. My grandmother knew the little girl as a very old lady. I wonder'—Jytte gave a fleeting thought to the roast in the oven—'I wonder if 1850 would fit? Grandma told me the girl in the picture was seven. Her name was Amelie. I used to ask Grandma lots about her, I was pretty crazy about that picture.'

The woman looked at Jytte.

'I can certainly understand that', she said. 'It's a wonderful little portrait. Very pretty, but also very *skilful*, no?'

Jytte nodded. The woman sent her a bright smile, then became absorbed in the picture again. We need to get the place painted, Jytte quickly thought, seeing the wall where the picture had hung. She went out to the kitchen, set the oven door ajar, and then went back to the two guests who, along with Leif, were still absorbed in the little portrait.

'You have *no* idea who painted it?' asked the woman, signalling with a little movement of her head that she wanted Jytte to come and look at it with them. 'Was there never any talk of the painter in your family?'

'No. It was just Grandma and me who thought the picture was anything special.'

'It's incredibly well *handled*', said the woman. 'Not just anyone could capture the eyes in that way.'

'Grandma had the same eyes. When I was the girl's age she used to say I had those eyes as well. But it was probably just because I was so in love with the picture.'

'Not just anyone', repeated the woman. It took a moment for Jytte to realize she meant the painter.

'Oh no', said her husband, smiling. 'It must have been someone. And someone quite special.'

The woman did not reciprocate his smile. Carefully she turned over the picture, quickly tightening her grip when she realized the canvas wasn't very well fixed inside the heavy gold frame. Jytte gazed at the woman's fingers, dirtied now from handling the picture. The woman peered a long time at the grimy and slightly dented back of the canvas before she turned the picture round again, placed it on the oval sewing table and pulled the work lamp right down over the picture.

Leif caught Jytte's eye and mouthed something, presumably 'the roast'. Jytte nodded that it was under control.

And then the new junior partner placed both hands on his wife's tensed shoulders and said to Jytte and Leif, 'My littl'un is reading art history. Just for fun, she said when she started four years ago. And blow me if she isn't on her way to doing finals now!'

'One step at a time', said the woman without looking up from the picture.

Jytte glanced at the woman. Straight away she had thought there was something different about her. The chunky modern jewellery, for one thing. Also she had to be a good deal younger than the junior partner who, Jytte had thought in the hallway, looked just the kind of man who would be called in to revamp failing businesses. Except that kind of man wouldn't normally call his wife 'my littl'un'—or had that become fashionable?

The woman opened her handbag, produced a pair of glasses, and after putting them on began to study the lower edge of the picture.

'Anything written there?' asked her husband in a low voice.

'Have a look yourself.'

The woman made room so that her husband could get his face right down into the corner. For a moment it seemed the two of them had forgotten their hosts.

'By God, there is something there!' said her husband.

He picked up the picture, held it out at arms' length, and passed it back to his wife.

She looked at it for an unbelievably long time.

'Have you got a magnifying glass?'

Her husband cleared his throat meaningfully. She glanced up at him.

'I know', she said, 'I know. All the same...'

Smiling, Jytte lifted the picture off the sewing table, opened the lid of the table and took out a magnifying glass, which she handed to the woman. The woman began studying what might be a signature, but next moment the magnifying glass was lying across Amelie's eyes, and Jytte for some reason stood there feeling there was something wrong about what was happening. Perhaps it was just that the picture might get damaged, though there was no fear of that, for the woman moved the magnifying glass from one eye to the other with the greatest of care.

'Should I *carry* my wife to the table?' said the junior partner.

Jytte shook her head. The woman became aware she was standing with a magnifying glass in her hand, and put it down.

'It's not really my field', she said. 'But definitely it's what we call Danish Golden Age, right?'

'And if this happened to be a TV quiz, and you *had* to guess?' asked her husband.

'Well luckily it isn't. I just want to say: some day you should get an expert to look at it.'

She closed the sewing table and set the picture on top of it, as though she didn't think it should go back on its nail.

'Just for fun,' she said.

'And for the sake of the insurance', said her husband.

'That too.'

Jytte considered returning the picture to its nail before they all sat down to dinner. But she let it be. During the meal she realized why the junior partner called his wife his littl'un: her name was Lillian. They talked of this and that at the table, and towards the end Leif and the junior partner started discussing the reorganization of the firm, and conversation livened up; but Lillian appeared preoccupied and barely reacted to Jytte's two or three attempts to speak about something else, across the men's shop talk.

When all were settled on the three-piece suite with coffee and a brandy, Lillian got up and went over to the picture on the sewing table again. The men's conversation stopped. Jytte got up and went to join Lillian. After a while the men came over and stood behind her once again.

'Just say it!' said the junior partner. 'You reckon it's one of the really big boys! Am I right?'

She laughed and shook her head.

The junior partner cleared his throat, and then said very softly:

'Koebke?'

'No, no.'

The junior partner broke into a grin.

'*Then* they'd bloody well have to insure', he said. 'And put in locks and alarms.'

'And yet...' said Lillian. 'And yet...'

'Say the name!'

'Okay, pretend it's a quiz. At the risk of making a complete fool of myself, alright? It *looks* like Constantin Hansen. Those very, very sharp eyes. The very *sharp* gaze.'

'She's looking straight into camera', agreed the junior partner.

'Perhaps one of his pupils. Could I borrow the magnifying glass again?'

Jytte handed her the magnifying glass, and again Lillian placed it down in the bottom right hand corner of the picture.

'Something's written there', said Lillian. 'But the picture needs a bit of TLC. A gentle clean.'

'And now no doubt we're all remembering what happened to Rembrandt's *Night Watch*', said her husband.

Lillian glanced at her husband and then once more focused all her attention on Jytte.

'Probably it would be best to start very carefully down in the corner with the signature', she said. 'And now the quiz is over, and the little girl goes back on her nail.'

She passed the picture to Jytte, and Jytte hung it back in place, and the yellowish bit of wall was finally covered again.

The guests left early. Leif gave Jytte a hand filling the dishwasher; he had fixed himself a whisky and water and was sitting on the kitchen table, tapping his nails against the side of the glass.

'Great things are about to happen', he said.

He emptied the glass and put it in the machine a moment before Jytte banged the door shut and started it.

'They're nice', he said. 'Both of them. We could get to be friends with them.'

While he was in the bathroom, Jytte went back down to the living room. She stood there a while, gazing into her seven-year-old great-great-grandmother's eyes. Were they *sharp*? She didn't think so. The gaze was strong, but not sharp. If anything it was mild. Amelie was a very obedient little girl. She looked the painter in the eye firmly but kindly.

In her right hand, which rested on a red tablecloth, Amelie held an apple—or was it an orange? The child's hand gently squeezed the fruit, which very probably never got eaten.

'Maybe we *should* have it cleaned', thought Jytte.

She tore herself away, but turned round at the door. She could just make out Amelie's eyes. From this distance it could perhaps be said the gaze was 'sharp'.

Curious?

Jytte turned off the light and went upstairs.

The summer rain drummed against the fabric roof of her 2CV when, a couple of days later, Jytte drove the picture into Copenhagen. She had wrapped it in brown paper and was already regretting she hadn't put it in a plastic bag, for the roof wasn't completely watertight and a couple of raindrops were running along the inside and threatening to drip right on to the brown paper parcel lying on the back seat. While she had to stop for the red light in Glostrup, she quickly pulled off her raincoat and spread it over the parcel.

In Bredgade she couldn't find a parking space, she had to go all the way to the Marble Church to get rid of the car. There she stood in the heavy summer rain with the parcel inside the raincoat under her arm. She started running, stumbled on the pavement and only just managed not to fall or lose her grip on the tightly rolled coat with the picture inside. With beating heart she continued more steadily on her way; the rain was milder now, she just hoped she wouldn't look in too much of a state when she had to show the picture.

She had to sit and wait a while with the parcel in her lap. You were served in turn at a counter, she had chosen a busy day. At the counter the people from the auction house assessed what was put in front of them. A woman put a wonderful and incredibly large doll on the counter, and demonstrated to an interested young man how the doll could say 'Mama!' when you leaned it back, while at the same time it closed one eyelid.

'We haven't tried to repair the other one', she said.

'You mustn't even think of doing so', answered the man. 'That's expert work.'

Another woman placed a whole set of pretty little boxes on the counter, opened them one by one and held jewels up to the light. Two men left an enormous cardboard box standing on the floor but revealed its contents, a gigantic chandelier with eight amber-coloured PH-shades.

A young man in a soaking wet Marco Polo jersey got the thumbs down for a picture of Kongens Nytorv. 'It's a lovely picture', said the lady who kept rotating it in her hands, 'very well painted, but it's *not* a Paul Fischer. The tram is too recent...'

In the end the young man shoved the painting under his arm and stomped out.

Now it was Jytte's turn. She put the parcel on the counter and opened it. The young man picked up the picture and held it at arm's length.

He stood there for an exceptionally long time, studying it. Then he looked round toward the back of the room, caught the eye of an older man and with a nod of the head summoned him over.

The older man, who was very well dressed and very tall, came and stood behind the young one and inspected Jytte's great-great-grandmother. The two exchanged a glance, and Jytte became aware that it had gone very quiet everywhere behind the counter.

The lady who had discovered the wrong tram in the painting of Kongens Nytorv took a couple of steps to the side, leaving a man with a bronze clock to his own devices in order to have a look as well.

For a moment the silence was so total that Jytte could hear the rain at the windows.

'It's not that I want to sell the picture', she said softly. 'But I've been told I ought to have it valued.'

And when the two men and the lady failed to look up from the picture, she added:

'For the insurance.'

'Yes', said the man who had joined them, 'that would be wise.'

Finally he looked up at Jytte.

'Do you have any idea yourself who the painter might be?' he asked.

'No. But she is my great-great-grandmother. And recently we had a guest who was of the opinion—'

The man with the bronze clock coughed discreetly.

'That it could be a good painter', Jytte finished.

'That's for sure', said the tall man who by now had taken control of proceedings. 'So good that we would like to be allowed to keep the picture for a couple of days. The gentleman whose verdict we would like to hear happens to be in London, but he's coming back at the weekend. May we be allowed to keep it that long?'

The man with the bronze clock had stopped clearing his throat. He had edged closer and was now also peering at Amelie's head.

'If you *dare* leave it with us', said the tall man, smiling.

A little later Jytte was on her way out of the room with a receipt. She was starting to feel cold now. She turned round at the door and saw how the little portrait was being very carefully carried into an office. In the big man's hands it looked very small, but Jytte managed to catch one last glimpse of her great-great-grandmother's strong grey eyes. Then a door closed, and Jytte walked down the steps.

In Bredgade she unrolled her raincoat and put it on. Now she was shivering with cold, and she walked as fast as she could to warm herself up.

A week later she was reunited with her great-great-grandmother in the office of the tall auctioneer. He made no secret of the fact he had had it hanging in such a way that he could see it from his desk. He took it off the wall, held it for a moment in the light from the window, and then placed it on the table between Jytte and himself.

'Well', he said, 'all week I have enjoyed the lovely little girl. Do sit down, please. Now, personally I am fairly certain that the painter is...'—he lowered his voice—'is Constantin Hansen. But our expert is a little less certain. He is more inclined to say: Constantin Hansen, *question mark*. And somehow that is not quite so satisfactory. Cigarette?'

Jytte shook her head. The very polite man turned the picture so that Jytte could see it the right way up. It was a little smaller than Jytte remembered, also a little darker, and it suddenly struck Jytte that little Amelie's hand was squeezing the orange as though she feared she might lose it.

'Unfortunately our expert has a way of being right', said the auctioneer. 'But we were in agreement about one thing. In order to value the picture correctly we need to be able to study the signature, which we believe is to be found in the bottom righthand corner. That corner needs to be carefully cleaned, and in that connection one might suggest...a very gentle cleaning of the *whole* picture. What would you say to that idea?'

'I can't imagine the picture any different to how it is.'

'Not even a little closer to how it actually was, when the painter painted it?' Jytte looked at the kind man, defenceless.

'We have a good friend at the National Museum of Art, who occasionally, purely for his own pleasure, occupies himself with an interesting picture', he said. 'We've had a word with him. We suggest you now carry off your great-great-grandmother and entrust her to him for a couple of days. Perhaps he can take photos through the old varnish with infrared rays or whatever kind of devilry he uses. But we think...oh dear, are you unwell?'

'Just a cold.'

Jytte stood up and gripped the back of the chair very firmly.

'One must listen to the experts', she said resolutely.

'Not at all.' The tall man also stood up, and smiled. 'You listen to your heart. But you came for some advice—'

The tall man turned a large book her way, which he had opened beforehand. He showed Jytte a reproduction of an Italian scene, and directed her gaze down into the corner. 'This *is* a definite Constantin Hansen. It sold for three-quarters of a million at Sotheby's in London a couple of years ago. It would fetch more today. And here we have his signature, or one of them. His first name he shortens to *Const*. The surname, which...'—the tall man looked as though he felt he might be speaking out of turn but couldn't stop now in mid-sentence—'which he may not have been quite so proud of, he limits to a capital H. *Const. H*. It is something of that nature we think we can make out very faintly in the corner beneath your charming great-great-grandmother. The painting could not be any lovelier than it is, but it would satisfy me personally—and perhaps annoy our expert a bit—if it were the abbreviated first name and the somewhat...bare capital H hiding there in the corner!'

The picture was carefully packaged up and placed in a very elegant plastic bag, before Jytte was sent off. Today the wrapping was not so necessary, as a heat wave had replaced the summer rain. Jytte risked rolling back the 2CV's fabric roof after depositing her great-great-grandmother in the plastic bag on the floor by the back seat—at least it couldn't fall from there. She drove to the National Museum of Art, where she hadn't been since school when her class had visited a basement full of grubby plaster casts.

The lilacs were in bloom around the museum. Jytte stood for a moment with the picture under her arm staring straight ahead at the vast building bathed in the oversweet scent of lilac. She turned round and stood with her back to the museum. Turned back again and walked swiftly on.

Shortly after, she was following a museum attendant—who kept glancing back at the plastic bag as if he yearned to peer inside to make sure it didn't contain a bomb—down a steep and narrow spiral staircase whose perforated metal steps kept threatening to snag her heels. Then along some long corridors through a veritable labyrinth before she was finally deposited in front of a prisonlike iron door. The museum attendant stepped inside and shut the door, so that for a moment she found herself alone in the corridor waiting for her next sneeze to come. Then she was admitted to a room which was as light as the corridor had been dark. A man in a blue smock greeted her with an iron handshake which she could still feel several minutes later. His hand felt like one large icy bone. He relieved her of the bag and fished out the contents, whistled a short sequence of three or four notes, and looked her in the eye with a gaze as firm as his right handshake.

'Good', he said. 'So now let's see if we can lighten things up a bit here—'

'Just the signature.'

The young man eyed Jytte with his penetrating stare. He cautiously ran a finger across the canvas, hummed, fell silent, hummed again. Studied his dusty forefinger under the light from a powerful lamp, and with a little wave of the hand motioned to Jytte to sit down. After this he produced a couple of paint brushes which he dexterously arranged between the fingers of his left hand. He set three small glasses containing a clear liquid on the table.

There was a sharp chemical odour in the room, which made Jytte think of brain damage and of the local cleaners which had had to close down since the husband and wife who worked there had died within months of each other. The man in the blue smock dipped a brush into a glass, let a few drops run off, and looked up at Jytte.

'Listen', he said, 'I won't be able to get it done today. All I can do is see how far there is to go. And it's only the varnish we'll just *begin* to lift, isn't that so?'

With the almost dry brush he carefully touched the canvas where the signature was lurking. The movements of his hand were light and precise. After each stroke he painstakingly studied both the brush and the place it had touched. He was an expert. Jytte got through a sneeze and sat a little further back in her chair. The restorer reached for the next brush, which he dipped in the next glass and again carefully squeezed almost dry before using it in the same small spot.

'Nope,' he said after working on the place for a couple of wordless minutes. 'It won't budge—'

He moved on to the third brush, the third liquid. This time he squeezed the brush a little less dry. As he swung it in over the canvas a phone in the room rang and he lost concentration for a fraction of a second. A drop fell from the brush. Jytte thought it fell so slowly that she could follow it in its fall. It settled like a tear in the corner under Amelie's right eye.

The young man laughed and quickly wiped away the drop with a rag. He had caught the panic in Jytte's eyes, for he laughed again very briefly, but for the first time in an almost friendly fashion.

'It'll take more than that', he said.

Again he went to work for a couple of minutes, concentrating with the brush down in the corner where the signature was supposedly hiding. Then he abruptly stood up and set all the brushes on a small tray.

'We'll get there', he said. 'But there's quite a way to go. At least I've made a start.'

He picked out the last of the paint brushes and showed Jytte how the light brush hairs had turned a pale grey.

'A hundred years of dust and tobacco smoke.'

'Only a hundred years?'

'Or a little more. But there *is* a signature, and we'll get to it. The question is—'

He raised the picture.

'We really ought to give the whole painting a gentle clean. Believe me, it will be all the better for it.'

'It mustn't be any different. The eyes—'

'I'm not talking about *butchery*. I'm actually talking about *protecting* the little lady. She is *suffering*. This kind of rubbish works away at a picture, and ends up breaking it down. In ... in a hundred years, or five hundred ...'

Jytte sneezed again. It appeared to her the man contradicted himself when, after handing her a very soft, lush tissue from a box on his table, he went on to say:

'In all likelihood you'll barely be able to *see* that the little lady and her apple have had their life prolonged, when we meet again.'

'It's an orange.'

The restorer looked down at the picture. Turned it this way and that with minimal movements.

'You are quite right. A rather pale orange. I promise you—it will continue to be an orange! But the eyes. Such a little girl's eyes should be white, isn't that so? She wasn't painted with advanced conjunctivitis. You know what— perhaps you're thinking this will be expensive, but in actual fact I'll do it for free, for I have quite lost my heart to our little friend, and frankly we can let the public purse pay for the hours I put in.'

'I hadn't thought about the money', Jytte heard herself reply. Halfway through the sentence she tried to make it sound less angry. The restorer nodded slowly, glancing a couple of times from the picture he held in his hands to Jytte, as though comparing the two.

'No need to worry', he said.

He placed the picture on the table and pulled it towards him.

'What do you think the painter was paid by the hour for this picture?'

Jytte shook her head uncertainly. His hands now grasped the picture frame in a very possessive way. The smell of the chemicals made her nostrils itch, but the expected sneeze failed to come. It would be impossible now for her to take the picture away from him and put it back in the plastic bag, she thought.

'Whereas the little girl', said the restorer. 'It's not hard to guess what the little girl's reward was for sitting days on end for the painter. Isn't that so?'

Jytte found she had got to her feet, but her legs weren't supporting her as they should.

'She got the orange of course, and ate it!' said the restorer without letting go of Jytte with his smiling eyes.

It would be more than a month before Jytte was to see her great-great-grandmother again. Not until one day in August did the restorer call to say the picture was ready for collection. He said no more than that on the phone, and Jytte couldn't bring herself to ask the relevant question. Instead she drove into town to collect the picture.

He received her in the museum foyer with a completely neutral expression, and she followed after him down the corridors, down the narrow perforated metal spiral staircase which again snapped at her heels. Then into his workshop, where the whiff of chemicals once again made her nostrils itch.

'Now where has the little lady got to?' he said, and went around lifting up any number of pictures. Then he found her, and laid her on the table between them so that for the present she faced his way. He put a magnifying glass to his eye and pulled a lamp down over the picture, apparently to check one last time that he had not been mistaken.

Then he turned the picture round, pushing it towards Jytte with one hand and passing her the magnifying glass with the other. Jytte accepted the magnifying glass, but immediately put it down on the table.

'What's happened to the picture?' she said.

'Happened?'

'You cleaned it?'

'Not really. Just what we agreed. The very worst of the dirt.'

'But the eyes.'

'Yes?'

'Aren't they completely wrong?'

'Perhaps they are a tiny bit more how the painter painted them. Do you really think they've changed?'

Jytte stared at the hard eyes.

'It just isn't the same girl', she said.

The restorer sat there regarding her for a bit in silence.

'Normally one would remove *more*', he said. 'Seeing one was doing it anyway. But as for the signature, because that after all was what we wanted to throw a little more light on... have a look for yourself with the magnifying glass.'

Jytte delayed the moment. She tried to meet her great-great-grandmother's new and strangely indignant gaze. Then she held the magnifying glass to her eye and studied the signature.

'I make it out to be *Conrad* Hansen', said the restorer.

'And who is he?' Jytte heard herself ask. Conrad was not something he 'made out', but very definitely the name now written in the corner.

'If you ask me—an absolutely brilliant artist.'

'But...'

'I haven't been able to find out a thing about him. But that doesn't make him any the worse. Of course I'm a restorer, not an arbiter of taste, but personally I think—'

He smiled at Jytte.

'Personally I think this picture is rather too *good* to be a Constantin Hansen. Personally I've always found his portraits a little wooden. Over the years there were a lot of commissions, bread-and-butter work, and at times quite a bit of assembly line production. And the man got old and tired. While this unknown artist...'

The restorer turned the picture round so that he could again admire it for himself.

'This man certainly wasn't tired.'

'But what have you done to her eyes?'

'Just gone over them with the minutest amount of cleaning fluid on the brush. I honestly believe at the very most it's the strong light from the lamp here.'

He pushed the lamp away and got up. But little Amelie's eyes did not change; they continued to gaze up at Jytte, angry and indignant, until she preferred to look away.

'Will you still send it to auction?' asked the restorer quietly.

'It was *never* meant to go to auction. It's a family portrait.'

'It's definitely not without value. It's certainly worth something—on the open market as well. You don't need to get *angry* just because I tell you so!'

'Can you make it look like it did before?' asked Jytte.

The restorer slowly shook his head.

Of course he couldn't do that.

'How much do I owe you?' said Jytte.

'Not a penny. As I told you before. It's been a pleasure to work with the little girl. And I believe it won't be long before you get used to the fact she is free of the worst of the tobacco smoke and varnish.'

He wrapped the picture and Jytte went off with it. At home she left it in its packaging until Leif got back from work. Then they both studied it under the dining table lamp.

'Conrad!' said Leif and laughed. 'Just a couple of letters out, what?'

'That's not the point. It's the eyes. Look how she's staring at us!'

'If you hadn't told me it had been cleaned, I simply wouldn't have noticed.'

'Can't you see—she's *totally* changed?'

'Oh lord. Let's look on the positive side. We avoid raising the insurance and having to put burglar alarms all over the house. Should we put her back again?'

Jytte hesitated. But of course they should. Amelie went back over the sewing table which had once been hers. Leif stood for a moment, looking at her.

'Welcome back,' he said gently and turned away.

As she hung there, between the two west windows, not much light fell on her. But even in the twilight, before they lit the lamps in the living room, Jytte felt that her eyes were following the people in the room with a new attention, which all the time bordered on hostility.

'We could move her', she said while they were laying the table.

'Where to?'

That was the nub. Preferably gone altogether. Leif stopped in the middle of laying the table and looked over at her.

'Now I can't see any difference at all', he said. He lifted a glass. 'Welcome back where you belong', he saluted her.

But Jytte did see a difference. And the next day too, and the day after that. The little girl had been given new eyes, and she kept them. Angry, suspicious eyes, as though she would never again feel safe amongst her descendants.

Conversation One Night in Copenhagen

Karen Blixen

It was raining in Copenhagen one November night of the
year 1767. The moon was up and well into its second
quarter—at intervals, when the rain abated as though
pausing between two verses of an endless song, its pale,
painfully upended mask showed high in the sky behind
layer upon layer of shifting copper-green vapours. Then
the rain's dirge resumed, the moon mask would retreat
deep into space, and only the lamps in the streets and an
odd window here and there would be discernible amid the
dark mass of houses, like phosphorescent jellyfish at the
bottom of the sea.

There was still some sporadic night traffic in the streets. Out to sea, a few solid solitary barques headed homewards, and restless privateers and buccaneers on dubious errands beat upwind between black crags streaming with wet. A chaise was hailed, took aboard its load and lurched off toward a destination deep in the city and the night. A heavily gilded coach with winking torches, a coachman high up on the box, footmen behind and precious contents inside, pulled away from a reception, wheels spraying rain water and street filth to all sides as the spirited horses' trotting hooves struck long sparks from the cobblestones.

In the narrow streets and lanes Copenhagen night life continued in high spirits. Music and song filled the air to the steady accompaniment of revelry and rowdy disputation.

Suddenly the hubbub increased, a brawl had broken out like a fire. Many voices were raised, smashed window panes tinkled on the pavement, and heavy objects hurled from one or two storeys above crashed and thumped down on top of them. Shouts and gales of laughter mingled in a whirling maelstrom from the middle of which women's cascading shrieks soared high into the air.

Two Copenhagen burghers, one tall and thin, the other shorter and big-bellied, with their greatcoat collars turned up and their hats pulled down over their ears and a lad with a lantern preceding them, paused a little way into the alley. The rain had driven them to take this short cut home, and they had become so absorbed in talk of vessels rounding Africa laden with spices for Copenhagen that a thin sweet wake of cinnamon and vanilla seemed to trail after them through the alleyway's restless swell of stenches. As the uproar ahead grew louder and nearer they had told the lad with the lantern to halt, and now together they peered pensively down the lane in the direction of a house whose door stood open and around which pressed a howling wrestling mass; and at the spectacle their faces grew longer and their limbs heavier. But they said not a word.

For it was by no means certain that this time the disturbance ahead of them was one more late-night riot for which one could call upon the forces of law and order, and the wrath of God. On the contrary, it almost certainly spelled their shame and sorrow. The mob down there in the alley was no rabble—these were important folk, fine gentlemen from the court bent on wreaking havoc. And it was not impossible, sadly all too likely, that the country's young king himself, still barely more than a boy, was running around at the head of them.

Aye, still barely more than a boy, and one whom it was rumoured had been raised excessively severely. Loyal subjects could be expected to turn a blind eye to a royal youth's excesses. All the same, he did after all have his creamy pink young English queen back home in the palace, who within but two months would be delivered, God willing, of a crown prince for his father's two hereditary realms. Yet here he was, raving in the night, fuddled and wild with wine, helping his mistress wreak revenge on other women of her profession with whom she had old scores to settle. What evil folk they all were, these servants and favourites of the king, these counts and equerries and royal councillors, leading astray the Lord's anointed, a beloved dead mother's son. The two Copenhageners called to mind, as their feet froze where they stood, the story of how only recently on a night such as this in a scuffle with the city's watchmen this young king by the grace of God had collected a black eye and in return had personally borne off to his palace a spiked mace by way of a trophy. What was said abroad these days about Denmark and Norway's sovereign? As for his own people who over many hundreds of years had prided themselves on their loyalty to their King and his house, how in the humility of their hearts were they to put up with such a wretched state of affairs?

Still not uttering a word, both mutely swallowed their own and their country's disgrace. They, at least, would remain silent as the grave.

A long authoritative blast from a watchman's whistle cut through the din. The brawl broke up, and within two minutes had dispersed in all directions. Some crashes and shouts, the sound of a yard door banging to, and a rush of running feet followed the flare-up. Light from a window for an instant caught the rose lining of a cape and caressed a speeding turquoise silk ribbon, and a moment later the street lamp lit up the braid on a naval officer's uniform which appeared to enclose very round young limbs. A laughing exclamation in French was flung over a retreating shoulder, and a handful of biting saucy Danish oaths were hurled back in return. Then colours and voices spilled into the side lanes, and the adventure was over. Now only a pair of heavy watchmen's cloaks were outlined against the hazy radiance of the open street door.

The two burghers continued on their way, directing their steps around the nearest corner and their thoughts back to happier waters, to the Cape of Good Hope and the price of pepper and nutmeg. The faint stream of fragrance behind them acquired a dash of stoical self-righteousness.

A very young man, a fine little figure in a heavy cloak, who in the confusion had become separated from his companions, had lost his way in a long series of back yards, passageways, and steps. He looked round him, ran, looked round again, and finally fetched up on the topmost landing of a steep, narrow, mouldering staircase. Here he halted, breathless from the ascent, remaining on his feet with his small person pressed into a corner. After regaining his breath a little, his hands went to his throat to undo the clasp of his cloak. In one hand he held a naked rapier, the sheath was gone and the weapon was in his way. He set it down, reeling a little as he did so. Still unable to loosen the clasp, he groped about for a while with outspread fingers on the filthy floor before retrieving the hilt. Once it was back in his hand, he made a few passes in the air with the blade. During all this he remained as silent as a fish, no complaints or oaths, no sound at all escaped him.

But in the darkness, within the silent house, his eyes were wide open. He did not know—and in this place felt there could be no way of knowing—whether his madcap dash had been a splendid idea, a game of hide-and-seek up and down the houses, or more of a flight from deadly danger, the Evil One himself out after him. There was no one here to tell him whether the next moment he would be hailed and hugged by flushed, laughing friends, or if a pitiless hand, dreaded in dreams and in reality, would suddenly descend upon him. He was alone.

He was alone, and in all his life he could not remember ever having been alone before. The realization of his utter isolation slowly but powerfully took hold of him, at first making him giddy, but then lifting him up as on the crest of a wave. It swelled into an immense and fitting revenge over all who until now had confined him. A triumph. At last, at last the apotheosis he had been promised!

Passionately he clung to the person he had become in this place, here in the dark, a statue of himself, pure as marble, all of a piece, invulnerable and imperishable. But after a while he began to shiver, until his teeth were chattering in his mouth.

A little higher up, where the staircase ended, a light shone out from beneath a door. The narrow beam, which moved back and forth and seemed to multiply in strength, had to mean something. Slowly he came to the realization that just inside, behind the door and in the light, there must be someone. But who? There were many hundred faces in the dark city around him. There were, he had been told, starving people who preyed on others, people who murdered and people who gave themselves up to the dark arts. Creatures from his boyhood fantasies appeared to him, and it was possible, even reasonable, to suppose they lived right here, where he had never been. But now he became aware of sounds too, behind the door a woman was crying, and a young man was comforting her. In a trice—with surprising assurance and agility, and managing to avoid placing his hand on the greasy banister rail— he mounted the last few steps, placed two fingers on the door handle, and pressed it down. The door was not locked, it opened.

The room he entered was small, peat-brown in the corners since the only illumination came from a tallow-dip on a table, but with a vivid play of colours as far as the light could reach. Beside the candle stood a clear pinch-bottle and a couple of glasses. Apart from the table and a three legged stool next to it, the room contained an old chest, an armchair with worn gilding and shabby silk upholstery, and a big four-poster bed with faded grey-and-red striped cotton hangings. The whole little chamber glowed with the heat of a pot-bellied stove against the wall, and the air was filled with the good smell of apples baking on top of the stove, sizzling and spitting once in a while.

The hostess in the room, a big flaxen-haired girl, heavily powdered and rouged and stark naked under a negligée with pink bows, was seated on the three-legged stool and rocking it a little to and fro while inspecting a white stocking which she had drawn over the outspread fingers of her left hand and up her arm. As the door opened, she ceased moving and turned a swollen, sulky face towards it. A young man in shirt and breeches, with buckled shoes and a bare foot thrust inside one of them, lay across the bed gazing up at the canopy. Lazily he turned his gaze upon the newcomer.

'A pity, my lovely', he said, 'it seems we are no longer free to discuss the nature of love in privacy. We have a visitor—', he eyed their guest again. 'And a distinguished visitor too—', he continued slowly, sitting up, 'a gentle-man, a gallant gentleman from the court. A—' Breaking off abruptly, he paused a moment, then swung his legs over the edge of the bed and stood up.

'We have,' he exclaimed, 'a visit from the ruler of all faithful Muslims, the great Sultan Orosmane himself! It is common knowledge that at times his glorious Majesty will don disguise and visit even the humblest dwellings in his good city of Solyme in order to get to know his people without being recognized. Sire, never could you have found anywhere better suited for such investigations than right here!'

The stranger blinked at the light and the faces. Then he stiffened and turned pale.

'*L'on vient!*' he whispered. Someone is coming!

'*Non!*' cried the young man in the one stocking, announcing he would allow no mortal soul to cross the threshold: '*Non, jusqu'ici nul mortel ne s'avance!*'

Brushing past his guest he turned the key in the door. The faint grating of metal sent a shiver through the youth in the cloak. But soon after the certainty of having a locked door behind him seemed to lift his spirits. He heaved a deep breath.

'*O mon Soudane!*' said his host. 'As you see, Venus and Bacchus hold equal sway in our little temple—and though it be not the noblest of their grapes that we press here, it is at least the pure stuff! That pair are the most honest of all the gods, and in this place we put our trust in them entirely. You must do likewise.'

The newcomer looked around the room. Recognizing in what sort of premises he found himself, a faintly lascivious little smile flitted across his face.

'Does the gentleman take me for a poltroon, perhaps?' he asked, still with a trace of that smile.

'For a poltroon?' cried his host. 'Why no! For a sentimental traveller, your lordship. What is it one of my beloved masters says? "The man who either disdains or fears to walk up a dark entry may be an excellent good man, and fit for a hundred things, but he will not do to make a good sentimental traveller!" I suspect that you, like myself, have before tonight set foot—alas, I suspect, like myself, *after* this night will again set foot—inside many a dark and unknown entry! Moreover I suspect that you and I will tonight make a true sentimental journey together!'

A brief silence descended on the room. The girl, who still sat with the stocking on her fingers, glanced from one young man to the other.

'What are your names, you two?' asked the guest.

'Ah yes, of course,' answered his host. 'Forgive me that contrary to all good manners I failed at once to introduce your humble vassals, so close to heaven. Even though you elect to remain incognito, it would plainly be most improper for us to withhold anything of our true nature and condition from you.'

The host had reached more or less the same stage of intoxication as his visitor. It made him somewhat unsteady on his feet, and to some extent appeared also to encumber his tongue, for he lisped a little. But at the same time it lent wings to his speech and opened up his soul to powerful and generous impulses. He bestowed an open, bright, and loving gaze upon their visitor, and perceiving that still more time and palaver were needed before the fugitive would feel completely at home in the room and with the company, he continued:

'The name of our charming hostess', he said, 'is Lise. I have called her Fleur-de-Lys after that deeply enchanting heroine of a novel whom she resembles. But vulgar folk in this neighbourhood, by altering a letter in her name, have given it a bad odour. I mention all this purely *en passant*, and as a matter of no consequence, for my friend may in fact be called by whatsoever pet name her worshippers may care to choose, and thus in her person represent the entire sex. As my aforementioned master has said, "That man who has not a sort of affection for the whole sex is incapable of loving a single one as he ought." Lise is thus, as I have but now had the honour of explaining to you, her sex incarnate!'

'And I?' he continued, 'I flatter myself you will already have perceived I am a gentleman. Beyond that I am, *sauf votre respect*, a poet—which is to say a fool. My name? As a poet I have, God forgive the Danish public, no name as yet. But in my capacity of fool I may, like the master whom I have already twice cited, take the liberty of calling myself Yorick. "Alas, poor Yorick! A fellow of infinite jest, of most excellent fancy! And now—in this place and in this state! How abhorred in my imagination it is! My gorge rises at it. To what base uses"—my friend and brother—"we may return!" ' He stood for a moment lost in thought. 'Return!' he repeated to himself, then bitterly exclaimed: ' "You came to see my father's funeral, and instead I think it was to see my mother's wedding!" '

He collected himself quickly, and shook off his morose mood.

'And now', he said, 'now, Sire, be assured you are quite safe with us, as safe as in heaven, or the grave! For who, anywhere on this earth, would be less likely to betray a King *par la grâce de Dieu* than—by His same grace—a poet? And by His same grace again, a...but Lise abhors the word, so I shall not pronounce it.'

Again he fell silent a while, but remaining alert, observant, his entire being absorbed in the present moment, and finally took a step forward. Seizing the pinch bottle, he filled the glasses, and with a smile extended a ceremonious arm to pass one of them to the stranger.

'A toast!' he cried. 'A toast to this hour! It is by its very nature everlasting, and by that same token therefore non-existent. Our door is bolted—hear how it rains!—and no one in the whole world knows we are here! And the three of us together here are equally favoured in that tomorrow we shall have forgotten this hour, and never ever will remember it again! Therefore in this hour shall the poor speak freely with the rich, the poet conjure up his visions for the prince, and even Sultan Orosmane himself—oh, in ways that he never could before, and alas, in ways he never will again—entrust his lofty and to mere mortals incomprehensible woes to the hearts of two human beings, the hearts of a fool and a whore! Thus does this hour become a pearl in an oyster shell at the bottom of the dark flood of Copenhagen all about us. *Vivat!*—friend and mistress—long live this our stillborn and death-doomed hour!'

He raised his arm high in the air, emptied his glass and stood very still. Obedient as a reflection in a mirror, his guest repeated his every movement.

This last glass, coming on top of all that each had downed already that evening, had a powerful and mysterious effect. It caused the two small figures to grow, pumped a deep and appealing flush into both pale faces, and kindled a sparkling light in their two great pairs of eyes.

Host and guest beamed at each other and stepped so close that for a moment it appeared they were about to wrestle or embrace.

Then it became apparent the guest wished to be liberated from his cloak: '*Ôtez-moi donc*', he said softly, '*ce manteau qui me pèse.*'

He stood very still, his chin raised and his eyes fixed on his host's face, while the latter fumbled with the clasp and finally freed him of the heavy encumbrance. Beneath, the stranger wore a pearl-grey silk coat and a waistcoat with aquamarine embroidery, the lace at the neck and cuffs was torn. The pale costume gave his whole figure the effect of something incorporeal and shimmering, as though he were a young angel visiting the hot and close little room. But as the cloak fell backwards and spread out across the back and seat of the armchair its deep-gold velvet lining gathered up all the colours in the room, transfiguring them into a radiance of pure glowing ore. The young man who called himself Yorick watched wide-eyed as the air about him turned to gold, and in his delight squeezed his guest's delicate fingers.

'Oh most welcome!' he cried. 'Oh long awaited! Our lord and master, we are yours! See, we now offer you our best chair, and can offer none better. Lise never cares to sit in it herself for fear of straining the webbing with her charms or wearing out the upholstery. So now it is yours, if you will deign to leave your imprint on it. Make it this night a throne!'

Under the speaker's powerful gaze the fugitive's features trembled for a second, then softened into a serene calm. From having not long before searched so fearfully on all sides, he became collected, self-possessed, exhilarated by one joyous conviction. Yes, he was among friends, such as he had read about and had sought but never found, such as would know and understand who he truly was. Aided by his host's graciously raised hand, he allowed himself to be guided a step backwards to the chair, and rather abruptly sat down in it, without in any way damaging his dignity. Bolt upright against the golden velvet, his fine hands resting on the arms of the chair as though already holding sceptre and orb, he surveyed the room as from a great height.

Yet when he spoke he changed again. His voice in his few brief phrases in French had been fluid and melodious. When he changed to Danish it was plain he had acquired the language through mocking his tutors and plotting pranks in the company of pages and stable boys.

'Yes', he said, 'yes indeed, Poet! This is what I want. I wish to hear my people's complaints with my own ears. Never have I been able to because you are kept from me. Tonight I had to run away from the others, through dark rooms and up long black staircases to find you, you who are poor and who suffer injustice. Tonight you may come to me and speak freely.'

He stopped, searching for words, and then went on in a raised voice:

> '... *dans ces lieux, sans manquer de respect,*
> *chacun peut désormais jouir de mon aspect,*
> *car je vois avec mépris ces maximes terribles,*
> *qui font de tant de rois des tyrans invisibles!'**

'Well, come along now,' he said reverting to Danish. 'Complain away! Are you unhappy?'

The one who had called himself Yorick pondered a while, then laid a hand on his chest and pressed it against his collarbone, where his shirt lay open.

'Unhappy?' he repeated slowly. 'Tonight of all nights we cannot be unhappy. However, neither would we wish to appear objects of pity to your eyes. A true-born courtier does not insult his king by making himself smaller in his presence, as though such were necessary to heighten a sovereign's majesty. No, he straightens his back and makes himself as tall as he can, and says to the world: "See, what proud men are this master's servants!" All credit to his Catholic Majesty of Spain that he has servants

---

* Not without due deference, in this place / henceforth may all safely behold my face, / for I scorn dire maxims where kings have been / in most part portrayed as tyrants unseen.

so grand that they have the right to keep their hats on before his throne! And similarly do we honour our God, not by crawling, but by holding our heads up high before him!

'Nevertheless', he continued still more slowly, 'some petty human woes we shall always have, since we are humans and fools. Would you care to hear them?'

'Yes, that is what I said', answered the one called Orosmane.

'Then hear', said Yorick, 'the first of our woes. You would see, were you to look closer, that Lise's salt tears have worn pathways, two noble runnels through the rouge on her cheeks which recently she took much trouble to apply. This for the simple reason that in a squabble another young lady in this house called her an alabaster whore! If I had just two rixdollars—which alas I do not—I should this very night go into town to procure some object of alabaster so that Lise might comprehend with what a feminine masterstroke her normally uncommonly good friend Nille described her person. Ah, how I long to console Lise! For you must know, Orosmane, that I owe a great deal to this girl, far more than the paltry four marks which in her goodness she has allowed me to have on credit for the time being. What a boon and blessing for the likes of myself, and solace to our souls as well as our bodies, that such girls exist!'

Orosmane looked at Lise, who tossed her head and turned away.

'Your debt with Lise, Poet', he said, with a gracious movement of the hand, 'shall be borne by us. Tomorrow she will receive an alabaster jar containing 100 rixdollars. For know this: no whore shall ever weep in our city. No, they shall hold high office—*comme d'un peuple poli les femmes adorées*. No less of a boon and a blessing is it for the likes of oneself that such girls exist.'

'*Bénissons le seigneur*, Lise', said Yorick.

'And now', said Orosmane, 'now let *les prudes*, all righteous dames weep over their hymn books in resentment at our generosity to Lise. For there is no generosity in them at all. They mince and flounce and simper just to dupe and ruin us. And'—he burst out, his face suddenly twisting with anger and bitterness—'and in bed they want to talk!'

'Well said, Sire!' said Yorick. 'In bed they want to talk, the impossible creatures! At the very moment we have granted them our entire being up to—and beyond—the limits of our strength, granted them our life and our eternity—then they want to talk! They know nothing of man's, of mankind's unutterable longing for silence, and the relief of silence. Instead they wish to hear from us whether there is life after death, or if that *adrienne* model which they wore yesterday became them!'

Orosmane thought long, and again that little grin played over his face.

'Do you know something?' he said. 'Something Kirch-off told me?—Well, in paradise Adam and Eve went on all fours, just like the dumb animals they lived among. There-fore in those days Adam kept his sex beneath him, in the shelter of his body, in accordance with his perception of *les décences*, which far exceeds that of women. But his lady wife could hide nothing, went about entirely exposed to his gaze. Then one day Madame Eve got up on her two legs, and assured her husband that only this posture and this manner of walking befitted human beings. And thereby immediately she concealed her own sex, and from that moment could practically deny all knowledge of it. But lo!—from that day on Adam had to carry his own on full display before him, revealing for all the world how very accurately his maker had shaped and crafted him for his wife's secret little crucible. So then Madame was able to strut about and make the sign of the cross and shrill: "Oh my God, what is the world coming to?!"—Good, eh? But yes, yes, tell me, isn't that precisely how it is? And therefore', he finished, with a fleeting but intense grimace, 'therefore the more inoffensive a woman and the more inclined to resemble a dumb animal and go down on all fours, the greater ease man finds in her company. Is it not so?'

'It is! It certainly is', answered Yorick with a laugh. 'You put it well! And in fact I too have thought the same before tonight. For see here, Orosmane—I have never had the opportunity of observing Lise at her meal, but whenever I have pictured her it has been plain to me she does not dine or sup like the rest of us, but of necessity must graze like a white lamb in the meadow. Down by the murmuring brook—down there in the shade!'

Orosmane studied Yorick for a while, and then his young face smoothed over.

'Not here', he said with dignity, 'not tonight will we speak of Kirchoff. He is a scoundrel, a *valet de chambre* who should definitely not put his words in Lise's ears, or in yours or our own! What were we talking about?'

'About our woes', said Yorick. 'And about your munificence which has drowned Lise's sorrows.'

'Yes', said Orosmane. 'Lise's sorrows. And now yours. How many sorrows do you have?'

'I have two sorrows', answered Yorick, 'since Lise has almost finished mending my stocking, and thereby most lovingly removed my third. And one of the two is this: there is a hole in the sole of my shoe and it lets in a great deal of water—but never mind, I have more or less grown used to it. My other sorrow, Orosmane, is this: that I am not almighty.'

'Omnipotence?' said Orosmane slowly. 'You want omnipotence?'

'Alas', said Yorick, 'forgive me for coming to you with so worn, so banal a complaint! But all we sons of Adam have an unutterable longing for omnipotence, just as though we had been accustomed to it, born and bred to it—and afterwards had been grievously and cruelly deprived of it.'

'So you wish for absolute power, do you?' asked Orosmane as before, fixedly regarding his host. 'Ha! Then come to me—I have it! I have it, so everyone tells me. Didn't they put a crown on my head and a sceptre in my hand—Danneskjold and the Lord Chamberlain himself carried my train. They even swore to it in rhyme—wait a moment and I shall remember it and quote it to you.' He bethought himself a while, then calmly and clearly recited:

'What shall I call thee, our young Solomon?
A King, a God?—Oh both, for see, your seal
Is stamped with wisdom and omnipotence:
Almighty Monarch with a mind divine!

'Did you perhaps create this verse yourself, you who are a poet?'

'No, not this verse', said the poet.

'Well, so would you like to be me?' asked Orosmane in a high merry voice. 'Should we swap roles tonight, and see if we feel any different? For do you know what? Just now, when you handed me the glass, I was of the opinion it was you who was all-powerful.'

'You are right once again, Sire', said Yorick. 'Of all here in Copenhagen, probably you and I, the monarch and the poet, come nearest to possessing absolute power. No, we should feel no difference.'

At this point in the conversation Lise got up to remove the apples from the stove before they started burning. She put them on the table and sprinkled sugar on them with her fingers, so that her guests could regale themselves at their leisure. From time to time, while the others talked on, she took a mouthful herself, leaving a trace of crimson on the apple flesh, and licked her fingers. Orosmane followed her movements with his eyes, but absentmindedly, as if only half-seeing her.

'All sons of Adam, you said!' he exclaimed. 'Then what of his wife's brood, what about the females of this world? Do you honestly suppose they have no craving for omnipotence? You may be certain my sweet Katrine would love nothing more than to govern the world, just as our consort's *preneuse de puces* would like nothing more than to determine our own bedtime!'

'No, probably they do not crave it', said Yorick. 'But for one reason alone: in her heart every woman believes herself all-powerful already. And they are right to believe so. Look at Lise here! She hasn't spoken a word during all our conversation, nor will she. And yet it is she who allows our conversation to arise, and had she not been in this room it would never have happened!'

'Well now,' said Orosmane, 'what would you do with your omnipotence? Because I', he announced, and for a moment his delicate face assumed an astonishingly wild and fierce expression, 'know very well what I should most like to do with mine!'

'*Mon Soudane*', said Yorick humbly. 'I should like to live.'

Orosmane considered a moment. 'Why?' he asked.

'Well', said Yorick,.'It is genuinely the case, *sauf votre respect*, that people would like to live. First of all they would like to live from today until tomorrow, and what they need for this to happen is food. It is not easy to procure. And when we starve we moan and we howl, not from the pain precisely, but because in our stomachs we can feel our life itself is threatened. That is why a baby cries for the breast, because it wants to live from today until tomorrow—though it knows not what that means!

'But next', he went on, 'we desire to live longer than from today until tomorrow, and somewhat longer than the lamentable span of years called a lifetime. We desire to live down through the generations, through the ages. For this to happen we need to take another in our arms, we need a beloved who will receive, house and bring forth this our earthly everlasting life. That is why a youth will moan and howl—even in verse, some of us—because he yearns for his own blood to greet the dawn and the rising moon a hundred years hence. And because with all his blood and in every limb he feels that if he is denied a loving embrace his very life will be denied him.

'But lastly', he concluded very slowly, 'lastly and most powerfully man desires life everlasting.'

'Ah yes', said Orosmane, 'life everlasting, I know all about what that is. Much praise was heaped on my old tutor Nielsen when I performed so well in my catechism.' And quickly he reeled off: 'The forgiveness of sins, the resurrection of the body, and the life everlasting! Is that what you want?'

'More or less', said Yorick. 'Even though my body is not what I take most pride in. Light enough in itself, and yet often a burden and terribly painful to carry around. As far as I am concerned it can stay where it is, and I could then contemplate it from a distance and gloat a little. Even so—I never cease to hope for everlasting life and can't resign myself to being without it.

'But you, Sire, being the Lord's anointed', he continued, 'are sitting very pretty, being assured of eternal bliss amongst your hallowed forbears. My own poor soul, though, blunders about in uncertainty, both blinded by the light and shrinking from the dark, and in this wise must duly suffer both the gnawing hunger and the unquenchable longing for the loving embrace. Alas, and I would so like to help it!'

Orosmane, his fond memories of former glories re-awakened, now proceeded to declaim these lines from an old Danish hymn:

'How sweet to taste
All that His house doth own,
To know no waste
Who stand before His throne!
And there to see
The persons three
Who reign above alone!'

Losing the thread of the verse, he broke off and gazed intently first at his own hand, and then at Lise and Yorick.

Yorick too grew thoughtful, pausing a while, before taking a sip from his glass.

'Yes', he said at last. 'It may well be very sweet to taste, and the house up above undoubtedly has much to offer. But what I would never dare confide to anyone I shall tonight confide to you, Orosmane—because you understand everything one says to you: never shall I quite be able to turn my back on this earth! Yes, I have kept it ever alive in my thoughts, just as when I was a boy I kept a bird in a cage alive, and a plant in the window, by giving it water when it was thirsty, turning it towards the sun, and covering it at night. This earth has been so delectable and precious to me. From up there I would ever be on the lookout to see if it could survive without me. Oh, and I would insist it preserve me, I would so long to see my heavenly bliss reflected far down there, as in a mirror. Do you know what that sort of reflection is called?'

'No, I do not', answered Orosmane.

'It is called *mythos*!' cried Yorick, in a transport. 'My *mythos*—that is the earthly mirror of my heavenly existence. And *mythos* in the Greek language means *speech*. Or at least—for I'm not so well up in Greek, and learned folk might think me wrong in this—you and I, just for tonight, will agree to interpret it this way. Uncommonly pleasing and delectable is speech, Orosmane, so we feel tonight. Yet, before speech, and higher than speech, we must recognize a greater phenomenon. *Logos! Logos*, which in Greek means the *word*. And the Word created all things!'

A certain rhythm to their mutual happy intoxication had, like some unimpeachable law, guided and borne along the speakers throughout their conversation. It now subtly seemed to part them, as when two dancers separate, and one, though still at hand and indispensable to the figure, momentarily stands inactive to one side to contemplate his partner's big solo. With a mighty movement, the room's host swung away from his guest and took the stage on his own.

'Oh!' he cried. 'Oh how I have always loved the word—
few have loved it so much as I! The secrets of its nature and
its ways are familiar to me! Which is why I know and
understand more than any other that at the moment my
Almighty Father created me with His Word he also de-
manded and expected of me that in time I should return to
Him, bringing back His Word in the form of speech. This,
and only this, shall be my work during my sojourn here on
earth. Out of His divine *logos*—the creative force, the
beginning—I will fashion my human *mythos*—the lasting
record. Yes, and when through His infinite mercy I am
once more united with Him in heaven, then the two of
us—I abjectly and in tears, He with a smile—will gaze
down and expect and demand that my *mythos* remain
after me on earth.

'Terrible', he continued in an altered, and slower, more
oppressive tempo, 'terrible is the recognition of our obligation toward the Creator. Heavy and unremitting is the
acorn's obligation to yield Him the oak tree—yet it is
lovely too, with its young leaves after the rain. And crush-
ing in its weight is my own covenant with the Lord! Yet
joyous too, and magnificent! For if only I can hold to it, no
adversity or privation shall ever make me bend. No, on the
contrary, I shall bend every adversity and privation, all
poverty and sickness and my enemies' heartlessness when

they betray and persecute me, bend them to work with and for me. And all things will be of service to me!'

He came back to his fellow dancer, who had still not moved, and made ready for their *pas de deux.*

'What happiness!' he called to him. 'What happiness, Orosmane, that tonight I have you to talk with. Anyone else would think I have drunk too much and speak without knowing what I'm saying. But you! Let me again bless you for understanding! Now, now in this our hallowed hour your sympathy makes me realize most powerfully that my *mythos* really will one day be found on earth. People down here, the people of Copenhagen, will know nothing at all about me two hundred years from now—and yet when they meet me they will recognize me! Terrible and joyous is my covenant with the King of heaven and earth. *Dignum et justum est* that the hand of an earthly king should seal it.'

Orosmane received him as gracefully and harmoni-ously as a dancing partner, and fell in with his rhythm.

'*Ainsi soit-il!*' he said. 'My hand shall seal your covenant.'

For a moment, in confirmation of what had been spoken, both speakers were at rest and expectant.

'But what of myself!' burst out Orosmane, in a new movement. 'What of me? Will I ever obtain the earthly reflection of my heavenly glorification which you tell me is called *mythos*? Do you believe so?'

'Yes, I believe so', said Yorick.

'*Oh là là!*' cried Orosmane. 'You believe so because your whole life you have associated with decent people, never the king's teachers and advisors, and so you have no conception of real villainy! Because everything you have said, Poet, is nothing less than what I have always known, and always wanted. What else have I ever desired other than—what you spoke of, what you called—what did you call it?'

'*Mythos*', said Yorick.

'—than *mythos!*' said Orosmane. 'I have wanted to harden myself—and a *mythos* is certainly hard, and an oak tree certainly no less—I have wanted to be all of a piece, the same as them. But let me tell you something, my friend! At court, and in council meetings, people are afraid, all are afraid, and not one of them will ever come out with what it is they fear. They might tell you they fear God—but they don't fear God! Or that they fear the king— but they don't fear the king! No, they run about, they tattle, they argue, they bow and scrape and flatter, they dress up in uniforms and vestments, they make a bonfire of a king's day and peace of mind, and all because they fear one thing—what was it called?'

'*Mythos*', said Yorick.

'*Mythos!*' said Orosmane. 'Women they procure me, both royal and out of the Danish stud-book, so they can watch them walk all over me! But one of their silk slippers wouldn't fit even the toe of a King's *mythos*! And the only boot in which it could freely march they whisk away from me. They would so love to give me an epitaph—no doubt the sooner the better—and no doubt they'd even settle for putting up an equestrian statue of me. But never, ever would they grant me a—say it again—'

'*Mythos*', said Yorick.

'Never, ever a *mythos*!' said Orosmane. '*Tu l'as dit!* I can't escape my hallowed ancestors. But the magnificent mirror reflection of my exalted person here on earth, and here in Copenhagen, this they smash into a thousand pieces, even before it has come into existence, and in my ears I hear the splintering of glass!'

Yorick regarded his visitor at length and with great attention, and at last he spoke.

'No,' he said slowly, 'no...

> ... if God deserves respect,
> He must show justice in the law,
> In judgment and in punishment and more!

'Your *mythos* will be this, that you have been unable to create a *mythos* for yourself! Your subjects in Denmark, in Copenhagen, two hundred years from now will know little, perhaps nothing, of you. And yet you will be the one—out

of all your illustrious forbears and your glorious sons—
whom they will first of all recognize.'

Orosmane too remained silent a while, with all his
attention drawn to something, perhaps something in
himself.

'Give me a drink', he said.

The schnapps, which could be said to have been the
musical accompaniment to the scene, infused his being
with a mighty earnestness and power. Now was the time
for his own big solo. Straightening his back, and with a
singular freedom of movement, light as a bird, he rose up
on tiptoe. Not one of his movements was hasty or disjointed, even in their boldest leaps there was body and
weight. He glided across the stage, and across the pause,
straight for Yorick.

'What happiness, you said, Yorick, my poet and my
friend!' he cried. 'What happiness for you that tonight you
have myself to speak with. So listen! Your happiness is
greater than you know. I want to share my knowledge with
you. I wish to tell you who I am and who you are yourself!

'For here on earth there are some people—and I think
we number seven in all—some people who see the whole
world as it truly is in essence, the world which the rest
unceasingly seek to misrepresent to us, for they want no-
one to understand its proportions and its harmony. And
what is more they must unceasingly seek to separate us

and keep us apart—because they know that if we come together we will be stronger than our enemies. I have sought out these others, but my guards have not allowed me to find them. They are not yet aware I have reached you up here. But soon, very soon, they will find their way here and again tear us apart. This very moment—you didn't know—they are out there after me, chasing through backyards and passageways, and up stairs. Yes, well may you now think and cry out:

> ... *o nuit, nuit effroyable,*
> *peux-tu prêter ton voile à de pareils forfaits!**

'But in that hour of which you spoke, and which we still share, we can speak the truth to each other. Let me then in this hour, as I speak truly to you, have your true answers.'

'Yes', said Yorick. 'Speak, Sire. Your poet and fool is listening.'

'Then listen!' said Orosmane. 'Listen, my poet and fool. The world is far more beautiful than others would have us know.'

'Yes', said Yorick.

'Humankind', Orosmane continued, 'is created far better, far greater and more beautiful than they say.'

'Yes', said Yorick.

---

* Oh night, oh dreadful night, / now draw your veil over such monstrous crimes.

'And are not', cried Orosmane, 'our pleasures far more enjoyable than they would have us feel?'

'Oh yes', said Yorick.

'And are not actors on the stage', asked Orosmane again, 'far less wretched than they appear to us?'

'Most certainly they are', said Yorick.

'And is it not far pleasanter', said Orosmane, 'to go to bed with a woman than we yet know it to be?'

'I guarantee you that, *mon Soudane*', said Yorick.

'Then we three know it!' said Orosmane. 'We know all this, you and I and Lise, even though from tomorrow we must keep it to ourselves. And we know too how truly exquisite is the quality of schnapps. Yes, we know', he cried, gliding into a graceful repetition of an earlier passage in the conversation:

> 'How sweet to taste
> All that this house doth own,
> To know no waste
> Who stand before His throne!
> And there to see
> The persons three
> Who reign above alone!'

Graciously he extended a hand, with the fingertips joined, towards the other two in the room. The intention was not that they should take the hand, neither did they make any move to do so. Yet this gesture of lofty regal favour made the three of them in the room into one.

'And', he said very slowly, '*il y a dans ce monde un bonheur parfait.*'

Yorick rose on his toes and fell into step with his partner.

'Yes, Sire', he said equally slowly. 'Perfect happiness does indeed exist. On this earth, in this human life, there are three kinds of supreme happiness. And you and Lise and I will come to know all three in the course of our lives.'

'As many as three!' exclaimed Orosmane joyously. 'You see how a single thought, when we three are together, can double and treble. Put my own thoughts into words now, you who claim to love the word! I shall demand no more of you. Name these three for me.'

'The first supreme happiness', said Yorick, 'is this: to feel in oneself an excess of strength.'

'As now!' cried Orosmane and laughed aloud. 'As we do now, when in our beautiful fellowship we can soar free up into the air—like kites attached only by a string to wet Copenhagen! You are a real poet—you say what I think, and your word makes everything visible to me. Now I see before me a glass filled to the brim with wine from Bouzy or Epernay, foaming over the edge and down the stem— and yes, in such abundance that it foams even in the dust. That time I proclaimed to the people in wigs that I intended rampaging for a year, that was when I too foamed and frothed like that. "An excess of strength"—glorious words, like a song. And truly, that whole year the entire court charade was transformed into a drinking song. Swelling through all our palace halls, and in our streets of Copenhagen you could hear the mighty sound rampaging! And you say there is still another supreme happiness to equal that. Name it then!'

'The second supreme happiness', said Yorick, 'is this: to know for certain one is fulfilling the will of God.'

A brief pause followed this.

'*Mais oui!*' said Orosmane proudly. 'Now you are talking prettily and as befits a King by God's grace. The burden of the crown is heavy, you know, but our own insight and knowledge, *par la grâce de Dieu*, can swing the balance. They wrote a verse about it which I shall recite for you:

And we saw God's anointed did possess
The wisdom of an angel of the Lord.
Thrice blesséd is the land whose great King knows
God, the good of his country, and himself.

How right you were, the king in his own country is also blessed. But let me say something else. You, who have painted your second supreme happiness so unforgettably for our soul—"to know for certain one is fulfilling the will of God"—you too assuredly shall fulfil God's will in your own calling. And Lise, who has granted us her room for our meeting, who listens to what we say and with her sweet charms sweetens our conversation, shall in her own calling also assuredly fulfil *la volonté de Dieu*. And now you see, my good friends, how very happy it was we met. For henceforth you will remember my words and find comfort in them.

'But now—my soothsayer—now for the third supreme happiness of which you spoke.'

Since Yorick did not answer at once, he repeated: 'The third one, what is it?'

Yorick answered: 'The cessation of pain.'

Orosmane's face instantly brightened, assuming an almost luminous pallor. In a last flying, utterly weightless leap—of the kind that in the language of ballet is called *grand jeté*—he completed his solo.

'Ha!' he cried. 'You utter all that our own heart holds dear! This, your third happiness, I know it well and have explored it in depth! It was the reason I first of all desired omnipotence! So I should no longer have to feel the cane— old Ditlev's cane!'

Yorick rocked back a step, as though Orosmane's flying leap had cannoned into him. Slowly his own face too grew white and shone. His intoxication dropped away from him, or within a couple of seconds so greatly increased it steadied him.

The silence which followed was not an absence of speech, but an affirmation so strong it suspended all speech.

Finally the host took a step forward as far as he had stepped back, and bent a knee before the chair. Lifting one of his guest's delicate hands from the arm of the chair, he brought it to his lips and kept his mouth pressed to it for a long time. Orosmane, motionless too, lowered his eyes to the bowed head before him.

The kneeling man stood up. He went over and sat on the bed and starting pulling on his stocking and his shoe.

'Are you not staying?' Orosmane asked.

'No, I am going', said Yorick. 'My business here was already at an end before you came. But stay here a while with Lise. In the lap of the people', he added after a little pause, 'king and poet may mingle their innermost beings like sworn Nordic brothers of yore who to seal a lasting pact would manfully mix their two bloods in earth's mute and bounteous womb.

'Goodnight, Sire', he said. 'Goodnight, Lise.'

From a peg on the wall he took an old cloak which had once been black but after seeing many years' service now showed patches of green and grey. He buttoned it on, listened to the weather outside, and turned up the collar. His hat had fallen to the floor, he retrieved it and pulling it down over his ears went out of the door, closing it after him.

As he took the steep stairs he heard muffled voices from below. On the next landing he came upon a small company of men ascending in single file. A young man wearing a uniform under his cloak led the way with a lantern, and an elderly gentleman who was evidently having some difficulty with the uneven steps came close on his heels, followed by another two figures. All faces looked pale and solemn in the lantern light.

When the company met the person coming down they came to a stop, thereby also halting him, as he could not get round them in the narrow space. They regarded him in some perplexity for a couple of seconds, seemingly keen to ask something but uncomfortable about doing so. Anticipating them, Yorick whistled softly and aimed a thumb back over his shoulder and upwards.

'Yes, that's where Lise lives', he said. 'A fine wench. I've just paid her off and left.'

The small group on the stairs pressed against the wall to let him pass. But as he went by the elderly gentleman asked in a hushed, slightly hoarse voice with a German inflection:

'And nobody else is up there?'

'Nobody!' said Yorick, whistling once more, this time a snatch of a song.

He continued his somewhat unsteady course to the ground, and before reaching the bottom could hear that the company above had turned round and was following him down.

The Night of Great Shared Happiness

Merete Bonnesen

On the evening of 4th May, the Norwegian writer Johan Borgen was holed up in the cellar of a house in Gentofte. That same morning he had been smuggled across the Sound with instructions to prepare for the establishment of a Norwegian legation the moment peace was declared. He had listened to the heavy tread of Gestapo boots on the hatch over the hold where he had lain concealed during the crossing.

Around 8 o'clock, wearied by a hectic day's work among his Danish contacts, he had managed to doze off in his hiding place under the house, falling into a dream-ridden fitful sleep from which he was awoken after only half an hour by sudden new noises in the unfamiliar building which harboured him. From the floors above came indistinct sounds whose explanation could only be the muffled cries of fear and confusion betokening a raid, or the more unusual one—an outburst of joy. In any event, so peculiar was the noise that he stole up the cellar steps into the hallway. There he saw a man, presumably his unknown hospitable host, coming down the stairs from the first floor and proceeding in a fashion hitherto unrecorded in the annals of bodily movement. He clasped an armful of bottles to his chest. The man's face radiated a delight which could well have been mistaken for open-mouthed idiocy, a kind of ecstasy of bliss.

'So it's actually *happened!*' said Borgen.

At the sound of this Norwegian voice the man with the bottles gave a start. He stiffened as though he had quite unexpectedly received a slap in the face. Then he said:

'You're *Norwegian*! Then I must ask you to forgive me.'

And down the stairs rolled the bottles, bumping and banging.

Just minutes earlier news of Denmark's liberation had been broadcast from London. Even so, in this Danish home there now happened to be a Norwegian, the official representative of a Norway which was not part of the peace agreement, and as the bottles went sailing down the stairs his Danish host was apologizing for an elation which now struck him as utterly improper, like laughing in a house of mourning.

Johan Borgen has often since described this scene for Norwegians as an expression of a Danish reaction which was not just supremely tactful, but which, uttered by a Dane, was also the spontaneous expression of what was felt by thousands: *Norway wasn't part of it*. It should also be said that in poverty-stricken and exhausted Norway Borgen's account was always followed by the more prosaic question:

'What about the bottles? Were they all right?'

They were. And once they were emptied Borgen set off, like the journalist he is, for the office of *Politiken*, the daily paper. It was a long tramp along suburban roads where the fruit trees were wrapped in clouds of blossom, and on through swarming streets which had abruptly burst into colour with thousands of flags. Around midnight, grey in the face from lack of sleep, and the excitement and rejoicing, but also anxiety for the fate of his own country, he reached the Town Hall Square through a sea of people. There, in the paper's dazed and chaotic main office, he managed to leave his congratulatory article on a desk in the compositors' room. What he had experienced on a strange staircase in a strange house, the extremes of emotion which that night forged a bond between the lone individual and the community, was borne out when he heard the Norwegian national anthem *Ja vi elsker dette landet* soar up from the Town Hall Square toward the light-filled windows, while Gestapo soldiers stood by their machine guns on the roof of their headquarters in Dagmarhus. Whether the choice of song was the final straw for the Germans has never been determined, but soon after midnight the happiness which like an inrushing sea had flooded the city was shattered by machine gun fire. In seconds the square was empty of all but the wounded lying flung across the pavements.

No one could possibly sum up the many moods of that night. Leafing through the enormous newspapers of the time once more confirms the old adage that there isn't much of a story in happiness. All they are really saying, in every column, is a barely suppressed HURRAH.

Yet every single person will have his or her memories of those intoxicating seconds and hours, unless they have been erased as happens sometimes with emotional shock, for no one is capable of absorbing them all, let alone formulating them. Are there diaries out there, I wonder? From such jottings it might some day be possible to piece together that mosaic to which each person brought their own small, glittering, precious piece, so that a full picture could be reconstructed of this day of days, the night of great shared happiness.

But desperation and anger find an easier outlet on paper than joy. Its more immediate release found expression in a way everyone remembers: *light*. These battered grey streets, dark chasms of danger where throughout the years fear had been the only sure companion, were transformed within minutes. It wasn't just that the stiff unwieldy blackout curtains were torn to shreds so that light from the rooms within came streaming out. Nor was it because the little black cardboard coverings over the tram light bulbs were ripped away, or that all of a sudden the Town Hall stood there fresh and radiant with its facade and tower floodlit, so that even in the middle of the night you could once more set your watch by the hands of the Town Hall clock. Neither was it because the electronic newspaper above the *Politiken* building again set its band of text travelling against the black of the sky. No, the unforgettable thing was that in less than an hour the whole city was alight.

Without prior agreement, without anyone knowing where so much light could possibly have come from in a country where for months everyone had fumbled about in the gloom of little 5-watt bulbs, all at once along every windowsill stood little candles which from house to house propagated their flickering blaze of joy across the entire land.

It's often said that by then all of us knew the end was coming. But that is only true in part. The city that awoke on Friday 4th May was a disappointed city which somewhat sullenly got down to yet another day of occupation, puzzled as to how much longer it would last. Capitulation had been expected from one hour to the next ever since that moment on Monday 30th April when the news of Hitler's miserable death was broadcast. When it did not come, and it had to be faced the country could become a theatre of war, people, wiser after their experiences of the days of the general strike, started to prepare for the worst by filling their bathtubs with water and queuing up outside chemist's shops to buy chloramine. Furthermore, the Hipo[*] squads of young thugs still stalked the streets even at this eleventh hour, attacking from their open cars.

Thursday 3rd May, a day in which a certain dejection could be felt in the air from early on, had drawn to a close in a mood somewhere between disappointment, fear, and frustration. For on the radio that evening Reichsminister Albert Speer had made a speech to his countrymen in which he described the hopeless situation in such a

---

[*] In the last months of the war the Germans formed Danish Nazi sympathizers into a Hilfspolizei ('Hipo') corps, to replace the disbanded regular Danish police force.

startlingly frank fashion that all were left waiting to hear the only logical conclusion to such dismal premises. But no, right at the end, as we listened with bated breath, he announced that in the light of all he had said it was plain that Germany could *not* surrender.

The atmosphere had been so upbeat, expectations so whipped up, that immediately after Speer's speech the Danish radio service in London delivered an urgent caution against the flood of rumours:

'The German defences have not collapsed. The situation now is no different to 48 hours ago. The fight continues until unconditional surrender. Very possibly the Germans would like to leave Denmark, in that case let them run straight into the arms of the British or the Russians. As they please! But an arrangement between the Germans and the Danish authorities does not exist. They have only two possibilities: surrender to the Allies, or annihilation by force of arms. There is no third option.'

This was followed by an urgent exhortation from the Freedom Council to maintain discipline, withhold our jubilation, and not take any independent action. That was one of three proclamations issued by the Freedom Council on the 3rd May. Another was addressed to members of the resistance, and a third, composed in German, to all German soldiers. This impressed on them that the war was lost, and there was nothing for them to do other than remain in their barracks and lay down their arms. The proclamations were disseminated all over town, passed from hand to hand, even posted on walls; one hung for a while in the window of the German Travel Agency on Strøget. The staff had packed up, all signs had been removed, the window displays emptied.

Thus, after a night punctured by blasts from fresh acts of sabotage, Friday 4th broke with brilliant May sunshine, and utter uncertainty. The beeches had burst into leaf, fruit trees were in blossom, and Tivoli opened. News spread through the city that from early morning Montgomery's troops had started moving north out of Schleswig. Great crowds were gathering at the border in expectation of the British troops' arrival.

But on their way to work that morning Copenhageners were again reminded that much was still unchanged. At 9 o'clock, and again at 10, the sirens wailed; and at 4 in the afternoon, as offices were about to close, there was a full-scale air-raid warning. People's only reaction was to stop in the street and gaze up in the air as though they expected parachutists to descend from the skies and free them. But not one plane was sighted. On the other hand, around 6 p.m. the city echoed to the sound of an explosion from a sabotage attack on the St. Annæ Palace in Dronningens Tværgade, the Germans' new headquarters,* where a cupboard had just been carried in with a bomb in a false bottom of one of its drawers.

The day was waning, and by and large nothing had occurred. The shops emptied and people went home, unless they intended to shorten the evening by going to the theatre, which started at six, or in the case of the Royal Theatre which was putting on one of Oelenschläger's plays as early as five in order to finish at eight-thirty at the latest. Some went to the cinema to sit through the rather tedious movies, whose titles just hours later came to sound startlingly symbolic. For on that 4th May there was a choice between 'Yesterday and Tomorrow', 'A New Day Dawns', 'All Hands On Deck', 'A Day without Lies', and 'This Way Please For Happiness!'

And then the city settled to a kind of calm, albeit a peculiarly restless calm, if to all appearances no different to so many other long days in those years. It was not as though anyone expected anything to happen just at that moment. The ministries emptied too; government officials went home, and presumably like most others during the half hour between eight and eight-thirty were intent on

---

* On 21 March 1944 the RAF had bombed Shell House, the Gestapo head-quarters, in order to free gaoled Danish Resistance fighters. Among the escapees were Freedom Council members Mogens Fog (see p. 344), a leading doctor and founder of the Socialist People's Party after the war, and the journalist Aage Schoch (p. 346).

tuning their radios to receive the BBC as clearly as possible, trusting it would not be jammed when the Danish broadcast began.

And then it came. It had started in such an ordinary way that people were soon only half listening after all the anticipation. After four minutes of relaying the usual reports from the front came a brief communication, and one which only a week earlier would have come as a considerable shock: 'In the Deer Park and on the square outside Gentofte town hall German troops have been engaged in fighting amongst themselves.'

That was all well and good, but now our hopes were very different. And at this point the reading stopped. There was a short pause, with no forewarning, simply silence. And then we heard:

'At this very moment we are informed Montgomery has confirmed that the German forces in Holland, North West Germany and in Denmark have surrendered.'

What was the effect? Presumably that is a question of how fast are each individual's reactions. But we had help. For the newsreader, Johannes G. Sørensen, now said:

'This is London. We repeat: Montgomery has this very moment reported that the German forces in Holland, North West Germany *and in Denmark* have surrendered.'

The Reuter's telegram had been received in London at 8.29 p.m. on the BBC's teleprinter from Montgomery's head quarters. It was relayed to all departments over the building's internal loudspeaker system, and the young Flemming Barfoed heard it in the Danish editorial office. Flying downstairs, three flights above ground, two more down into the basement, and on through a labyrinth of corridors, he reached the studio and beat the unsuspecting Johannes G. Sørensen on the back with clenched fists. White in the face, out of breath from his dash, he said:

'Capitulation, North West Germany, Holland and Denmark. Say it, say it!'

Thus did the most joyous message of the last five years come to be broadcast, against all the rules of the BBC's strict wartime regulations, improvised and without text. It left two lone Danish journalists in a country where the war was not yet over, a country which that very day had despatched fresh troops to an unknown fate on distant battlefields, a country where life continued to the harsh rhythm of the daily struggle. In the radio control room the few Danes sang and danced, while the English looked on bemused. They shrugged their shoulders in a friendly manner and said:

'And the war in the East? That will carry on for at least another year.'

So then the Danes went off to the one place that it was most natural for them to go, to Christmas Møller's, a home oppressed by its own dark clouds of war,* where one could be glad but not rejoice.

But in Denmark there was rejoicing. If we use the term in its fullest sense to mean a *state of being*—an all-encompassing, all-engrossing exultation which now ran through the city like a sudden effervescence and manifested itself in song, in light, in colour. All had happened so bewilderingly fast that it was hard to take in. In this too reactions differed widely. Some sat paralysed in front of the radio, others shot out of their seats as though they'd received an electric shock. Some were in floods of tears, others were in such a state of confusion that almost angrily they started asking everyone around them what the voice had said, and if it could possibly be true. But even for the paralysed it lasted but a few seconds, though it felt so long, that instant of stillness which for many remains in memory as the most unforgettable thing of all.

---

* Christmas Møller's son had been killed in April while serving with the Grenadier Guards. As an outspoken anti-collaborationist, Møller had been forced to surrender his seat as a Conservative member of the Danish parliament. With the communist Mogens Fog and others he founded the non-partisan underground Resistance paper *Frit Danmark* (Free Denmark), and in 1942 fled with his family to London where he became a famed broadcaster to occupied Denmark.

Then everyone regained, in the most literal sense of the term, their freedom of movement. It carried them in one bound to the windows, where breaking voices could be heard shrilling rather than shouting from house to house across the streets: *We are free, we are free! The Germans have capitulated, Denmark is free!*

From that moment on everything unfolded in wondrous confusion. People raced out of doors, consumed by the one desire to be together in their joy and share this ecstasy with each other. From the city's outskirts, from suburban roads and from side streets, people came running with flags in their hands—from wherever they could lay hold of them in a hurry—large and small, one so long that it waved like a tongue of fire from the hand of a young student who like a relay runner for peace dashed through the narrow streets round the university, drawing everyone along in his wake. Singing crowds followed after him with Danish and Allied flags in quantities and sizes which normally only conjurers can pull out of top hats.

But this was indeed a kind of magic which flew in the face of all norms. Trams were held up and carried on towards the city centre with knots of people clinging to them or sitting right up on the roof. Somewhere, or in many places simultaneously, the cry went up: *To Amalienborg!* To the royal palace! But Amalienborg that night was a barred fortress, not yet liberated. It was under guard, albeit by the Danish police unit which had defended the palace during the battles of 19th September 1944, and now lay blocked off by barbed wire defences thrown across Frederiksgade, the Colonnade, and Amaliegade, so that the forerunners, the fastest among the throng of people, had to halt at the Yellow Palace. All the way back to St Annæ Plads, along Strandstræde to Kongens Nytorv pressed the crowd of tens of thousands growing wilder and ever more threatening as they joined together in a great clamour for the King. But by agreement the capitulation could not be made official until 8 o'clock next morning, and so the King's aide-de-camp had to resort to extending the King's greetings from the roof of a car along with a plea for patience, and his request to go home was later reinforced by the chief of the Amalienborg police.

So it was back to the Town Hall Square. On the way through Kongens Nytorv a vast swallow-tailed national flag could now be seen suspended from the balcony of the Royal Theatre. The actors, who at 8.30 had been sitting in their dressing rooms removing their make-up after the evening's performance, had heard the shouts of peace travel from the radio in the porter's little lodge in the lobby right up through all the corridors of the wardrobe department, and with flowing robes and wigs askew they pressed together faces shiny with greasepaint, in ecstatic embraces.

Elsewhere in the city things were very different. Ambulances sped off to hospitals with sirens blaring, transporting the wounded from locations where the Hipos or SS soldiers were still active even now they knew the game was up. There was shooting all over the city, in Østerbro, by the school in Alsgade, on Knippelsbro, and ward windows in the Kommune hospital were shattered by gunfire in Farimagsgade. The hospital was immediately put on a state of high alert, and so many wounded were brought in that the lighter cases had to wait for hours on their stretchers.

In Store Kongensgade a crowd was going berserk in front of the editorial office of *Fædrelandet*.* When it looked most ominous, a group broke through in a surprise attack and occupied the hated paper. It was people from the famous underground paper *Information* who went into action.

All this time Christiansborg was springing to life too. At 8.30 prime minister designate Vilhelm Buhl, appointed by the liberation government, was sitting in the parliament restaurant together with a couple of MPs, and this is where he learned what had happened from a pair of breathless Christiansborg police who came hurrying over to them. He went straight to the Ministry of Foreign Affairs, and

* The Danish Nazi Party newspaper.

from there attempts were made to contact as many of the new government's 18 members as possible. It was not at all straightforward. The fact that they were still spread out across the city, a good number of them in hideouts known to very few, the fact that they were not together and that many hadn't even heard the announcement on the BBC, whose word was normally wolfed down every night like our daily bread, shows better than anything how unexpected was the news.

Hans Hedtoft* was dining at the Nordland with his contact man Herman Dedichen, the engineer, when the news was broken to them by the waiter, who served it up together with the dessert. Hedtoft set off for Christiansborg, and on the way chanced to see the German sentry on fortified Vesterport reverse the order of the day, lay down his gun, and walk back into the fortress which now became his prison.

After much searching and telephoning, Mogens Fog was collected in a ministerial car from his undercover address in Charlottenlund where the clamour in the street had disturbed him in the midst of drafting the very Liberation proclamation which, as spokesman for the Freedom

* Social Democrat Party leader, twice prime minister in the post-war years. Like Christmas Møller, forced to resign his seat in parliament due to his stand against the Nazi occupation, and later instrumental in the rescue of the Danish Jews (October 1943).

Council, he would deliver on the radio when peace came. He too was taken by surprise—in the middle of a full stop.

In another safe house on Strandboulevarden, the leader of the armed resistance, Frode Jakobsen,* had just concluded a meeting with members of the military command, in addition to three representatives from the army, the navy, and the police, together with Ole Lippman, the British forces liaison officer—and alone again in his hideaway Frode Jakobsen, too, had received the news through an open window. All that hectic night he spent between meetings in Christiansborg and the command centre in the 'Stjernen' brewery, while also working on the announcement which at eight in the morning of 5th May he would read anonymously over the radio, to the effect that from now on members of the resistance would be taking over responsibility for law and order.

But by then they had already seized power. For during the night these young men with their blue-red-and-white armbands, steel helmets, and Sten guns had occupied every street corner and all large buildings. A hidden army had sprung out of the pavement armed with weapons which many of them had had a hand in concocting in their clandestine factories.

* Journalist and politician, author of an important memoir of the Resistance.

Even so—they weren't to be used in war! And it was probably this sense of what the country had almost miraculously been spared that lent that night its undertone of profound thankfulness. In Denmark there were 110,000 heavily armed German soldiers, and one can only guess at what horrors a battle between a small intrepid force and those 110,000 veterans of war would have led to.

That is why it was not simply a jubilant but also a mild and kindly city which celebrated those first hours of freedom. All that filled our hearts was released in songs and rejoicing in the Town Hall Square. Around midnight chief editor Niels Hasager spoke to the crowd from the *Politiken* building. On 9th April 1940, he said, the American papers had broken the news of what had befallen us under the headline 'Denmark Murdered'. But tonight we could look out over the square and see we were still alive and join in the cheers for our country, and the wish for *Norway*'s happy liberation.

He then handed over to Aage Schoch, a prominent member of the Freedom Council, who now found the words to express what lay deepest in everyone's mind— thoughts for the young dead, the sailors, the soldiers, the airmen, the paratroops, and those who had fallen as saboteurs or perished in the concentration camps, and those the Germans had executed and tortured without mercy up to very last hour. It seemed a great sigh rose into the night sky, and a long silence fell like a blanket over the throng of people.

Through tears, at that midnight hour, peace had come at last, a painful, hard-earned peace—with a morning still to follow, when, as three hundred years earlier when the siege of the city was lifted, we could lay down our heads without fear 'every time a gate or a door opened', and where all hearts could share in the fulfilment of the 300-year-old prayer:

> May this lovely land
> Now flower and fruit
> Let truth have dominion
> And justice be done.

Notes on the Authors

1. **Hans Christian Andersen** (1805–1875) H. C. Andersen, as he is always known in Denmark, is the country's best loved storyteller. The son of a cobbler and a washerwoman, he came to Copenhagen at the age of fourteen to be trained at the Royal Theatre, but was finally rejected as lacking 'both the talent and the appearance necessary for the stage' (see Tale 14!). He went on to become one of the greatest literary celebrities in Europe. No works other than the Bible have been translated into more languages than Andersen's fairy tales. Although these are what he will always be remembered for, he also wrote a number of plays, vivid travelogues from his many journeys, as well as poetry and an acclaimed autobiography.

2. **Henrik Pontoppidan** (1857–1943) After breaking with the narrow Lutheranism of his childhood in Jutland, Pontoppidan worked as a teacher and journalist in Copenhagen, allying himself with the cultural radicalism of

Georg Brandes and the political left. His many novels and stories are imbued with a desire for social progress, though often despairing of its realization. 'Twice Met' is set in the political crisis following the attempted assassination of the long-serving right-wing chief minister Jacob Estrup in October 1885, an event which gave the autocratic Estrup a useful excuse to consolidate his regime by tightening press censorship, criminalizing opposition politics, and setting up the hated 'Blue Gendarmes', a special police surveillance force. In 1917 Pontoppidan received the Nobel Prize for literature for 'his authentic descriptions of present-day life in Denmark.' *Lykke-Per*, his greatest novel, has finally appeared in English as *Lucky Per* (2010).

3. **Bjarne Reuter** (b. 1950) Bjarne Reuter was born in Brønshøj, a suburb of Copenhagen and the location for many of his hugely popular stories for children and teenagers. As well as over 60 books for young readers, he has published novels, thrillers, short stories, plays, an autobiography, and film and TV scripts. 'A Tricky Moment', with its mixture of humour and despair at contemporary society, is typical of his adult stories. The 'shabby' TV City was the forerunner of the present DR Byen (Denmark Radio City) near Kastrup airport, opened in 2006.

4. **Eugen Kluev** (b. 1954) Eugen (Evgeny) Kluev. born in Russia, has been resident in Denmark since 1996. In Russia he is considered a master of the absurd, best known as a novelist, playwright, and children's writer. In Denmark he has published widely on Russian and Danish social questions. 'To Catch a Dane' is from the 2009 Danish PEN publication *Herfra min verden går* (From Here My World Begins), an anthology of work by foreign writers living in Denmark.

5. **Dan Turèll** (1946–1993) Prolific poet and journalist, popular thriller writer, and TV performer, 'Uncle Danny' Turèll believed that an artist's work is all of a piece, a unique 'oeuvre'. He was into the American Beat poets, jazz, drugs, anarchism, and Zen Buddhism. Above all he loved his city of Copenhagen, its life and noise and all the little stories that lurked everywhere. When he died of cancer aged 47, the city lost one of its most beloved inhabitants. His friend Peter Laugesen is today one of Denmark's leading poets, who like Turèll performs his poetry with backing from his own band. '*Rex regulus*', Willadsen's favourite bird in Turèll's story, is presumably *Regulus regulus,* the goldcrest.

6. **Tove Ditlevsen** (1917–1976) Tove Ditlevsen, who started writing poetry at the age of twelve, was born into a poor working class family in the Vesterbro district

of Copenhagen where the biggest employer was the Carlsberg brewery. Though she considered herself primarily a poet, it is often in her short stories that she is at her most lyrical, and at the same time most precise. Her work often concerns children and young people and the damage inflicted on them by adults and by society. Later in life, when she had become a household name for her journalism and memoirs, she suffered from a sense of having betrayed her working-class roots, and the work circles round the subsequent loss of identity. Her themes of insecurity and depression, love and pain, reflect her own life experiences. She was married four times, and committed suicide in March 1976.

7. **Søren Kierkegaard** (1813–1855) Søren Kierkegaard, the 'father' of existentialism, was the author of numerous works of philosophy, religious thought, and social criticism. His daily walks through Copenhagen made him a familiar figure (see illustration), and like Dan Turèll 150 years later he drew inspiration from the city and its people. In his first great work, *Either/Or (Enten-Eller*, 1843), from which I have chosen a passage from the section called 'Diary of a Seducer', Kierkegaard lets two types of men speak with equal conviction: the godless aesthete who lives purely for the pleasure of the moment, and the ethical man whose principles are

duty, the norm, and the rules. Here are a few Kierke-gaard sound bites: 'I see it all perfectly; there are two possible situations—one can either do this or that. My honest opinion and my friendly advice is this: do it or do not do it—you will regret both.' 'Life is not a problem to be solved, but a reality to be experienced.' 'People demand freedom of speech to make up for the freedom of thought which they seldom use.'

8. **Jakob Ejersbo** (1968–2008) Jakob Ejersbo, who died of cancer aged only 40, was the most promising writer of his generation. His first novel *Nordkraft* (2004) was hailed by readers and critics alike as a great new Danish work of gritty realism. 'The Bra' is from the short story collection *Superego* (2000), which deals with issues of youth culture, fashion, and alienation. Most of his early years were spent in Tanzania. The superb 'Africa trilogy' (*Exile*, *Revolution*, and *Liberty*), now also available in English, was a publishing sensation when it came out posthumously in Denmark in 2009.

9. **Hans Christian Andersen** In a much-quoted comment on his stories, Andersen wrote: 'They lay in my thoughts like a seed-corn, requiring only a flowing stream, a ray of sunshine, a drop of wormwood, for them to spring forth and burst into bloom.' It is the 'drop of wormwood', so evident in the two tales I have

chosen, that is all too often missed in the popular conception of the author. This tale is illustrated with 'Flower Man', one of Andersen's many paper cuts.

10. **Jan Sonnergaard** (b. 1963) Jan Sonnergaard, a novelist and playwright who has also published five short story collections, was born in Copenhagen. Like his contemporary Jakob Ejersbo, his debut collection of stories aimed to break with what he saw as the impoverished self-regarding literature of the 1980s, replacing it with a raw and concrete realism. His voice is often cynical, oozing with black humour. 'Is there Life after Love?' (2000) bears out one of his literary credos: 'Exaggeration furthers understanding.'

11. **Katrine Marie Guldager** (b. 1966) Katrine Marie Guldager, another contemporary specialist of the short story, was born in a suburb of Copenhagen. She has received many awards for her poetry and prose works, including the critics' prize for her collection *København* (2004), from which 'A Bench in Tivoli' is taken. It contains eleven 'Copenhagen' stories in which a character who takes centre stage in one tale can reappear as a minor character in another. Central to the book is the sense of loneliness experienced by them all, the way people pass by and through each other's universe in the big city.

12. **Naja Marie Aidt** (b. 1963) Naja Marie Aidt, who now
    lives in New York, was born in Greenland, where her
    father was a teacher. The extreme contrasts she expe-
    rienced there between light and dark, and the contrast
    between Greenland and Copenhagen, where the fam-
    ily returned when she was 7 and the parents later
    divorced, have had a major impact on her work. She
    has written poetry, song lyrics, plays, children's
    books, three volumes of short stories, and more
    recently a novel, and is the recipient of many literary
    prizes, including the prestigious Nordic Council's Lit-
    erature Prize, which she won in 2008.

13. **Benny Andersen** (b. 1929) Benny Andersen was born
    in Vangede, a suburb of Copenhagen, and initially
    earned his living as a light music pianist. Like so
    many of Denmark's contemporary writers he is a
    jack-of-all-trades: musician and song writer, prolific
    poet and short story writer, and author of many pieces
    for theatre and radio. He writes for adults and children
    alike and is the most widely read, most often sung,
    and best loved of modern Danish lyricists. He is also
    an outspoken campaigner for the rights of new immi-
    grants, publishing *Rubbish and Lies about Islam* in
    2012. A life-affirming sense of humour permeates his
    work (his poetry collections include *The Musical Eel*

and *The Inner Bowler Hat*), and on his 70th birthday in 1999 Copenhagen honoured him with a torchlight procession through the streets.

14. **Meïr Goldschmidt** (1819–1887) Meïr Goldschmidt, a contemporary of Hans Christian Andersen and Kierkegaard, was born into a Jewish merchant family in North Zealand and educated in Copenhagen. He was the first writer to explore the problems facing the Danish Jewish community from the inside, most notably in his first novel *A Jew* (1845). His novels and novellas with Jewish protagonists deploy a special mixture of irony and sympathy in their exploration of his recurring themes of social rejection and nemesis, 'Nightingale' being a fine example in a lighter vein. As a journalist Goldschmidt battled against social injustice and the absolutist monarchy. and was imprisoned for a short period. He is now regarded as one of the pioneers of modern and independent Danish journalism. The linguistic notes to 'Nightingale' are Goldschmidt's own, as is the Yiddish spelling.

15. **Anders Bodelsen** (b. 1937) Anders Bodelsen, born in Frederiksberg, Copenhagen, is a prolific professional writer who in clear, realist prose examines how the forces of competition and consumerism affect individuals, often clashing with their human values. In

addition to over a dozen short story collections, he has published many novels and thrillers in which, as he says, 'ordinary members of the steadily growing Danish middle class are put in extreme and painful situations' where issues of motive, ambition, guilt, and fear are explored. Many of his bestsellers have been made into films, radio plays, and TV series. The illustration is from Constantin Hansen's 'Portrait of Elise Købke' (1850) in the National Museum of Art.

16. **Karen Blixen** (1885–1962) Karen Blixen, who also wrote under the name of Isak Dinesen, was the most internationally renowned Danish writer of the twentieth century, best known today for *Out of Africa* and 'Babette's Feast', both of which have been filmed. Proud to call herself above all a storyteller, her many stories and novellas (*Seven Gothic Tales*, *Winter's Tales*, etc.) are set back in time, often in exotic and imaginary environments, and told in a somewhat archaic and colourful language overflowing with images and symbols. Her main themes are life, art, love, fate, and identity. 'Conversation One Night in Copenhagen', the very last story in *Last Tales*, clearly had special personal resonance for an author looking back on her life's work. 'Sultan Orosmane' is the male lead in Voltaire's play *Zaïre* (1732), a role played in real life by the young king

Christian VII himself, whose citations in French all come straight from the play. Rungstedlund, Karen Blixen's home just outside Copenhagen, now a museum devoted to her life and work, had previously been an inn, and here Johannes Ewald, the poet in the tale, spent his happiest years before his death from ill health and alcoholism aged 38 in 1781. Laurence Sterne (aka 'Yorick'), author of *A Sentimental Journey* and *Tristram Shandy*, was a favourite writer of both Ewald and Blixen.

17. **Merete Bonnesen** (1901–1980) Merete Bonnesen, born in Copenhagen, was an all-round journalist who worked all of her professional life for *Politiken*, the left wing daily paper founded by Georg Brandes and his brother Edvard in 1884 with the motto 'the paper of greater enlightenment'. One of the first women journalists to work in the traditionally male areas of politics and foreign affairs, she became foreign editor of the paper under the German occupation, and was for a short while interned in the Horserød camp along with several hundred other leading cultural figures. Her passionate commitment to the people and events she describes is obvious from this commemorative article she wrote for *Politiken* on the 10th anniversary of Denmark's liberation.

Further Reading and Viewing

Books

The usual guide books such as *The Rough Guide to Copenhagen*, *Lonely Planet Copenhagen*, *Time Out Copenhagen*, and *Politiken's Travel Guide: Copenhagen* are all useful for a first-time visitor. The City Museum (Københavns Bymuseum) on Vesterbrogade follows the history of the city from its medieval beginnings to the present day, with special sections on Søren Kierkegaard and new immigrants to the city. The Museum of the Danish Resistance (Frihedsmuseet, beside Churchill Park, under renovation after a major fire in 2013) is devoted to the history of occupation and liberation 1940–5 (see Tale 17).

For those wanting to find out more about the country and its capital the following books will be useful:

Patrick Kingsley's *How to be Danish*, part reportage, part travelogue, is a fun and easy introduction to contemporary Danish culture. Stig Hornshøj-Møller's *A Short*

History of Denmark is an ideal companion on a first visit. Knud Jespersen's *A History of Denmark* covers the story from the Reformation, focusing on how the modern Danish state has evolved. Torben Ejlersen's *Copenhagen: A Historical Guide* is a very helpful introduction. Pernille Stensgaard's *Copenhagen: People and Places* has lovely pictures and a lively text. Henrik Sten Møller's *Copenhagen, A Love Affair*, also beautifully illustrated, is a personal reflection on the city's architectural heritage and recent town planning.

Highly recommended novels by Danish authors with a Copenhagen setting, all available in translation, are Henrik Pontoppidan's *Lucky Per*, Tove Ditlevsen's *Early Spring*, Hans Scherfig's *Stolen Spring*, and Peter Hoegh's *Miss Smilla's Feeling for Snow. Copenhagen Noir* is a collection of contemporary Danish crime stories, including one by Naja Marie Aidt (see Tale 12).

Edmund Gosse wrote an entertaining book called *Two Visits to Denmark, 1872, 1874*, telling of his meetings with many famous Danes, including Hans Christian Andersen and Georg Brandes, describing the enormous development taking place in the city right at that time. Rose Tremain's *Music and Silence* is a hugely entertaining historical novel about seventeenth-century Denmark and the court of King Christian IV, the 'architect king' whose vision shaped much of the old city centre. Each of Thomas

E. Kennedy's fine 'Copenhagen Quartet' of novels (*Falling Sideways*, *Kerrigan in Copenhagen*, etc.) is in one way or another a homage to the city and its citizens. Patricia Berman's *In Another Light: Danish Painting in the Nineteenth Century*, now also available in paperback, is a very attractive survey (see Tale 15).

Cinema and TV

Lars von Trier and Thomas Vinterberg's famous 1995 'Dogme' manifesto for movie-making without technical wizardry relaunched Danish cinema, gaining it the international audience it had lost since the films of Carl Dreyer over fifty years before. The classics are Vinterberg's *Festen* and von Trier's *Idioterne* (The Idiots), a no-holds-barred satire on Danish middle-class conformity (see Tales 3, 8, and 12) set in the wealthy Copenhagen suburb of Søllerød. Von Trier's *Riget* (The Kingdom) is a wonderfully whacky TV series set in Copenhagen's main hospital, Rigshospitalet (see Tale 5).

Susanne Bier, who initially worked in the Dogme mode, has made a number of Copenhagen-based films of great appeal, notably *Open Hearts*, *Brothers*, and *After the Wedding*. Ole Madsen's *Flame and Citron* is a powerful film about resistance fighters against the Nazi occupation set in Copenhagen. Nikolaj Arcel's Oscar-nominated film *A Royal Affair* concerns the 'mad' King Christian VII (see

Tale 16) and his German physician Struensee, whose affair with the king's English wife, Caroline Mathilde, led to his fall from favour and public execution.

The master of Copenhagen *noir* cinema is Nicolas Refn, whose *Pusher* trilogy explores the dark underworld of the city's drug and gangland cultures. His influence is evident in the best of the currently very popular Danish *noir* TV thriller series: *The Killing* (series 1–3), and *The Bridge* (series 1 and 2, with series 3 due soon), a Danish–Swedish collaboration with at its heart the great Øresund bridge between the two countries. *Borgen* is an excellent 3-series TV drama about political and personal intrigues in and around Christiansborg, the Danish parliament (see Tale 3).

Publisher's Acknowledgements

1. H. C. Andersen, 'Vanddråben' from *Nye Eventyr*. Reitzel 1848.

2. Henrik Pontoppidan, 'To gange mødt' from *Skyer*. Gyldendal 1890.

3. Bjarne Reuter, 'Et tricky tidspunkt' from *Halvvejen til Rafael*. Gyldendal 2006.

4. Eugen Kluev, 'At fange en Dansker' from *Herfra min verden går*. Danish Pen 2009.

5. Dan Turèll, 'Willadsen' from *Onkel Danny fortæller*. Borgen 1976.

6. Tove Ditlevsen, 'En æggesnaps' from *Dommeren*. Hasselbach 1948.

7. Søren Kierkegaard, extract from *Enten-Eller*. Reitzel 1878.

8. Jakob Ejersbo, 'Brystholder' from *Superego*. Gyldendal 2000.

9. H. C. Andersen, 'Den uartige dreng' from *Eventyr fortalt for børn*. Reitzel 1835.

10. Jan Sonnergaard. 'Er der liv efter kærligheden?' from *Sidste søndag i Oktober*. Gyldendal 2000.

11. Katrine Marie Guldager, 'En bænk i Tivoli' from *København*. Gyldendal 2004.

12. Naja Marie Aidt, 'Som englene flyver' from *Vandmærket*. Gyldendal 1993.

13. Benny Andersen, 'Bukserne' from *Puderne*. Borgen 1963.

14. Meïr Goldschmidt, 'Avromche Nattergal'. Christian Steen. 1871.

15. Anders Bodelsen, 'Amelies øjne' from *16 noveller*. Gyldendal 1957.

16. Karen Blixen, 'Samtale om natten i København' from *Sidste fortællinger*. Gyldendal 1957.

17. Merete Bonnesen, 'Den store lykkes fællesnat'. *Politiken*, 4 May 1955.

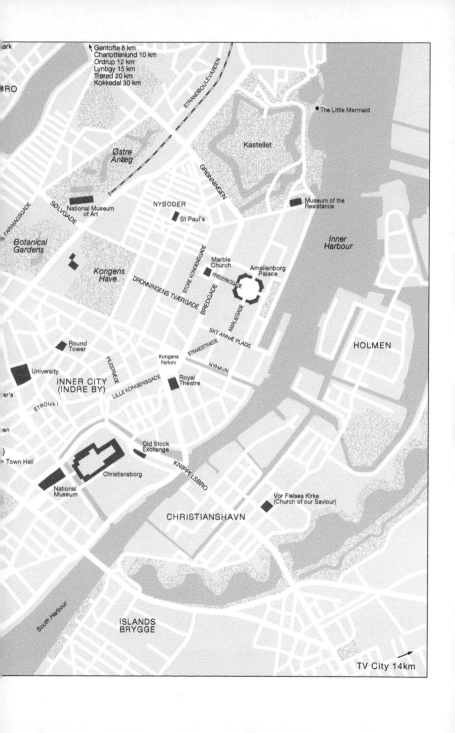

ark

Gentofte 8 km
Charlottenlund 10 km
Ordrup 12 km
Lyngby 15 km
Trørød 20 km
Kokkedal 30 km

RO

STRANDBOULEVARDEN

The Little Mermaid

Østre
Anlæg

Kastellet

GRØNNINGEN

Museum of the
Resistance

FARIMAGSGADE

SØLVGADE

National Museum
of Art

NYBODER

St Paul's

Inner
Harbour

Botanical
Gardens

Kongens
Have

STORE KONGENSGADE

Marble
Church

FREDERIKSGADE

Amalienborg
Palace

DRONNINGENS TVÆRGADE

BREDGADE

AMALIEGADE

SKT ANNÆ PLADS

HOLMEN

Round
Tower

PILESTRÆDE

Kongens
Nytorv

STRANDSTRÆDE

NYHAVN

University

INNER CITY
(INDRE BY)

LILLE KONGENSGADE

Royal
Theatre

er's

STRØGET

en

)

Town Hall

Old Stock
Exchange

KNIPPELSBRO

Christiansborg

National
Museum

Vor Fielses Kirke
(Church of our Saviour)

CHRISTIANSHAVN

South Harbour

ISLANDS
BRYGGE

TV City 14km